miss FIX-IT

EMMA HART

NEW YORK TIMES BESTSELLING AUTHOR

miss
FIX-IT
EMMA HART
NEW YORK TIMES BESTSELLING AUTHOR

For Alexia-Belle and Cobie.
The very real inspiration behind all my very fictional kids,
but in this book more than ever.

Thank God, you're not twins.

1

Stereotypes were a bitch.

I knew it. I'd lived it with it my whole damn life. As a child, it'd been, "Aw, it's so lovely that Keith brings his daughter to work. So nice that she's interested in helping him, too, even in that pretty dress!" As an adult, it was, "Huh. She's a builder. How strange. Doesn't she worry about breaking a nail or ruining her make-up?"

Well, screw stereotypes and your preconceived notions, you dick.

And for the record: I wasn't so worried about the make-up, but the nail thing? Yeah. I totally worried about breaking a nail now and then. Chipping polish was just *the worst.*

There was a damn good reason all the advertising for Hancock Handyman Co. eliminated the fact I was a woman. When my dad semi-retired, I'd learned pretty quickly that people were willing to overlook our company just because I was a woman.

Several surprises later, word had gotten around our small, coastal town of Rock Bay, and most of the residents were no longer surprised when Kali, not Keith, showed up on their doorstep.

The people just outside of town? Still surprised. Still fun for me. Especially when wives and girlfriends and moms convinced the skeptical man of the house to give me a chance and I got to blow them away.

That would never get old.

"I got a call from the mayor today," Dad said, absently flicking through the TV channels.

"Mhmm," I replied, focused more on the cat article on Buzzfeed than another one of the mayor's complaints.

"He thinks you need to make it known on The Facebook that you're the 'K' in K. Hancock."

"So he's been saying for eighteen months. And it's just Facebook, not The Facebook."

"Kali, you should consider it."

I glanced up with a, "No."

He snorted. "Can I have him call you next time he wants to complain?"

"You can have him call me," I said, closing the app on my phone. "But that doesn't mean I'll answer it. I have other things to do than listen to Mayor Bennet's complaints."

"Kali—"

"Dad, when he fixes the five-inch wide pothole on Main Street, then I'll listen to him. He should be doing that instead of scrutinizing my Facebook page."

Dad sighed, muting the television. "I should have known you'd get your mother's stubborn streak."

Right. Because he was the most agreeable person in town. "She obviously left it behind when she died. You got the money and the house, and I got the attitude. I need a good, strong stubborn streak to deal with yours."

His lips twitched. "Mine is necessary. I have to field Mayor Bennet's calls."

"Like I said. He can fix the pothole, then we'll talk." I paused, tucking hair behind my ear. "Plus, everyone in town knows you're semi-retired. The only person who forgets is old Mr. Jenkins and that's because of his dementia. Hell, I saw him in the grocery store this morning and he called me Coral and asked me how my pet clownfish were."

Dad opened his mouth, then obviously decided against what he was going to say. A thoughtful look crossed his mind. "At least he made the connection between coral and clownfish. That's better than last week when he told Irma Darling that Mr. Pickles needed to be in a zoo all because the cat brushed up against his ankle."

"Stupid name for a cat," I muttered. "And that thing does belong in a zoo. She should have called him Mr. Prickles. Damn thing hisses at me whenever I come within fifty feet of the register."

Irma Darling—no, really, it was her name, and she insisted all gentlemen over the age of twenty-five refer to her as such. Except she wanted to be Irma, darling. She was also as mad a box of frogs on a trampoline…and utterly delusional if she believed Mr. Pickles was as sweet, cushy, cuddly cat.

"That's because you almost ran him over when she got him last month, sweetheart."

I held up my hands. "I was under the limit. Don't blame me if the dumb creature jumped in front of my truck."

Dad offered me a withering look. "You just hate cats."

"No, I hate that cat. There's a difference."

"Are we talking about Mr. Pickles again?" My step-mother wandered into the room, pasta sauce decorating the front of her white shirt. Her blue eyes scanned the pair of us from beneath thick, dark eyelashes, and her pale, pink lips curved, wrinkling at the edges. "That demon cat scratched my leg when I went to the store this morning. Irma told me not to stand on his tail, and I told her that if her cat attacked me again, I'd relieve him of the damn tail."

Dad brought his hand up to his face, closing his eyes before he pinched the bridge of his nose.

"Thank you," I said looking at her. "The thing sold its soul to Satan, no doubt about it. Along with Mayor Bennet."

"Oh dear," she said. "Has he been harassing your father again?"

I nodded.

"The man needs to focus on our potholes. I have half a mind to write a strongly worded letter to the council."

"I'll co-sign," I offered.

"I need a drink," Dad said. "Portia, honey, if you write another letter to the council this year, they might…Well, I have no idea what they'll do, but Councilor Jeffries will lose his mind."

Mom wiggled her finger at him, the bright red of her nail a quick flash of color through the air. "You can't lose a mind if you don't possess one in the first place. I've half a mind to run for council next year."

"Excellent," Dad drawled. "You have half a mind to run for council, and the other half is focused on writing them a letter. Do you think you could spare a little to focus on not burning dinner?"

I bit the inside of my cheek so I didn't laugh.

"Keith Hancock, I'll wash your mouth out with soap if you keep sassing me."

"You'd have to catch me."

"That wouldn't be hard, dear. You haven't moved from the sofa for three hours."

I burst out laughing, quickly covering my mouth with my hand. Dad shot me a look that was a cross between "shut up" and "don't validate her." Of course, I didn't stop laughing—I'd stopped being afraid of that look ten years ago—and got a wink from Mom for my troubles.

"Can I help you in the kitchen, honey?" Dad asked, now all sweetness and light.

"You can lock the workshop. Don't think I didn't notice the door open, and you're not sitting there until two in the morning building that coffee table again."

"Ooh," escaped my mouth. "Are you almost done?"

Dad's expression brightened. "I am. Do you want to see?"

I nodded, getting up as he heaved himself out of the chair. "I haven't seen it since you started carving the first leg."

"The first three are done now. They just need a bit of sanding and varnishing. Come see."

I followed him out of the room to an eyeroll from Mom, but it was a fond one. After all, she'd come into our lives when I was thirteen. She knew my father's true passion was carpentry, and she knew that all the aspects of building and handiwork were engrained into my very soul.

And my dad? Well. He was the best damn carpenter in the whole state, and this coffee table had been his pet project for months.

My phone beeped with a notification right before I could enter the barn. I held up a finger so Dad knew

I'd be inside in a minute. The notification bar showed a new email to my work address, so I clickedit to open it.

To: Hancock Handyman Co (khancock@hancockhandymanco.com)
From: Brantley Cooper (brantley-cooper@gmail.com)
Subject: re: Website Contact Form

Dear Sir/Madam,

I'm contacting you to discuss the possibility of a consultation. I recently moved to town and I would like to have someone come in and fix up my children's bedrooms. They're not in great condition at present.

I was recommended your company by someone earlier today. Because of the condition of the rooms, I would need someone to come by sooner rather than later. Is this something someone from your company would be able to accommodate?

If not, I completely understand, and would appreciate any recommendations for other local companies.

Regards,
Brantley Cooper

I clicked my tongue and responded.

To: Brantley Cooper (brantley-cooper@gmail.com)
From: Hancock Handyman Co (khancock@hancockhandymanco.com)
Subject: re: Website Contact Form

Dear Mr. Cooper,

Many thanks for your email. Could you provide some more information as to the condition of the bedrooms? Perhaps pictures if possible?

Best wishes.
K. Hancock

I tapped 'send' and headed inside to view Dad's coffee table project. The legs were all laid out on the worktable, and one was noticeably less-carved than the others. Still, that didn't take away from the intricacy of his carpentry, and I ran a finger over the rough surface of one of the completed legs.

"They still need sanding and treating, but I should be able to start that next week." Dad picked up the unfinished leg and stared at it. "I hope so, at least."

"They're beautiful, Dad," I said honestly. "This is going to be incredible when it's finished."

He set down the leg and smiled at me before he pulled me close and kissed me on the cheek. The salt-and-pepper whiskers that dotted his jaw and chin tickled my skin with the sweeping peck, but I smiled all the same.

My phone beeped again.

"That's a lot of beeps," he remarked. "Anyone important?"

"Potential new client. Just moved to town and wants his kids' bedrooms looking at. Apparently, they're run down."

"How run down?"

I waved the phone. "That's what I'm, hopefully,

about to find out." I dropped my attention to my phone and opened the newest email.

To: Hancock Handyman Co (khancock@hancockhandymanco.com)
From: Brantley Cooper (brantley-cooper@gmail.com)
Subject: re: Website Contact Form

Dear K. Hancock,

Please see the attached.

Regards,
Brantley Cooper

I downloaded the attachments and pulled them up on my gallery. Dad peered over my shoulder as I swiped through them. They were mostly peeling wallpaper and cracked paint, a light in need of fixing, the floors in need of decent carpeting or flooring, but the last few were the ones that held the real problem: the mold on the walls.

"That's pretty bad," Dad said, tilting the screen. "They might need new windows, and they certainly can't sleep in those rooms or they'll get sick."

I nodded in agreement. "And it could be his lucky day. Well, he'd have to wait a week, but I can do it next Saturday and probably start the following Monday."

"Quiet on the books?"

"Once I'm done with the repaint of Susie Michaels' guest house, yep. That's no bad thing, though. I could have used the break, but he obviously needs my help."

Dad patted my shoulder and moved away. "Sure does, Kali. Want me to come and help you check the place over?"

"No, it's fine. I'm not sure Mom would be too impressed if I dragged you away next Saturday."

A puzzled look flitted across his face. "Why?"

I blinked at him. "Uh…Dad? It's your wedding anniversary."

He froze, eyes widening at my words sank in. "Oh, shit."

I smirked, leaning against the worktable. "There's a bunch of her favorite flowers reserved at Nova for you to collect at seven a.m., and I booked you a table at The Coastal Boulevard. Seven-thirty reservation, and yes, they already know it's your anniversary."

He visibly deflated, sighing out in relief. "What would I do without you?"

"Get in a lot of trouble with your wife."

"I can't argue with the truth. Talking of—we should go back inside before. Dinner is probably ready."

I nodded. "Let me just reply to this email. I'll be right in."

Dad left me to it, and I opened my email.

*To: Brantley Cooper (*brantley-cooper@gmail.com*)*
*From: Hancock Handyman Co (*khancock@hancockhandymanco.com*)*
Subject: re: Website Contact Form

Dear Mr. Cooper,

Thanks for the photos. I can see your problem. Unfortunately, I'm booked this week, but I'm free for a consultation next Saturday. Is that soon enough?

I can point you in the direction of other relatively local contractors, but I doubt many would be able to get you in so quickly.

Hope to hear from you on this soon.

Best wishes,
K. Hancock

His response within seconds—before I'd even left the workshop.

*To: Hancock Handyman Co (*khancock@hancockhandymanco.com*)*
*From: Brantley Cooper (*brantley-cooper@gmail.com*)*
Subject: re: Website Contact Form

Dear K. Hancock,

That's sooner than I was expecting. Does ten a.m. work for you?

Regards,
Brantley Cooper

I responded, confirming the time, and advising him to not have his children sleep in the room. I also offered a common solution to remove the surface mold on the walls and the windowsill. He responded appreciatively, so I tucked my phone away and headed back inside for dinner with my family.

Mom handed me a glass of wine. I had to handle it carefully thanks to her tendency to actually make a glass of wine a full glass, and I was never more thankful than right now that I could walk home from my parents'.

"Any news on the dating front?" she asked, taking the other seat on the sofa.

Dad had long retired to the workshop to play with his table leg, so she was able to ask me the questions she really wanted to. I was twenty-six, but that didn't mean my father was comfortable around these questions.

"Do you mean news other than "oh, look, another date with a fuckboy?"" I replied, sipping my wine.

"At this point, honey, fuckboys aren't news. They're the norm."

I groaned in agreement. "It's all the same, all the time. And the guy I went out with on Wednesday? He just proved he didn't read my bio at all."

"Oh, dear."

"Oh, dear? Oh, shit, is more like it." The thing I loved about my stepmother: She had a potty mouth to rival a sailor's, and while I had to watch it most of the time, when we discussed dating, all bets were off.

Besides, crapboy just didn't sound as good as fuckboy.

"That bad?" She looked at me with sympathetic eyes.

"The worst yet, maybe." I pushed my hair from my eyes. "First, he was late, which I forgave because he said he'd got caught in traffic."

"In Rock Bay? Was the traffic seagulls on the road?"

"He said he lived out of town, so whatever. Even though he never apologized." I sipped again. "Then, five minutes in, he asks me what I do. I told him I ran the family building business since Dad is semi-retired, and he goes, "Oh, you're the secretary?""

Her eyes widened.

"I said, "No, actually. I'm the builder," and if I could have captured the look on his face, I'd have blown it up and taped it to the side of the mayor's building."

"What did he say to that?"

My face wrinkled up as I said it. "He complimented me on my excellent bicep muscles and went to "take a phone call.""

"He stiffed you with the bill?"

I grinned, shaking my head. "He'd booked the table, and you know how Marcie started collecting addresses of bookers since the Coastal became the 'it' place?"

"No!"

"She's forwarded him the bill. I got to enjoy a great dinner for free."

"How did she do that?"

"Apparently, he booked on the website, and there's small print that states the booking party is liable for the bill in the event of a date gone wrong. Well—

probably not that, but enough to cover poor little women like me who get stuffed because the guy is a dick."

Mom shook her head and sighed. "At least Marcie has a plan in place for those dicks."

"Only because the last guy she dated thought their date would be free because it was at Coastal," I reminded her. "Marcie thought he'd be gentleman enough to pay, but nope."

"I'm so glad I don't have to date now," Mom said. "I don't think I could stand it. I'd likely be locked up for murder."

"You've been married to Dad for ten years next weekend. Isn't that similar to jail?"

She'd been drinking her wine when I'd said that, and she snorted, clapping her hand over her nose. I burst out laughing as she squealed and choked.

"Damn it, Kali. How can I drink properly if you keep making me laugh?"

I grinned.

"And for the record, no, marriage is not like jail." She paused. "Most of the time. At least in jail there'd be a rotation of whose turn it is to load the dishwasher."

"Mom, please. Every time Dad loads it, you redo it."

"It's not my fault if he does it wrong. I keep hoping he'll take the hint."

I tapped my finger against my chin. "Do you think if I wrote, "NOT THE SECRETARY" on my bio on the dating site people would get it?"

"No. I think you should say you are the secretary, then shock them when you can build Ikea furniture without swearing."

"And without the instructions."

"That's just cocky."

"Exactly."

She rolled her eyes, but her wine glass hid a smile. "Whoever marries you better have the patience of a saint, Kali Hancock."

"They'd better have more than the patience of a saint. I want the cock of a God, too."

She blinked at me for a moment. "Do you ever think I should be less of the best friend kind of parent and more of the "don't speak like that" parent?"

I twisted my lips in a wry smile. "You tried that once. It lasted a week."

"Maybe it's time to try again."

"Fifty bucks says you last three days."

She tapped her fingers against her knee. "You're right. Besides, you have your dad for that."

Once again, I grinned, thankful for having a mom and best friend wrapped into one.

2

One week later

Note to self: a girls' night out the day before a consultation with a potential client was not the best idea I'd ever had. Neither was the vodka.

Really, I knew better. Me and vodka weren't friends. By this point in my life, I should have been able to say no the allure of any cocktail with it in—and I definitely shouldn't be giving in to peer pressure when it's the shots round.

All things considered, I was a pretty lousy adult. But, hey. My best friend was back from a work trip that took her away for a month, and the night out had been planned long before I got Brantley Cooper's email.

Thankfully for me, right now, I'd drank enough water to quench the thirst of a herd of elephants, had scarfed down—ahem—three bagels, showered, and brushed my teeth at least five times to kill the alcohol grime the drinking session had left behind.

I was feeling almost human. *Almost.*

My professional head would take over when I walked inside the house. I had my toolbox, even though I didn't think I would need it. It was mostly for the tape measure that I would undoubtedly lose if I took it out of the box.

I was always losing the damn thing. I was about

ready to buy them in bulk and store them in my basement.

I swallowed a mouthful of water before I started up my truck. The bright-pin freshener swung from the rearview mirror as I pulled out of my driveway and away from my modest, two-story house.

The address Brantley Cooper had given me wasn't too far from my own house. A five minute drive, a ten minute or so walk, since you could cut through the park that separated our neighborhoods. I also knew it to be part of a block of houses that had mold issues ever since they were built. The original buyers had been given compensation for the problems it had caused, but that didn't count when you were buying it from one of them.

In other words, Brantley Cooper was in for the long—and potentially expensive—haul if he'd bought this house, and I was almost certain he had.

I pulled onto his street. It was easy to pick out which house was his. Flattened boxes were piled on the grass by the mailbox, stacked somewhat haphazardly. I pulled up to the curb and killed my engine. Another drink of water and I grabbed my toolbox—and drill case, just in case—and headed for the front door.

I rang the bell.

A scream answered.

I took a step back.

"No, Ewwie!" a young voice shouted. "Nooooo!"

"Eleanor. Elijah!" a deeper, gruffer voice said over the noise of them fighting. "Can you stop for two minutes so I can answer the door?"

"But she said—"

"But he—"

The door swung open, revealing to me the man I presumed to be Brantley Cooper.

Holy mother of orgasms.

Dumbly, I stared at him. At the dark hair that curled over his forehead and ears. At the turquoise-blue eyes that were currently sizing me up. At the sharp cheekbones, the full lips, the stubbled jaw…The arms that looked like they could lift a tank over his head.

"Can I help you?" he said in a low voice that I could hear over the unruly fighting in the house behind him.

My mouth was too dry to answer.

He cocked an eyebrow. "I'm sorry, I have an appointment in…" He looked at the watch on his wrist. "Any moment, actually, and I have to sort my kids, so…"

"Mr. Cooper?" Thank god. Hi again, voice. Nice of you to show up.

He stopped, mid-turn, and peered at me. "Yes…"

I held out my hand. "Kali Hancock. I'm here to consult with you on your children's rooms?"

"Kali Hancock." He said my name slowly, rolling it around his mouth as if he were trying it on for size.

Deep, rumbly, and…suspicious.

Here we go again.

"The K. Hancock I've been emailing with?"

"That's me."

"Is it common for your company to send someone who isn't the builder for the consultation?"

I took a deep breath and motioned to the toolbox by my feet. "Not at all. I *am* the builder."

He stared at me, eyebrows drawing together in confusion. I could see the exact moment understanding settled, because his eyebrows shot up and his lips parted oh-so-invitingly.

Damn it, no. I didn't get attracted to stereotypical people like him.

Someone needed to tell my vagina that.

"You're the builder," he finally said, slowly.

A gut-wrenching scream came from inside the house.

Brantley Cooper shook his head. "I'm sorry—come in. I'll be a minute."

"Thanks." I picked up my toolbox and drill and stepped into the hallway. There wasn't a lot of room—he'd either downsized tremendously or he'd failed to unpack a lot of stuff. How long had he been here for?

"Eleanor, Elijah, that's enough." He clapped his hands in the next room.

I leaned to the side so I could see through the door.

What? I was nosy. How else did I find stuff out?

He stood in front of two children, a boy and a girl. Despite the fact the little girl—Eleanor—was an inch taller than her brother, Elijah, it was obvious they were twins.

How?

They both had hair that was a golden-brown color that glinted almost copper in the sunlight that streamed through the window behind Brantley. They both stood in identical positions, too. Legs apart, arms folded, and the scowls that marred their adorable little faces… Well, you could have merged photos of those expressions, and you wouldn't be able to tell, even down to the freckles that appeared to dot their noses.

"I mean it," Brantley said. "The builder is here to talk about your bedrooms. I'll send her home if you aren't going to behave yourselves."

In perfect sync, they dropped their arms, and their scowls changed into horrified expressions.

"No, Daddy!" Eleanor rushed to him and tugged on his jeans. "No, no, no, I need my pwincess woom!"

"No!" Elijah copied his sister. "*I* need my superhewo woom."

"No, I need—"

"I need you to stop shouting," Brantley said, extracting the twins from him. "Next time, you're both in time out, do you hear me?"

Two pairs of wide eyes gazed up at him, and golden-brown hair bobbed as they nodded in unison.

Man. That was creepy as fuck.

"Now," he continued. "I want you both to sit down with the paint charts and pick out the color of your walls." He pulled two charts off the practically-empty bookcase to the side of him and handed them one each. "I'm going upstairs with Ms. Hancock, and the second I hear fighting is the second Ellie gets the superhero room and Eli gets the princess one. Okay?"

If Ellie looked horrified, Eli was positively beside himself at the possibility.

Never had I seen two children sit down and stare at paint charts so intently in my entire life.

Brantley blew out a breath and ran his hand through his hair, joining me back in the hallway. "Sorry. We just moved from Denver, and this is a bit of a change for them. No preschool, they lost their nanny, my parents aren't around anymore… It's hard."

No mention of their mom.

Hmm.

Was he single?

Damn it, Kali. Put your thirsty vagina back in its cage.

"Don't worry." I smiled. "Shall we go upstairs?"

He glanced back in the living room. "While they're still quiet? Absolutely. I doubt it'll last long."

I swallowed a laugh and grabbed my things. I'd been here less than five minutes, and already I could tell that was totally true.

I followed him upstairs, and I swear, I tried not to look at his ass. It was literally a mantra inside my head.

Don't look at his ass. Don't look at his ass. Don't look at his ass.

It didn't work. It was hard not to look at his ass. It was round and peachy and goddamn it, I was a heathen!

What was going on here? Was it a hangover effect?

That was it.

It was a lingering, painful trace of that fucking vodka.

Still…It was a really, really great ass. And I was an ass girl. And an arm girl. And an eye girl. And a mouth girl. And a cock-like-a-god girl.

Basically, I was easy to please unless you *spoke* like a cock.

"…really worked," Brantley said, reaching the top of the stairs.

Oh, shit. I hadn't heard a word he'd said.

"Good." Was that the right thing to say? Goddamn his mesmerizing ass.

"Yes—the mold on the walls is almost completely

gone, but I think it's just staining now." He pushed open a door. "This is Ellie's room. Her's was a little worse than Eli's."

I stepped inside the room after him. The pictures really hadn't done it justice—the paper was ripping, the floor was in desperate need of an overhaul, and the windows still held the signs of the mold in the way it was etched into the edges of the windows.

I put down my things and went to take a closer look. "It's just staining," I confirmed. "I need to look more, but I think it's just black mold, which is a problem all the houses in this neighborhood have."

"Really?"

"Yeah. The original contractors screwed something up, but since you bought from someone else and not them, management is on you."

"Great," he drawled. "Is there anything you can do for it?"

"Honestly," I said, turning around. "If it's just surface mold, no. It really is just management. Making sure the room is aired out—especially in colder months—and that you give the windows a wipe down with the solution you already used."

"Really? That's it?"

"Well, since I'm painting… There is a mixture you can get that you can put into paint. It won't help the windows, but it'll counteract the mold trying to form on the walls."

"Can you buy that?" His turquoise blue gaze settled on me intently.

"I can, but…" I paused. "It can be expensive, and if you need it for more than one room…"

"I can write you the deposit check today."

Well, that changed things. "I can order it as soon as it's cashed."

He nodded. "Perfect. Shall we see Eli's room?"

I nodded and followed him, feeling like one of those stupid bobby-head dogs people put in their cars.

Eli's room was much the same as Ellie's in terms of what it needed. New floors, new walls, mold treatment. That was all standard, though. It was everything else I needed to know that wasn't.

"What else are you thinking? I can see you're hoping for more than just a bit of paint and new carpet fitted."

A wry smile twisted his lips. "How did you know?"

"It's my job to know."

He motioned toward the stairs. "I need to check the twins. Can I make you a coffee?"

"Sure." We both went down. By some miracle, at least judging by his relieved sigh, the twins were quiet and still picking their paint colors. Who knew it was such a complicated job for such tiny people?

He led me into the kitchen and waved his hand at the table. "Take a—hold on." He shifted two boxes from a chair and put them by the back door. "Sorry. Unpacking is damn hard with two kids around."

"Are you by yourself?"

He nodded briskly and turned on the coffee machine.

"You don't have family here?" I frowned. Nobody moved to Rock Bay if they didn't have family here.

He gripped the edge of the counter. "No family. The twins' mom passed away two and a half years ago."

I opened my mouth, closed it, and opened it again. Nothing came out.

Oh, that's right. Nothing came out because my foot was in my mouth.

"I'm sorry," I finally managed to eke out. "I shouldn't have asked."

He waved his arm dismissively, setting a mug in front of me. "Two and a half years is a long time. You didn't know. I can see why you asked. Rock Bay is a little…quieter…than I'd expected."

A wry smile assured me he wasn't too annoyed at my questioning.

"Cream and sugar?"

"Please," I said. "Sorry. I'm a little nosy and sometimes have a habit of putting my foot in my mouth and chewing on my toes."

"Hopefully not literally."

"Not since I was at least three."

He half-grinned. "Got any tips to stop that? Eli is a fan of his toenails."

I wrinkled my nose up. "Oh, gosh."

Brantley pulled his mug from the machine and sat opposite me. He piled three sugars and a dash of cream into his coffee, then smiled again. "If somebody had warned me how gross kids are, I might have reconsidered."

"Well, that's the reason I'm not a kid person," I admitted. "I can't deal with the toenails thing."

"Ellie doesn't do it, so there's that."

"Yeah, no. Have you ever been a teenage girl?"

"I'm one hundred percent sure I haven't."

I bit the inside of my cheek. "Well, my apologies

for what will happen to you in ten years."

"Thanks." He fought an even wider smile. "So, the other stuff for their rooms…"

"Sure. Go on ahead." I pulled my phone from my pocket and opened my Notes app.

He glanced at it with a quirked eyebrow, but didn't acknowledge it otherwise. "The rooms aren't huge, so I'd like to get them a higher bed, but not a really high one."

Technical.

"A mid-sleeper? With room for a desk or something underneath?"

"That's it, but I think Ellie would prefer a dress-up wardrobe with space for books, and Eli would prefer a "bat-cave" type thing."

I smiled and nodded as I tapped that onto the app. "I can definitely do that. My dad is an excellent carpenter, and he'd be thrilled to take on that challenge."

"Really? He's a carpenter?"

"Family business." My smiled turned wry. "Don't think you're the first person to be confused when I show up."

"The K.Hancock throws you, that's for sure."

I sucked my lip between my teeth so I didn't grin even wider. "Is there any other furniture you'd like built? Dad can build beds to match anything you'd be buying from a store."

"I actually have their furniture. I planned to build it, but then the mold…Then parenting happened, and I'm starting to feel like I'll never have time."

I held up my hands. "Don't worry. I can handle that for you, too. All I'll need is you to get me photos of the furniture or links to them. I'll pass it on to my father." I paused. "You know that's a little extra, right? The beds."

He nodded. "It's fine. They've had a rough time, and I want them to be happy."

Something deep inside me warmed at that statement. "Why don't you give me your phone number? I can pass all this onto Dad, and he can call you with a quote."

"Sure. Do you mind?" He pointed to my phone.

I brought up the contacts and hit the button for a new one.

He input his name and number, then slid the phone back to me.

Well. That was the easiest I'd ever gotten a hot guy's number.

"When do you think you can start?"

"Monday," I replied, finishing my coffee. "I'll need to come by a couple times this week to take some measurements for the bigger things and drop off some brochures for you. I'll call ahead to let you know, but I'll be here at eight-thirty on Monday morning to start tearing out that wall paper and flooring. Is that good for you?"

"That works. Can the kids go in their own rooms now the mold is gone?"

I stood, tucking my phone in my pocket. "Wipe the walls every day and leave the window open so it can dry out. If you do that, I don't see why not."

"Perfect. I need some peace back. Talking of peace…" He got up and darted into the front room.

I hovered awkwardly before I grew the courage to peek inside the room.

"Oh my god." Brantley covered his face with his hands. "Where did you find the pens?"

"Ewi did it," Ellie said.

"No! Ewwie did it!" her brother replied.

I edged a little further inside. On the lovely, cream wall of the living room was a dodgy looking fairy with one wing, all drawn in pink. Next to her was a strange dinosaur with purple spots that were half-colored.

As if he knew I was there, Brantley dropped his hand, blinked, and looked at me. "Can we add the living room to painting?"

He looked so helpless, so…exhausted…yet also like he was trying not to laugh at their artistic streak, that it took everything I had not to laugh, too.

"Good thing I have a lot of dust sheets."

3

"So." Jayda leaned back on my bed and wriggled her toes in her stripy socks. My best friend had skipped out early on a bad date, promptly deciding to show up at my house with wine, ice-cream, and candy. "How about you tell me about your last date?"

"Nuh-uh." I pulled a Twizzler from the packet and bit off the end. "You know about my last horror date. You're the one who ran away tonight, and if you showed up with all this, it must have been bad."

"Aside from the fact I know better than to show up at your house without Twizzlers—"

"True story."

"—You're right. It was terrible. Probably the worst one ever, actually."

I turned my head away from the *Friends* re-run and stared at her profile. She was the blond to my brunette, and I had no idea how she was single with her cute button nose, full lips, and large, blue eyes.

"Worse than Johnny Knox?"

She groaned, leaning her head right back against the headboard and reached for her wine glass. Instead of the glass, she grabbed the bottle. I smirked when she took one look at it, shrugged, and swigged straight from it.

"Wow." Wow was the right reaction here. If it was worse than Johnny Knox, Mr. Handsy himself who tried to get her off right there in the middle of the restaurant, it was bad.

"It was a string of bullshit, Kali. First up, he shows up late."

Been there.

"Then, he didn't look anything like his picture. Claimed the only different was the fact he didn't have a beard or dark hair anymore." She waved the bottle and put it down, switching it for the glass before changing her mind again. "Fine, whatever. He was still cute. I sucked up the fact I'd spent thirty minutes getting sympathetic looks because everyone thought I was being stood up. You know what? I wish I had been!"

Oh, boy.

"So, he finally sits down. We order two drinks and our meals. He refuses to get starters or a dessert because of the price, and that's the first hint he's a total fuckboy."

I "hmmed" in agreement.

"He doesn't ask what I do or how I am. He doesn't even apologize for being late. Instead he launched into a monologue about how stressed he is at work and how lonely he is since his pet rabbit, Cheeto, died."

"He named a rabbit Cheeto?"

She held up a pink-tipped finger. "Not to mention his budgies, Ben and Jerry, are fighting colds."

"Budgies get colds?"

"Apparently. So, he's heartbroken over Cheeto, Ben and Jerry are sick, and honestly, I wanted to ask him if he had an ant farm collectively named the Sour Patch Kids or something equally ridiculous."

"You didn't?"

"No."

"You missed a trick there."

"We're not all unfiltered like you."

"I'm not unfiltered." I paused. "I'm…quick-witted."

She raised an eyebrow at me, setting the wine bottle down—and leaving it there instead of picking it back up like she did before. "Sure. Quick-witted. That's one way to describe it."

"Why did I let you in?"

Jayda waved the Twizzler packet at me.

"Shut up," I muttered, snatching it off her. "Tell me the rest of the date."

"Where did I get to? Oh, yeah—the sick budgies." She wedged the tub of ice-cream onto her lap and wriggled. "So, I apologized, but before I could ask him anything, he dove into a spiel about how his mother never loved him."

Oh dear god.

"What did you do?"

"I downed my wine and excused myself to the bathroom. Marcie sent the new bar girl in to tell me to run on her signal."

"What? Why?"

"Marcie corralled him toward the bar with the promise of a free drink, because she'd heard his sad tale, and needed a new whiskey tried out."

"Did it work?"

Jayda nodded. "I left to the sounds of him regaling Marcie with a tale about how his mother kicked his first cat, Noodles."

"I don't know if the bigger concern is his

obsession with animals or his mother or the way he names them."

"The names. No grown-ass man should ever admit to having a cat named Noodles unless his sister named it." She sighed. "I think I'm destined to be single forever."

"No, you're just looking in the wrong places. I'm starting to figure out that online doesn't mean success."

"Starting?"

"Want me to make you feel better about your life?"

She nodded. "That's always helpful."

Sighing, I got up out of bed and went to fetch my laptop from downstairs. When I had it, I went back up and sat on the bed, loading it up. "I checked my messages before I went to work this morning. Some of them were so bad… And not even just bad, but some of them were the grossest things ever."

"Well, I haven't had those this week. I guess that's a plus."

"No kidding. Okay, here." I logged in to the dating website and went to my message box. "Look at this guy. "*Kinky sub for you to keep in chastity and make your little bitch.*" And if it wasn't enough, check the pictures."

I clicked on one and looked away.

"Oh god, my eyes! They burn! Get it off!"

I winced at the…portly…gentleman wearing nothing but leather straps and a collar on his knees and hit the 'x' button on the pop-up.

"I have two questions," Jayda said, peering at the screen from between her fingers. "The first one is, why do you get those and I don't?"

"Do you want them?"

"Shit—please, no." She snorted. "My next question is, why do they keep coming to you? What's in your profile that isn't in mine?"

"Dunno. Do you think it's the builder thing?"

"Maybe. Mr. Kinky Sub sound like he wouldn't mind you screwing him into a wall."

I stilled.

Turning to slowly meet her eyes, the twinkle in them killed me within seconds. We both burst out laughing, and I reached for my now-empty wine glass.

"Damn it."

Jayda waved the bottle. "I'll pour it if you tell me about the new guy in town."

"Brantley Cooper?"

"Is he the twins guy?"

"Uh, yes."

"Jesus," she muttered. "Even his damn name is hot."

I snatched the wine out of her hand. "You should see his ass."

"Do you need, uh, an assistant next week?"

"His kids were fighting when I got there, then drew on the walls right before I left."

Jayda wrinkled her nose up. "Hmmm. Let me know on the assistant thing. I mean, I might be busy."

Imagine that.

4

After a week of running back and forth between my booked jobs and taking measurements at Brantley's, I was more than ready to get to work on Ellie's room today.

I'd worked out a full game plan with my dad at Friday dinner and seen his plans for the beds. He'd been thrilled to work on some stuff for little kids, and had promptly reminded me that he'd been married to my mother at my age.

My stepmom had then reassured me—out of earshot—that there were way more fuckboys in my generation and not to worry about it, but babies would be nice soon enough.

So, with the little nugget of information that my parents wanted me to house a human being in my uterus pretty soon, I got into my truck and headed toward the Cooper house.

I was armed with all the things I needed to soak off wallpaper. Not only was eight-twenty practically the middle of a night on a Monday—and certainly not a time my brain was able to function past "coffee"—but removing wallpaper was the worst. Tedious, messy, and time-consuming, I hated it.

Nobody tell my dad.

Still, I was ready. At the very least, the monotonous scraping against the wall would hopefully do the same thing to my brain. Scrape away the dreadful and slightly painful messages I'd been receiving.

Oh, that's right.

Mr. Kinky Sub, as Jayda had named him, wasn't in fact the worst.

Nope, that was Mr. Hammer, who messaged me a very slick, "You're a builder. I'm a builder. Wanna hammer a hole the wall together?"

And to think—I'd almost been excited about the acknowledgment that I was, in fact, a builder, and not a secretary.

I should have known it would be too good to be true.

I took a deep breath as I pulled into the empty driveway of the Cooper's house. It didn't look as if anyone was here, and that had been par the course for the past week. We'd collided once, briefly, and that hadn't even been at the house. I'd been using the spare key under the pot of flowers next to the door all week.

I hated that. I always felt like someone was watching me pick it up and put it back.

This morning was no different.

I hopped out of the truck and checked my phone. I'd barely glanced up from it when I saw Mr. Ackerman walking his elderly Doberman, Dixie.

"Good morning, Kali," he said in his throaty, shaky voice. "Working for our nice, young neighbor?"

"Good morning, Mr. Ackerman." I smiled. "Yes, sir, I am."

"Good, good. Lovely young man. Cute kids, too. He'd be good for you."

Ahh, there it was. "That would be completely unprofessional of me."

"Only when you're working for him." He cackled,

winked, and tipped his ever-present tweed cap at me. "Have a good day, Kali."

"You, too, Mr. Ackerman." I smiled as he walked past the car, a whistle filling the air. When he'd gone far enough that he couldn't see me and nobody else was around, I bent down and retrieved the little, silver key from beneath the almost-empty flowerpot.

It clicked in the door, and when I pushed it open, I dropped the key in the blue dish on the side table and headed back for my things. Since I knew it would take me the best part of the day to strip off the walls and figure out the state of them beneath that paper, I'd only brought that stuff with me.

I dragged the box inside, shut the door, and headed upstairs. I was used to the house being quiet—a Barbie doll on the stairs? Not so much.

"Fucker!" I snapped, hissing as the sharp feel of the doll's nose dug into the ball of my foot.

You know what? Everyone always said about Lego being hell to step on—they never said a damn word about Barbie's face.

I wonder how she felt whenever Ken wanted her on his face.

Ouch.

I gently nudged the bitch doll to the side and finished my journey up the stairs and into Ellie's room.

Making sure there were no offending Barbies on the floor in here, I put my bag down, and got to work.

"But I wanna jooooosh!"

I startled, turning toward the door.

"Get inside, please," Brantley's voice echoed up the stairs.

"I. Wanna. Joosh!"

"Elijah Cooper, get inside right this second."

"No!"

Wide-eyed, I scraped a piece of wallpaper off.

"Fine, then you can stand outside on the front steps and everyone will see how silly you are."

The door shut.

My jaw dropped, and I looked Ellie's bedroom door.

Did he just shut him outside?

Banging against something downstairs confirmed that to be true.

"Dad! Daddy! Daddy, pwease let me in!" Eli's voice grew thicker. "Daddy!"

The door opened. "Are you going to come in nicely now?"

I didn't hear his response, but I heard Brantley say, a lot quieter, "Now, ask nicely for a juice and I'll get you on."

I heard nothing more, so I went back to scraping the paper off the wall.

"Is that Kawi's car outside?" Ellie's little voice asked.

"Yes." The sound of cupboards opening and closing accompanied Brantley's voice. "She's in your room right now."

She gasped. "Can I go say hi?"

Hesitation, and then, "No, let her work."

"I wanna say hiiiiii."

"I want to put the groceries away, but sometimes it sucks, okay? I'm sure she'll come down and say hi soon."

"I wanna say hi now."

I squeezed my eyes shut. Ugh—I didn't like kids. I never had, even when I was a kid. But here I was, contemplating going down there right now, because her little, lispy voice was making me want to.

"Ellie…"

I put down my scraper on the windowsill and turned to go downstairs. Honestly, I needed some water anyway, so it killed two birds with one stone.

"Daddy…"

"Hey," I said, stepping slowly into the kitchen. "Do you mind if I get some water?"

Brantley turned to look at me. Relief flitted across his face, mixed with the hint of happiness. "Hi—of course. There are some bottles in the fridge. Did we disturb you?"

"Not at all," I half-lied. "Thanks." I grabbed a bottle and looked at Ellie, smiling. "Hey, Ellie. Hey, Eli."

Eli's eyes widened. "Hi." He looked away and down at the floor.

"Hi, Kawi!" Ellie bounced on the balls of her feet. "Are you doing my bedwoom?"

"I'm pulling all the horrible paper off the walls." I uncapped the water. "Do you wanna come see?"

Eli narrowed his eyes and answered before she could. "Did you do my woom?"

"Not yet. One room at a time."

"Why you do Ewwie's first?"

"Eenie meenie miny mo," I answered, keeping my expression straight. "Next time, I'll do yours first, okay?"

He side-eyed me, putting the straw of his juicebox in his mouth and sucking on the apple juice instead of answering me.

Ellie rolled her eyes. "He's so gwumpy. Can I see my woom?"

Their inability to say 'r' correctly was nothing less than completely adorable.

Just like the dimple that indented her right cheek when she grinned hopefully at me.

I glanced at Brantley.

He shrugged a shoulder. "As long as it's not dangerous."

"Nothing can be more dangerous than my shock when I stomped on Barbie's face this morning."

"Welcome to my life." He smirked, his turquoise eyes glinting enticingly.

Lord, I hoped it wasn't.

"Come on, Ellie." I motioned for her to follow me. "Just look, okay? Don't touch."

"Okay, Kawi. No touching."

"That's right." I fought the smile as her tiny stomps followed me up the stairs. "See? It's not great. Just the paper from the walls."

She sighed heavily. "I fort you might be done."

I laughed. "No, not yet. It's going to take a couple of weeks."

"How many sweeps is that?"

"Sweeps?"

"Yeah. Sweeps." She put her hands together between her shoulder and head and fake-snored.

"Ahhh. Sleeps." I nodded, picking my scraper up in my right hand and my sponge from my bucket in the left. I squeezed. "I'm not sure. Sometimes, it doesn't go right so it takes a bit longer. Can I tell you when I'm nearly done?"

She blinked at me. "'Kay, but not too wong, okay?"

"Okay."

"Are you doing my woom first?"

"I'm doing both yours and Eli's at the same time."

She wrinkled up her face, causing her nose to crinkle in the most adorable way. "I want mine first."

I pressed my sponge against the wall and put it back in the bucket before I scraped the paper. "Sorry, Ellie. It's fair if I do them at the same time. Besides, I need to let your walls dry before I can get them ready to paint. It's a lot of work, so it's easier if I share it."

She sniffed. "What are you doing wight now?"

"Getting rid of this old paper. See?" I pulled the scraper away and took the edge of the damp paper between my fingers. I pulled it down, tearing it away from the wall and dumping it onto the floor.

"Wow," she whispered. "Can I had a go?"

The way she spoke killed me. "At pulling the paper?"

"All of it."

I shook my head. "The scraper is sharp. Come see." I bent to one knee and held it up. "Much too sharp for little girls. Why don't you have a go with the sponge, I'll scrape, then I'll let you rip some paper off?"

She clasped her hands in front of her body,

swayed, and looked away. Contemplation crossed her tiny features before she grabbed her dress. "My dwess might get dirty."

The princess room made a lot of sense.

"Nope. And if you're careful, it won't even get wet."

"Are you sure?"

"Sure as sure can be."

She sighed. "Okay, but if my dwess gets wet or dirty, I'm telling Daddy."

"I can't argue with that. Grab the sponge," I instructed. "And squeeze it really, really hard."

Ellie lifted the sponge as high as she could and squeezed.

Water splashed.

Everywhere.

She squealed as it splatted her dress.

"Okay, not that high." I lowered her hands. "Right there. It's okay, it's just water. It'll dry."

She looked at me dubiously, but tried again, albeit with a few scathing looks at the wet spots on her very pretty dress. "Like this?"

"Yes!" I smiled as she squeezed the sponge's excess water out a couple inches above the bucket. "Now, rub this bit of wall here and get the paper wet. You might have to do it a couple times."

She scooted over.

She kicked the bucket.

I just caught it before it splashed everywhere—not that it saved my booted feet, of course.

Awesome. I now had to spend the rest of the day with wet shoes and wet boots.

"I'm sowwy!" Ellie looked at me with wide eyes.

"I didn't see it!"

Reason number two I disliked kids. They didn't "see" anything.

"It's okay," I said, moving the bright red bucket out of the tiny tornado's path of destruction. "It's just water, right? You should wash the wall now before the sponge gets too dry, okay?"

"Okay. Here?"

"Right there."

Ellie wiped the sponge across the wall a few times. "Wet enuss?"

I touched my fingertips to it. Only just. "Perfect," I said to her.

She grinned.

"Fingers out the way," I instructed. "Just in case."

She held her arms above her head…And dropped the sponge into the bucket. Water splattered up my leg, but I ignored it and scraped the damp paper down the wall until it was big enough for her to grab.

"Okay, now, grab it." I gently held it out.

She pinched it with her finger and thumb. Slowly, she pulled, leaning backwards as she ripped the paper from the wall.

"Careful. You're going to—"

Thud.

She hit the ground with her full weight, her butt slamming into the floor and rocking the already-unsafe floorboard. She stared up at me with wide eyes, the bit of wallpaper tucked safely in the palm of her hand.

Footsteps thundered up the stairs.

"What the—" Brantley stormed into the room, stopping in the doorway, gripping either side, and staring at us both before his gaze homed in on Ellie.

"Ellie!"

"Look, Daddy! I helping!" She grinned and held up the bit of wallpaper. "Kawi said I could pull the paper offt!"

He blinked at her—again and again. Finally, he turned his gaze to me. It wasn't angry or annoyed, just…mildly amused and curious.

"She wanted to pull the paper off. I tried to tell her she'd fall, then she fell. She tore it a little too fast." I pinched two fingers together.

He sighed, running his hand through his hair. "Damn," he breathed. "That girl. I swear."

"Are you angwy?" Ellie whispered.

"No, princess. No." Brantley came over to her and crouched down, kissing the top of her head. "I heard a bang and got scared. Maybe you should come down for a snack and let Kali finish her work now."

"What if Kawi's hungry?"

"I have a lunch date with my best friend," I reassured her. "Don't worry. I'll go for an hour then I'll be right back."

Ellie looked at me. "Can I help you aster?"

I looked to Brantley for confirmation. I wasn't a fan of the idea, but if she agreed to pull the paper slowly and carefully, I couldn't say no.

"Paper only," he said to her. "And you do exactly what Kali says."

I nodded to agree.

"And you eat your fruit snack and all your lunch up before I say yes," Brantley agreed, sliding her hair behind her ear. "Is that a deal?"

Ellie sighed heavily before holding out her little hand. "That's a deal."

5

And that was how I ended up with two helpers on Tuesday morning.

Apparently, just taking one twin wasn't enough. Thanks to Ellie's help yesterday, I'd barely gotten through her room, never mind starting Eli's the way I'd planned to.

However, today was a new day, and that new day involved Brantley joining me with a scraper and sponge while the kids used their face cloths and plastic, toy knives he'd dug out of one of the mountains of boxes.

It was awkward. I didn't enjoy having help when I was working unless it was someone in the business or my dad, but it was even worse when the guy helping me was as hot as Brantley.

All the hot guys I knew, I'd known for years. We were friends, and aside from misplaced teenage crushes and a few—ahem—slightly inappropriate adult fantasies I'd since grown out of, I couldn't see them that way anymore. Our relationship was mostly business now, and it was pretty obvious that my dating life was severely lacking in the hot guy department.

Well, the decent hot guy department.

Not to mention we had nothing to talk about. I didn't know a damn thing about him, and after my foot-in-mouth moment yesterday, I was afraid to ask.

Honestly, I'd probably mean to say, "How are you?" and it would come out, "How big is your cock?"

That's just the way it was for me.

And it wasn't the least bit appropriate with the tiny people on the other side of the room. Who were making absolutely no progress with their paper scraping. But then they were using bright pink and blue plastic knives, so what did I expect?

"So," Brantley said, breaking the agonizingly awkward silence that had lingered between us for almost an hour. "What made you go into building? Handywork? What do you call it?"

"Handywork, generally, because we do a bit of everything." I peeled a long strip off paper off the wall.

God, it was so satisfying. Almost comparable to an orgasm.

Jesus. I needed to get laid. Or a life.

Preferably a life in which I got laid. Regularly.

"Interesting. Your dad is a carpenter?"

I nodded. "He loves it all, but that's his true passion. He's the reason I do this."

"It's different, don't you think? I've never met any woman who wanted to go into this field."

"Different is a word for it," I said slowly. "I don't think it's the career I chose. More in that it chose me, and I fell in love with it as a young girl. Now, I couldn't imagine doing anything else. I don't think I could do anything else."

"Really? You wouldn't do anything else?"

"I'm gonna be a superhewo," Eli said, knocking the knife against the wall.

Ellie blew a raspberry. "You can't fwy," she said in that way only four-year-olds can—sarcasm and sass wrapped up in innocence. "Superhewos have to fwy."

"Not true," Brantley replied. "Most of them can't actually fly."

Eli grinned. "I need a cape and then I can!"

"Capes don't make you fwy!" Ellie shouted, pointing her plastic knife at him. "Magic makes you fwy!"

"Superhewos aren't magic! They're super!"

Well. That was a good argument.

"Superhewos are stupid," Ellie carried on. "Who wants to be beaten up by bad guys? You should be a pwincess instead."

Eli wrinkled his face up as if the idea was completely disgusting. "Only girls are pwincesses!"

"Then I'll be a pwincess and you can't come in my castle!"

"I'll destroy your castle!"

"Okay!" Brantley put down his scraper and stepped between them, then crouched down. "Ellie, if you want to be a princess, be a princess. But it's only nice to let your brother in your castle, okay? And Eli—if you destroy her castle, that makes you a super-villain, not a super-*hero*."

Eli frowned.

"You'll be Loki and not Thor."

"I don't wanna be Woki," he said in a small voice. "Ewwie, if you wet me in your castle, I won't break it."

Ellie narrowed her eyes. "Will you save my castle from super-viw—super…bad people?"

Brantley fought a smile.

"Only if you have candy."

"Okay. I have candy."

"Shake hands," Brantley ordered. "Then it's the law."

I raised my eyebrows. The *law?* Wasn't that slightly extreme?

Their little hands met in the middle and they shook three times.

"Do they ever not fight?" I asked when he rejoined me.

He opened his mouth to answer, then paused, looking from the twins to me, clearly considering his answer. "I don't know…It's been a long time since we had a day without fighting. They're so similar, I don't think they know how not to disagree."

That made sense. "Well, I have to admit that's the strangest argument I've ever been privy to."

He dipped his head as he picked up his scraper and laughed quietly. "Don't put your expectations so low. There's every chance you'll hear something way weirder than that before you're done here."

"Really?"

He looked me dead in the eye and said, "Last night, after bathtime, we had an argument over who has the best genitals."

I blinked at him. "The best…genitals," I echoed.

What the hell?

"Eli insisted it was his because he can play with it. I told him we'd revisit this conversation in ten years."

I snorted, quickly clapping my hand over my mouth to disguise the dreadful noise.

Brantley had caught it, though, and he flashed me a quick smirk, his turquoise eyes shining with mirth. Then, he turned away, back to the wall he'd been working on.

My stomach flipped completely inappropriately at the brief eye contact we'd had then.

I swallowed had and focused back on my work.

The sooner this room was done, the sooner I got my space back.

Hours later, all the paper was off, and the first coat of base paint was on Ellie's room. An obnoxious shade of green had been the paint beneath the paper—yellow and red in Eli's room—and it was going to take several coats of white just to cover it up.

I hadn't been anticipating *that.* And that little detail had screwed with my plan, because I needed at least one more day to get that done, which pushed back my timeline by probably two or three. There wasn't a chance in hell I was putting that floor in until the walls were done, done, done.

I yawned as I dumped my stuff in the back of my truck. I'd left the paint and roller after cleaning it in the bathroom, because I knew that would be my day tomorrow: painting and more painting.

What I needed right now was a hot shower. My shoulders killed from all the scraping and holding my arms above my head, and my neck was aching from it, too.

And a nap. God, I needed a nap. Or three…or four…

The most terrifying thing about this was the fact I kept wondering…Would I have to battle the kids all the time? Or did Brantley hear my silent questions to keep them away? Soon enough, I'd be doing more work and bringing other people in to fit the floors and do the electrics. I had my friend, Eric, coming in on Wednesday to look over the electrics of their rooms.

With any luck, he'd keep them out of the way.

I had a burning question: What the hell was he doing here in Rock Bay?

I knew his wife died, but was that enough of a reason to move here? Colorado to California wasn't exactly the other side of the country, but it was far enough from his family, whom I presumed still lived in Denver.

I had no place wondering it. It was none of my business, but I had a big issue when it came to what was my business and what wasn't. More to the point: I didn't care. I was like a dog with a bone when there was information to be had, and I blamed that on living in such a small town.

I always knew everything about everybody, so when I was faced with a situation where I didn't…I didn't like it much.

In fact, I was kinda twitchy about it.

Brush it off, I told myself. Forget about it. It really, really was none of my business.

I tapped my fingers against the steering wheel as I pulled into my driveway. I pushed the stick into neutral and killed the engine with a twist of the key. The echo of my keyrings as they jingled through the cab of the truck, and I sighed, sitting back in my seat.

After staring at the side of my house for a moment, I pulled my cell out of my pocket and texted Jayda.

Me: *Are you at work?*
Jayda: *About to start. Got 5. What's up?*

Me: *Tell me that Hot Dad's reasons for moving here are none of my business.*

Jayda: *Hot Dad's reasons for moving here are none of your business*

Me: *THANK YOU*

Jayda: *But they are my business*

Me: *I take it back*

Jayda: *Why did Hot Dad move here?*

Me: *Idk. That's the point*

Jayda: *Find out*

Me: *You're supposed to be making sure I DON'T*

Jayda: *It's Hot Dad or Mr. Kinky Sub*

Me: *Don't even*

Jayda: *I know your MatchPlus password*

Me: *You're a bitch*

Jayda: **devil emojis**

Ugh.

I locked my phone, refusing to reply, and hopped out of my truck. This wasn't what I signed up. Had Jayda even seen him, or was she operating solely on the Rock Bay Gossip Vine?

Wait—no. I knew the answer to that. She'd probably been grocery shopping an hour after him and now she was a fucking expert in the Hot Dad.

Damn my life, I needed to stop calling him that. It wasn't going to help the awkwardness I felt around him.

I didn't know a hot guy that wasn't my friend. And I absolutely had no time in my life for someone with children.

Hadn't I just turned down a guy on the dating site because he had a kid?

Yes. Yes, I had. I was shallow and selfish, and I was okay with that. I didn't picture my life with kids in it. I was the person who, when asked, "When are you having kids?" said, "Never. I don't want them."

At least, not right now. Maybe that would change in the future, but right now, in the place I was in my life, I was happy with my choice. Jayda was desperate to meet Mr. Right and settle down, but all I wanted was Mr. Oh-Right-There unless he didn't want kids either.

I was weird and I was okay with that. At least, I was weird according to everyone in Rock Bay.

But I was a handywoman, so I was automatically weird in their eyes anyway.

I let myself into my house, dumped my keys on the side table, watching lamely as they slid over the back of the table and onto the floor with a clink.

"Whatever," I muttered to myself, leaving them there until I had to lock the door later.

This was Rock Bay. The closest thing to robbery that had ever happened here was when Mr. Jenkins forgot his pants—outer and under—and ran down the middle of Main Street with his manhood swinging side to side.

What was stolen?

My eyesight. Albeit briefly.

Actually, now I though about it, I didn't think I'd been able to look him in the eye for two years.

Maybe that was for the best.

I pulled water from my fridge and stared at the bottle before opening it. I was too tired to even do that. The work had been more rigorous, mostly thanks to the twins' major fail at getting any paper at all off the walls and Brantley having to finally leave me alone to get it done.

Brantley.

Turquoise eyes flashed in my mind.

I shook off the thought and swigged the ice-cold water. By the time I swallowed it, the memory of his eyes had disappeared, and I made the executive decision in the Life of Kali to order pizza from the local pizza place.

Ten minutes later, I was on my sofa in yoga pants. Discarding the water for wine—I'd give Jesus a run for his money if I didn't have to use my fridge to change it—I put my achy feet on my coffee table and leaned right back against the back cushions.

With *Friends* season five on my TV, I set my phone on my lap and tapped the dating site's app.

That was my first mistake.

My second was reading my messages.

The first was okay—cringey, but not bad, as far as it went.

The second?

"Hot, horny cuckold for you and your dom partner. Will let you chain me to your floor while he fucks you and pretends I'm your boyfriend."

I hit delete before my face had wrinkled in disgust.

Yep.

That was enough *MatchPlus* for tonight.

Maybe my entire week.

6

Two days passed without me seeing either Brantley or the twins. By the time Thursday lunchtime rolled around, I'd finished the base coat on Ellie's room and was about to start the final two coats in Eli's room. Eric was in Ellie's room measuring her floor and weighing up what he needed to do to fix it up.

"Kali?" He poked his head in Eli's room, his dark-blond hair swishing in front of his eyes. "I have a lunch meeting. Do you mind if I come back when I'm done?"

I put down the paint can and looked at him with a smile. "That's fine. You're working on your time, not mine." I winked at him. "I'd just like Eli's floor done so I know when I need to finish painting."

He held his hands up. "Don't worry, babe. I've got you covered. It doesn't take me half as long as it takes you to figure out some flooring."

"Do I look like flooring is my expertise?"

"No." He grinned lopsidedly. "Plenty of other things, though…"

I threw my cleaning rag at him. He caught it with one swift movement and tossed it back to me.

"Don't make me tell my daddy on you," I warned him.

"Your daddy would marry you off to me in a heartbeat."

"As long as you could abstain for six months

without sex with other random women."

He paused. "Point well made. See you in ninety minutes?"

Ha.

I rolled my eyes. "See you then, Eric. Come alone, won't you?"

"I can't promise I'll come alone, but I'll sure show up alone." He tossed me a wink before he headed out of the door.

So much for that *business* meeting.

I shook my head and dipped the paintbrush in the paint and began the arduous task of edging around the base boards between the wall and floor. It was the worst job, and not one I could screw up even now. I had to paint the base boards eventually, and cleaning them up was no joke. The less paint I could get on them now, the better.

I'd barely touched brush to wall when I heard the sound of the door opening and muffled voices downstairs. Since Eric hadn't left yet, it had to be Eric and Brantley.

Crap. I hoped Brantley didn't mind I'd had him here without telling him. In fairness, he was happy to let me get on with it. And by get on with it I meant navigate boxes until I reached the twins' rooms.

I made myself focus on the edging above the base boards before the door shut again. Silence reigned for a few moments before footsteps sounded on the stairs. It was suspiciously quiet for the middle of the day.

Where was the squabbling of the kids? Why weren't they yelling at each other? That was their M.O., after all.

"Hey," Brantley's voice came from the doorway.

"How are you doing?"

I shifted from my knees to my ass and looked over at him. Damn it, he looked good in a white polo shirt and light, ripped jeans. "Hey—good. You?"

"Good." He paused, pursing those full lips of his. "Shit, it's quiet."

"That was my next question," I said teasingly. "Did you leave them in the candy aisle at Irma's store?"

He laughed, a deep, rich sound that sent goosebumps up my bare legs. "No. I'm sure she wouldn't appreciate that."

"I don't know. It'd give Mr. Pickles something else to chase than customers' ankles."

"Mr—oh, that cat."

"Ah, you've met the town's resident sweetheart."

Another laugh. "Fortunately, I was wearing jeans. Protected myself well."

"Smart," I agreed. "Where are the twins, if not terrorizing Mr. Pickles?"

"Trial afternoon at daycare," he said slowly. "No preschool in Rock Bay apparently."

I shook my head. "Nothing until Kindergarten. Not enough kids in the area. Are they at Summer's?"

"How do you—never mind. Small town." His lips quirked. "Would you believe she knew everything about me before I'd even walked through the door?"

I dragged my lower lip between my teeth, grinning.

His eyes flickered down.

I think.

Damn, I'd been looking at plain walls for too long.

"Absolutely. Half the town probably know your social security number and birth weight by now."

His eyes widened, making the turquoise hue of his irises seem ten times brighter. "Seriously?"

The shock that saddled his expression made me giggle. "No. I'm messing with you. But don't put it past Irma…Or Marcie at the Coastal."

He relaxed, shoulders slumping, but he laughed lightly at the mention of Marcie. "Ah, yes. We just met for the first time. I saw she did take-out lunch on my way out of Summer's place and stopped in."

"My condolences," I offered. "It's always stressful to meet Marcie for the first time. So I hear. And see when she deals with people's unruly dates."

"Unruly dates?" He quirked a dark eyebrow. "Experience with that?"

I held up a hand and fluttered my eyes shut. "Don't. Just, don't."

He laughed. "Story for another time, right?"

"Sure, if by 'another time' you mean never."

A lopsided, half-grin took over his face, making his eyes sparkle. "She heard you're working for me—but you're not surprised at that, are you?"

"About as surprised as if you told me the temperature outside feels like we're halfway up Satan's ass."

That grin turned into another bout of laughter. Goosebumps tripled in quantity at the sound as they took over my arms. God, I wouldn't look colder if I were naked in the Arctic.

"Well, she gave me twice the amount of food she should have, and ordered me to make sure you were well fed. Apparently, she's able to make me wish I was never born if I don't."

"She's feisty."

"No kidding. Thanks for the warning."

"Write me a list of the places you need to go next, and I'll give you the rundown." I grinned.

"I'll make sure I do." He folded his arms across his chest. "So, I have lunch for you downstairs. It beats eating alone. Care to join me?"

I glanced over him quickly.

I'd had worse offers—and dates, lately. Not that this was a date. No, this was Mar—

Shit the bed. She knew what she was doing here.

I was going to kick her ass next time I saw her.

Just not too hard. 'Cause, you know. She saved my ass more times than she needed hers kicked.

"Let me finish up this edging, then I'll meet you downstairs," I said. "Is that okay?"

He nodded. "She said it's your favorite."

"Oh my god, she made her pasta?"

"I asked her what was the best, and she said the pasta you love."

I bit the inside of my cheek. "Is it unprofessional if I say screw it, I'll finish this after pasta?"

A smile crept back onto his face. "I won't tell if you don't. Take it as my apology for my kids terrorizing you at the start of the week."

"I wouldn't say they terrorized me," I said slowly, laying my brush on the side of the roller tray. I set the lid on the paint can and pushed it in just enough I'd be able to pop it off again without trouble.

"You're too nice." His eyes twinkled. "You can say it how it is—I won't be offended. Fuck knows they terrorize me at seven a.m. every day."

"I'm maintaining my stance," I replied, trying not to meet his eyes, because I knew I'd get butterflies if I did.

There was something about the way his damn eyes sparkled.

"It's best if I finish this edging." I picked the brush back up. "I'll be down in a few minutes. I don't have much left on this wall."

He glanced at the wall and where I was sitting. "Sounds good. I have some work to handle—I'll keep it warm."

"You don't have to wait for me."

"Kali," he said, smirking. "By the time I get stuck into my email, you'll the one waiting."

"Wow. You know how to charm a lady."

He laughed. "Come down when you're ready." He turned away, giving me another view of that tight ass of his.

I sighed, turning back to the wall.

Damn, that ass.

Twenty minutes later, I made my way downstairs.

Brantley sat at the kitchen table, his phone wedged between his ear and his shoulder, typing at his computer. "Yes, well I can't deal with this currently. I haven't yet been to the office here… I still have a week…I understand that, but—" He glanced at me. "Yes, sir. Understood. Can we continue this? I have a private appointment right now… Yes. Goodbye."

He pulled the phone from its perch, tapped the

screen and placed it face-down on the table. Offering me a tight smile, he closed the laptop and pointed to the microwave. "Sixty seconds and it'll be perfect."

I raised my eyebrows. "Did I interrupt an important call?"

His nostrils flared as he inhaled, but he shook his head. "My boss trying to get me back to work at my new office before I'm able to. The office managed before me, they can wait a few more days until I can get there."

"The twins?" I asked softly.

He hit the button on the microwave. The light came on with the whirr of the machine, revealing two of Marcie's pots of pasta. "Yep. I tried to source a nanny around here before I moved, but that was surprisingly difficult."

"Yeah, there isn't a lot here." I slid into a seat at the table.

"Let me guess," he said, amusement tinging his tone. "There's not a market for it."

"Oh my god, how did you know?"

He glanced over his shoulder, dark hair almost flipping into his eyes, and smirked. "Lucky guess."

I laughed, resting my chin on my hand. The table was hard on my elbow. "Summer is who we all use. It was her mom before her, and I think *her* mom before her."

"Is there anything in Rock Bay that isn't a family business?" Brantley pulled the two trays out carefully. He spilled the pasta onto two plates before setting them in front of me with cutlery.

"Thank you." I flashed him the hint of a smile. "Actually, that's a great question. I basically took after my dad because I didn't have much choice. I think the same was for Summer—her dad worked a lot so she was always with her mom, then worked for her when she got older. Hmm." I stabbed my fork into some pasta. "Have you been to Corkys? The Irish Bar?"

"No. I can't say that's a place I'd like the twins to explore."

"Because it's a bar or because they'd terrorize it?"

"Because I like to drink in peace," he replied wryly, a smile matching his tone stretching across his tone.

I fought not to snort as I ate and laughed at the same time. "Well, Corkys isn't. Paddy—not his real name, by the way—opened it about five years ago. Got pissed off with all the fake Irish in the North-East, apparently."

"I thought they were real Irish." Brantley paused. "And isn't that ironic given his fake name?"

"Kinda, but he's actually Irish. Accent and everything."

"Fair enough. What about the other businesses in town?"

I ate as I thought. "There's Delia's Diner. She's more on the road out of town, but still technically in Rock Bay. Her grandma was Delia, her mom Delilah, and her Della."

"I see the pattern there."

I rolled my eyes. "It's like the Kardashians heard of them and tried to out-name them."

"I can honestly say I couldn't give a rat's ass about that family."

"You should try it. It's a great stress reliever, because as long as you watch, you know your life will never be as much of a train wreck as their's."

Brantley laughed, sipping some water. "I'll remember that. Sorry—did you want a drink? I'm not used to guests who don't demand everything in sight."

"I'm fine." My lips twisted. "Anyone else in town you want to know about? That might be easier."

He inclined his head to me, eyes twinkling. "Mrs. Simpson at the Post Office."

"Ah! Family business there, too. Nobody but a Simpson has run that office for a hundred years."

"Seriously?"

"Ask Mr. Ibetger at the library."

Brantley finished his lunch and, pushing it to the side, wiped at his mouth with his thumb. "I have no intention of going near a library, with or without my kids."

"Shame. He knows everything there is to know about Rock Bay."

"Are you saying you don't want to tell me everything about this town?"

I stilled. When I met his eyes, the now-strangely-familiar twinkle of amusement shined back at me.

He was teasing me.

The shit.

"Absolutely," I answered. "This conversation is positively dreadful. In fact, if Slughorn's hourglass was sitting between us, it'd be moving slower than a sloth."

"Yet the sand will still fall quicker than when I argue with my kids about the benefit of drinking water over apple juice."

Oh. He just Pottered me.

Sigh.

"Well played," I replied. Then, I sighed. "That's

really a fight you have?"

"You're not around kids much, are you?" He smirked. "It's a daily conversation. I could record my responses and shower while the argument happens at this point."

"See—that's why I'm not around kids much." I put down my fork and wiped my mouth with a napkin from the center of the table. "Thank you for bringing back lunch."

He held up his hands. "Thank Marcie. I don't think I had a say in the matter."

"You'll find you generally don't where she's concerned. Don't worry. You'll get used to it." I stood and picked up my plate. "I need to get back to work now."

"Let me take it." His chair scraped along the floor when he got up. "Here." He took the plate from me and set it next to the sink. "By the way, Kali?"

"Yeah?" I paused, one foot in front of the other.

"You've got a little…" He motioned to his cheek. "Sauce. On paint. Right here."

Frowning, I rubbed at my cheek.

"No. Shit. The other cheek." He tapped his left one.

I rubbed there, too, but he shook his head, clearly fighting a smile if the twitching of his lips was anything to go by.

"No, hold on." He swiped a napkin and moved toward me. My breath hitched when he stopped right in front of me, just inches from me. His steady hand held the napkin, and my eyes followed its path as it came closer and closer to my cheek.

Gently, he wiped over my cheek, right by my ear.

His gaze glanced toward mine for a second. One that was somehow long enough to make my heart stutter.

"Well," he said, tilting his head to get a better look, "I got the sauce. I think the paint is dry."

"How did that even happen? I'm right-handed," I muttered, touching my fingers to where the napkin had just been.

Lips curved, he stepped back, crumpling the paper towel in his hand. "That's what I'd like to know."

"Let me know if you ever find out." I moved away from him, closer to the door. "I'll be painting. Maybe a bit of drilling to get rid of some stuff in Eli's wall. Let me know if I disturb you."

He waved his hand, setting his plate on the counter. "If you disturb me, I'll go out. I can work anywhere—you kinda need to be here."

Over his shoulder, he shot me a stomach-flipping smile that reached his eyes. One that made his eyes flash with laughter. One that put itself firmly in my "Must Resist" book.

"Good point."

He turned.

Our eyes met.

He winked.

Me?

I basically ran up the stairs.

7

"How's it going?" Mom put a box of chocolate cookies in her cart. It looked out of place among all the green, leafy veg that she currently had in there.

Yes, I was grocery shopping with my stepmother. I was guilted into it by my father who insisted I put chips in my cart then put them in her car. How he thought I'd do that, I didn't know.

"That's not on your diet," I pointed out.

She fluffed her hair. "What your father doesn't know and all that."

I grabbed a bag of his favorite chips. "You know these are going in your trunk, don't you?"

"And I shall pretend not to know when he unpacks the bags," she replied smoothly. "That's marriage, honey. We pretend we don't know that the other is cheating on our agreed upon diet."

I snorted. "I hope wedding vows are rewritten to include that."

"You and women everywhere. Now, tell me how this new job is going. I believe I saw him in the store yesterday. He's very handsome, isn't he?"

"I didn't notice," I lied, examining the nutritional values of a bag of Cheetos.

At least, I pretended to read it.

Mom snatched the bag out of my hand. "Kali Hancock, don't you lie to me."

"I'm not."

"Your ears are redder than a boiling lobster. He's cute, huh?"

"He's a little young for you." I took back the Cheetos and dumped them in my cart.

"We all have a little cougar in us." She chuckled, grabbing a bag for herself.

Wow. Talk about cheating on the diet.

"One, ew." I waggled my finger at her. "Two, yes, okay, fine. He's handsome. Are you happy now?"

"What's he doing in Rock Bay?"

"Ah, well, that I think I can answer." I paused. "I kinda put my foot in it the first time we met."

She mock-gasped. "And you didn't tell us at dinner last week?"

"Of course not. You were too busy dropping hints at Dad about your anniversary."

"Thanks for the evening, by the way."

"You're welcome. At least he paid."

She laughed. "Always a bonus. Now, back to Brantley."

I wasn't even going to ask how she knew his name. I was surprised she didn't know why he was here. "We were talking after I'd seen the rooms and I asked how he ended up in Rock Bay. He doesn't have family here, and he doesn't have a ring, so naturally…"

"Oh dear, Kali."

"Oh dear is a nice way to put it," I agreed. "I put my foot in my mouth and chewed up to my damn ankle. The twins' mom died two and a half years ago."

"Poor thing," she murmured. "And those poor babies. Is he here for a fresh start?"

I shrugged. "I didn't exactly carry on that line of questioning. I figured I'd screwed up enough for one meeting. Besides, it's none of my business."

"Does he work?"

"He mentioned it today. Something about his boss wanting him to go back. He's struggling with daycare options. I think he's used to having a nanny back in Denver."

"Hmm."

I side-eyed her. "What's that mean?"

"A nanny. If he can afford that as a single parent, he must be quite financially comfortable."

"No." I stopped smack-bang in the middle of the aisle and pointed my finger at her. "No, absolutely not. Do not even go down that line of thinking."

She giggled, a fake, tinkly laugh tickling the air between us. "What line of thinking, honey? I wouldn't dare."

"Work, Mom. It's just work. Besides, I have a date on Saturday night."

She stopped and jerked her head toward me. "You do?"

"Yes. I was giving up hope after a builder asked if we could hammer something else into the wall—"

"Ha!" she barked out. "That's a good one."

I shot her a withering look. "—When I got an email from a perfectly nice young man—"

"You sound seventy."

"—Who might actually be worth two hours of my time."

She rolled her eyes, carefully laying eggs at the end of her cart. "Whatever you say, Kali. You know as well as I do you'll reject him, too. I don't know what you're waiting for, but unless you lower your expectations, I doubt you'll ever find it."

"What's the point of lowering my expectations? I'm worth more than that. Look at me. Anyone would be lucky to have me."

"Your self-confidence is admirable," she admitted. "But you should make sure you don't have paint in your hair before you proclaim that to the world."

I stopped. Again. "I don't have paint in my hair...Do I?"

Mom leaned over and picked a loose curl out from my low ponytail. "Right here."

I grabbed the same lock of hair and tugged it into my eyesight.

Damn it. She was right. And the bright, white paint stood out like a sore damn thumb against the darkness of my hair.

Sighing, I flicked it back over my shoulder. "Well, I can't be perfect all the time."

"Yep," she said to herself, grabbing a bottle of wine. "You're your father's daughter. No doubt about it."

I smirked at her back.

Really...She shouldn't have been surprised.

I wasn't.

Friday came and went without fanfare. I didn't see Brantley at all. That wasn't ideal, since I'd taken over ordering the furniture for him to make sure Dad could match it, and it was all due for delivery the next day.

A week ahead of my schedule.

The house was still covered in boxes, and I was a total loss of what to do. There was nowhere to put it, as far as I knew. I had no idea what the garage was like or if there was any room there. It was obvious his cross-country move had been done by movers, so I had no idea how much stuff there was in this house.

Saturday morning dawned bright and early. Too early. My mom had plied me with her homemade sangria at family dinner, and once again, I'd made bad choices.

At least I didn't have such a huge headache…This time.

A text message at nine-thirty alerted me to the fact the furniture would be delivered in an hour. This was at odds—surprise, surprise—with the three-to-five p.m. window they'd originally given me when they'd told me it would be delivered early.

Because why not? I loved getting my whole schedule screwed up twice.

I filled my take-out coffee cup and tugged up my shorts. It was hot as hell outside, and I wasn't happy about having to work today. I'd planned to not actually do a thing except help Dad with Ellie's bed.

I sighed as I got in my truck. I dialed Brantley's number again, but the call rolled over to voicemail after ringing.

Awesome. I loved showing up at client's houses unannounced. Unexpected guests were about as enjoyable as a bout of hemorrhoids.

God, I was pessimistic this morning.

Ten minutes later, I pulled up outside the Cooper house. His car was in the drive, and my stomach rolled as I got out of the car.

I hoped that was because of last night's sangria.

Dear god, let it be the sangria.

I grabbed my coffee before I shut the car door and went to the front door. It swung open before I could knock.

"Kawi!" Ellie grinned. "Hiya!"

"Ellie!" Brantley stalked out from the kitchen, wearing nothing but gray sweatpants, slung low on his hips. He fiddled with a t-shirt, turning it the right way around. "What have I told you—Kali. Hi."

I froze.

Jesus, was there a part of this man that wasn't completely delicious?

I blinked several times as I took in the sight of his lean, toned torso. Perfect pecs, lightly shaded abs, a dangerous 'v' that teased way below the waistband of his sweats…

He pulled on his t-shirt, covering up his body and forcing me to come back to the here and now.

"Hi," I said, shaking myself out of the daze. "Sorry—I tried to call, but you didn't answer the phone."

"Inside," he said to Ellie, grasping her by the shoulders and directing her to the front room. "Come in. Yeah, sorry about that," he said, gesturing for me to follow him inside. "Eli was playing a game on it this morning and put it down somewhere safe, apparently."

"Ah." I stepped inside and closed the door, then went with him to the kitchen. "I have a lot of safe places. Not entirely sure where any of them are, though."

He snorted, stirring in a mug. "If you were a four-year-old boy who had to give back your dad's phone, where would you put it?"

I blinked. "Where all lost change goes to die. Down the back of a sofa."

Brantley paused, mid-stir. "Hold that thought."

The spoon clinked against the countertop as he dropped it and went to the living room. I watched him go, my gaze dropping to his ass two too many times for it to be appropriate.

Oh, whatever. Even once was inappropriate, but still.

Gray sweatpants—sent from the gods for the viewing pleasure of women everywhere.

"You're a genius, Kali." He returned, phone in hand. "You got a list of safe spaces for future reference?"

I laughed and shook my head. "If I had a list, I'd know where to find all the stuff I've put somewhere sa—damn it. I just remembered where I put my credit card bill so I wouldn't lose it."

His laugh was deep and rich. "Which is?"

"My underwear drawer. That's what I get for being lazy and not putting the laundry away." I sighed and leaned against the counter. "Hold on, let me email myself that."

More laughter. "I'd offer you a coffee, but I see you came equipped." He paused as I tucked my phone away. "I wasn't expecting you today."

"Well, I wasn't expecting to come either," I replied. "But the furniture delivery company let me know they're delivering today and not next week as planned."

He blew out a long breath and looked around

helplessly. "Shit," he whispered. "I have no idea where that's gonna go."

"I called them, but it's already on the truck and it's gonna be here within the hour, so they refused to redeliver."

"Didn't you specifically pick the date so it could go right upstairs?"

"Yeah…Uh, as a sidenote, you should probably greet them when it gets here. I think the delivery note might be a warning about the crazy, angry lady who ordered it." I bit the inside of my cheek when he raised a questioning eyebrow. "Off the professional record, my mom might have plied me with sangria last night and they contacted me very early."

He stared at me, turquoise eyes shining as his lips curved into an oh-so-sexy smile. "You don't look hungover."

"I'll write to Sephora to thank them for their flawless coverage."

He chuckled quietly and shook his head. "All right—I think we can do this. Would you just give me a hand in the garage to move some stuff around to make room for it?"

"Sure. I promise, I'll get out of your hair as soon as it's delivered and I've checked it all. It won't take long." I smiled.

He held up his hands and backed toward the garage door. "Don't worry—I plan to do nothing but try to get through some of these boxes. I figure we should have more than one cup in the cupboard at this point."

That was a hard fact to disagree with. "You do give off the impression you plan to leave at any minute."

"Yes, well, after meeting that damned cat at the grocery store, it's tempting."

"Ah, you've made the acquaintance of Mr. Prickles." I stepped into the garage. Fuck, it was like a sauna in here.

Brantley whacked a unit on the wall. A light flashed and it whirred to life, instantly shooting out cold air. "Damn thing," he muttered. "Prickles? I thought it was Pickles."

"It is." I smiled. "Prickles suits him better."

He lifted his sweatpant leg up and showed me his ankle. An angry, red scratch decorated it. "No kidding."

"Did you step on his tail?" I glanced at the scratch before meeting his eyes again.

"No, I dared to walk in front of him," he said dryly.

"Ah. Yes, such a thing will anger His Highness."

He snorted. "It might not have been my finest moment when I told Irma that if he scratched me again, I'd kick him."

"Been there, done that." I nodded. "Accidentally, of course."

His eyes twinkled. "Of course." We held eye contact for a minute—a minute that sent a shiver down my spine. "All right," he said, breaking it and looking around the full garage. "I have no idea where to start."

I picked my way between boxes, going up onto my tiptoes and balancing so as not to knock over a precariously balanced stack. "Well, usually I'd be snarky and say we should start at the beginning, but there doesn't appear to be one. Or a middle. Or an end."

His laugh echoed off the walls. "You're not wrong. I wouldn't recommend moving with twins. In hindsight, I wish I'd left them with my parents while I moved everything here."

"I can imagine." I smiled and straightened a pile of boxes. "Okay. Let's just shift some stuff around and see what room we can make."

"That's exactly what I was hoping you'd say. Let me check on the twins, then I'll start at this end."

"It is suspiciously quiet," I said over my shoulder.

"Exactly." Brantley's laugh lingered when he stepped back into the kitchen.

I had no idea how he did it.

I got started on moving the boxes. Some were light, so I stacked those first. They were labeled the most random things—towels, baby clothes, pillows, stuffed toys. It was chaos, to put it simply.

Mind you, if I were him, it'd be chaos, too. I guess keeping tiny humans alive was more important than unpacking stuff.

I shifted a box against the wall, hitting another in the process. I just about managed to grab it before it fell, and something clinked inside. This one wasn't taped like the others, and my awkward grab of the box had the top gaping open.

I set it down on top of another. More clinking came from inside it, and I paused.

A part of me wanted to check it, but at the same time, it felt like a bit of an invasion of their privacy.

I peered over my shoulder. Brantley was still in the house, so if I looked quickly…

I opened the box before I could question myself. It was full of unwrapped photo frames and a couple of vases. Pulling the vases out to check over them, I dislodged the frames. One fell flat forward where the vases had been.

I put them both on the floor and straightened the frame. Then, I paused. A young woman was in the photo, clutching two babies in her arms. I felt no recognition at looking at her face, so I pulled it out and looked at it properly.

The babies were dressed in pink and blue, and as I looked over the photo, it dawned on me. This was the twins as babies—with their mom.

She was beautiful. Short, honey-blond hair showed where the twins got their now-golden-brown locks from. Big eyes, a round face, light freckles on her nose.

Yet, the twins looked nothing like her. Except for the freckles and the tint in their hair, they were both the double of Brantley.

"Right, I can help now. Sorry. It's like being a referee sometimes."

I jumped, dropping the frame. Thankfully, it fell into the box and not on the floor.

"Are you okay?" Brantley asked, peering over the garage at me.

"Yeah. I—" I stopped. "You, uh, you have frosting on your nose. Just here." I rubbed the side of mine.

"Shit." He wiped his hand over his face. "Did I get it?"

I nodded. "Should I ask?"

His lips curled to the side. "Barbie and Iron Man

got married. Apparently, Superman started a cake fight, and Batman took offense to it. Rainbow Dash tried to save her, and that's apparently how frosting ended up all over the sofa."

"You had me up until Rainbow Dash."

"My Little Pony. Stupid names," he murmured, then shook his head. "Thanks. For the frosting." He tapped his nose. "How are you doing over there?"

"Oh, I…" I paused. "I almost knocked this one over, then something sounded like it smashed, so I was just checking it over."

He frowned. "Did anything? Smash?

"Oh, no." I bent down and picked up one of the vases. "All fine."

He picked his way through the boxes the same way I had and joined me. I hesitated, holding the vase close to my chest as he reached for the top and opened it.

Hesitantly, he picked up the photo. I peered up at him through my lashes, watching as a slight smile toyed with the edges of his mouth. "You're probably wondering why there's a whole box of photos of her, right?"

"No," I lied.

He looked at me, one eyebrow raised.

"I didn't know all of them were of her, so I didn't, but now I am," I admitted.

He laughed quietly, setting the frame back in the box. He took the vase from me, replaced it, and did the same with the other. Then, he folded the box flaps so it was completely closed.

8

"It's easier," he said, moving away. He lifted up a box marked 'gym stuff' and moved it like it weighed nothing. "The twins don't remember her, even though they know their mommy is an angel. I moved us here for a fresh start, and for now, keeping it all together, out of the way, is part of that."

I didn't know what to say to that. So, I said nothing.

He turned, half-smiling. "You look like you pity me."

"I don't know that pity is the right word," I said quietly, straightening the picture frame box up. "I feel bad for you. And the twins, obviously."

"I've accepted it. Honestly, the hardest part of everything was the adjustment after she'd died. She did most of the parenting while I worked, and all of a sudden, I had these two people who now needed me to do stuff I'd never done before. I had help, but…" He sighed and shrugged a shoulder. "Every time my family or friends looked at me, it was with pity. I'd proposed to her before she got pregnant, then when they were eight months old, we found out about her cancer."

"I'm sorry." I let my fingers fall from the box.

"I was ready for it. It was hard, but now I finally feel like we've settled." He shifted another box. "When they're ready to know about her, I'll tell them.

Until then, it's easier to start fresh."

"It kinda sounds like you're keeping her locked away for yourself."

"I am." He turned and met my eyes. "Like I said—easier. I'll never move on if I'm surrounded by her."

"Did you ever get married?"

"No. Honestly, we'd never even planned it, past getting engaged. Weird, right?"

"Not really. My best friend got engaged when she was nineteen and straight up said she never saw them getting married."

He raised his eyebrows. "Then why did she say yes?"

"She likes shiny things. Oh, and she was really shallow."

Brantley laughed, the genuine sound wiping any trace of sadness from his face. "Fair enough. Is she still shallow?"

I pinched my finger and thumb together, leaving a small gap. "Little bit. And she still likes shiny things, although she tends to collect them herself now. Bit like a blackbird."

"Isn't it crows that like shiny things?" He tilted his head to the side. "Along with small children, of course."

"Crows like small children?"

"What?"

"You asked if crows like shiny things, along with small children."

He stared at me, confusion clouding his eyes. "No, I meant that small children like shiny things as well."

I blew out a breath. "Oh, thank god. I was about to have nightmares over crows eating small kids."

"You're not the sharpest tool in the box this morning, are you?"

"Hey. I—" I pointed my finger at him, mouth open, and stopped.

I had no response to that.

Actually, I did.

I skirted the boxes and jabbed my fingertip in his arm. *Damn it, that bicep is made of rock.* "Move your own boxes."

He burst out laughing and reached for me when I tried to move away. "Kali—"

"I'm going to check on the superhero wedding party." I stepped back, waving my arm out of his reach.

And tripped.

A squeal left my mouth as I tripped over a box. Still laughing, Brantley darted forward and grabbed me before I could hit the ground. His hands were hot on my waist, and my heart thundered against my ribs—from the near-fall or his hands, I didn't know.

He pulled me up to standing straight, and the only thing stopping our bodies from touching was the way I held my arms to my chest. My fingers grazed my neck and the skin beneath my chin, and I swallowed hard when I looked up and met his eyes.

Inches.

That was how much distance there was between our mouths. Between my glossy, red lips and his soft, pink ones. So close that his breath tickled across my cheek warmly.

So close that I could see the hint of darker blue

flecks in the turquoise of his irises. So close that I could see the shadow his eyelashes cast over his skin whenever he blinked.

That I could see the dimple, half-hidden by the scruff on his jaw, as his lips pulled to one side.

"Sadly," he said quietly, still smiling, "You have to be a superhero to join the wedding party, and you just proved you aren't."

"Rainbow Dash doesn't sound like a superhero. Unless it's a superhero on a sugar high."

"But she can fly." His eyes danced with laughter. "You were not even close to that a second ago."

I opened my mouth to reply, but stopped short as the words caught in my throat.

He was teasing me again.

Except this time, he was touching me while he did it, and my heart was going crazy. *Boom, boom, boom.* It beat faster and faster until my pulse thundered in my ears, and I drew in a sharp breath. All it did was dry out my mouth, and my lips followed.

I wet my lips with my tongue.

He glanced down at my mouth. He just barely tightened his grip on my waist, his fingers twitching as he fought the battle between looking at my lips and meeting my eyes.

Oh god, this is wrong.

I wanted him to kiss me. Right now. Out of nowhere. In the musty garage where the air conditioner had stopped working yet again, because that was so fucking romantic.

What was wrong with me?

"Noooo! Ewi! Bwing back Twiwight! Noooooooo!" Ellie's voice reached a crescendo that slammed into me as the scream got closer and closer to the door.

Brantley and I parted like the other was on fire. I ran my fingers through my hair and looked away, my cheeks heating up furiously.

"What on Earth is going on?"

"He stole Twiwight," a red-faced, sobbing Ellie said by the door. She sniffed. "He won't wet Barbie get married, and I need Twiwight because she the bwidesmaid."

At least, that's what I thought she'd said. It was hard to tell between the snot and the crying.

Out of the corner of my eye, I saw Brantley get on one knee and sit Ellie on the step. As I pretended not to look, he lifted the hem of his shirt and wiped at her eyes. Then, he pulled it off, and wiped her nose with it.

Damn it. That should not be a sweet thing to do.

Shame my heart didn't get the message. It swooned right out of the garage.

"Okay," he said softly. "Is that a bit better?"

She wiped her nose and nodded. "I want Twiwight back."

He stood up. "Eli! Come here."

There was silence.

"I'm going to count to five," Brantley continued. "And if you don't come here by the time I get there, your sister gets the remote control all afternoon."

I rolled my eyes. "Such a man threat to make."

He looked over his shoulder and winked.

Okay. Back muscles, winking, and gray sweatpants?

Shoot me down and call me Sally. I think I just

came on the spot.

I was certainly a little uncomfortable down *there*, that was for sure.

I peered at him as he started to count. Yup. Definitely uncomfortable. From the shoulders right down to the dimples at the base of this spine…

"No! I am not watching Sofia all day!" Eli appeared as if from nowhere, and I suspected he was a lot closer than he'd pretended to be.

Brantley folded his arms across his chest, the snotty, tear-stained t-shirt hanging from one hand.

I gave up all pretense of not watching and, well, watched.

"Please give your sister back Twilight Sparkle."

Eli frowned and held the purple pony closer to him. "No."

"I'm not going to ask you again."

"She won't give me Eye-on Man!"

Eye-on Man. Oh, my god.

Brantley sighed. "Ellie, Barbie is going to have to marry Ken."

Ellie folded her arms across her chest. "But Ken was kissing her fwiend." She frowned. "Bad Ken."

I bit the inside of my cheek so I didn't laugh.

"Very bad Ken," Brantley agreed. "He'll have to stop kissing her friend so he can marry Barbie. If you give Eli Iron Man, he'll give you Twilight Sparkle back."

She tilted her chin up, peering down her nose at Brantley. As her little lips pursed into displeasure, you could almost see the cogs of her mind whirring to make the decision.

Then, she slumped. "Fine," she sighed. "Ewi can

had Iron Man."

God, I loved the way she talked.

"Here you go." Eli held out the pony.

Ellie scrambled and took it. "Fank you."

"Now, go get Iron Man, and leave each other alone, okay? You can have a snack soon."

They both nodded in perfect sync. They even turned and ran in sync.

"You'd think I'd be used to that," Brantley said, turning to me with a speculative look on his face. "But…Nope. Not at all."

I couldn't help the smile that stretched across my lips. "It makes me want to run for the hills, honestly. It's really weird."

"That's nothing. Not really."

"What does that mean?"

He threw his t-shirt through the door and moved for a box. His muscles flexed as he picked it up, and shit, this was not in my contract!

"They didn't speak until they were three. Not properly. I swear they can communicate with each other without speaking." He checked the side of a box and grunted when he picked it up.

"Isn't that a thing, though? Don't they say that some twins do have some weird connection where they can communicate without words?"

"I think I heard that somewhere, too." He huffed as he put down the box. "It's weird. I don't know if they couldn't speak until they were three, or if they simply chose not to. Whatever it was, when they started properly, it took them about two weeks to go from saying twenty words a day to having conversations with everyone, no matter who they were."

"I can't imagine them doing that," I said dryly. "They're so quiet."

He laughed. "And to add insult to injury, they can't pronounce the 'L' sound, but if you ask Eli to name dinosaurs, he can say half of their names perfectly. At seven a.m., he told me he was a "vewociwaptor" with "fedders" on his arms. I don't even know what a velociraptor is."

I paused, hands on a box, and gazed over at him. "It's a dinosaur," I said slowly.

He stared back at me flatly. "Shut up. I thought it was a breed of dog."

I tried to glare at him, but there was a playful glint in his eye that made it impossible not to grin. "Has anyone ever told you you're pretty sarcastic?"

"It's how I weed out the idiots from the people worth talking to." He winked and picked up a pink bike. "The idiots don't get sarcasm."

"Huh. That explains why I barely have friends. Most of the people in this town are idiots. Now, I feel better."

"I don't believe that."

"Oh no, they really are idiots."

"Not that part," he said through gentle laughter. "The part about you not having friends."

I shuddered. "I spend all my working hours dealing with people. I do not want to have to do that after work, too."

That gentle laughter got louder. "Then, I'm honored you're here and talking to me when you shouldn't be."

I mock-curtseyed. "As you should be."

He heaved a large box full of clinking things up and set it on top of another one. He looked over at me, a half-smile creeping onto his face, and shook his head. "How long until that furniture arrives?"

I opened my mouth to answer, only to be interrupted by the sound of something large pulling up outside. "I'm gonna go with right now."

"Shit," he muttered, looking at the garage.

"You the angry lady who called and demanded we not deliver this today?"

I glared at the delivery driver and held out my hand for a pen.

His eyes widened, and he extracted a pen from his chest pocket, clicked it, and handed it to me.

I scrawled my signature on the bottom of the paper on the clipboard to confirm I'd received the delivery.

"Wasn't it obvious when she insisted upon checking inside all the boxes to make sure everything was there before she'd do that?" Brantley nodded to the clipboard as I passed it back.

The delivery guy made eye contact with him and gave a quick raise of his eyebrows as if to say, "Yeah, it should have been."

I shot Brantley a hard look before clicking the delivery guy's pen and passing it back. "Then your company should pay attention to its customers. I booked the delivery for a certain day, and that's when I expected it. Not a damn week early."

Delivery guy shrugged. "Sorry, Miss. I deliver what they give me. Take it up with the manager."

"I tried. Hence your delivery note."

Brantley pushed off the side of the garage door where he'd been leaning as I checked all the boxes. "Thank you," he said to the driver, taking hold of my shoulders and steering me back inside the garage the way he had done with Ellie when I'd arrived an hour earlier.

He jabbed the button to shut the garage door.

"Why are you shutting the door?" I asked, doing my best to ignore the way his fingertips sent tingles across my bare shoulders.

"So, you don't terrorize the delivery guy anymore."

"I wasn't terrorizing him," I insisted. "I was simply informing him of all the things he does wrong."

"We can agree to disagree." He released me and stretched his arms over his head. "Let's get this furniture stacked against the wall we somehow managed to clear, then you can get on with your weekend."

I leaned against the wall, folding my arms across my chest with a smirk.

Brantley looked around, then stilled, sighing. "The furniture is outside on the drive, isn't it?"

My smirk got a little larger. "Yup."

"Shit."

9

I'd made a terrible mistake.

Sure, Declan was handsome. He had that dark, brooding look that was the reason so many people were attracted to Ian Somerhalder. He was definitely the kind of guy you'd look at four times in the grocery store and proceed to leave with a tingly clitoris and a hankering for a little time to yourself and Tumblr.

Also, he was perfectly nice. Thirty-two years old, had a great job in accounting, visited his mom once a week, loved to vacation in the mountains, and liked Harry Potter.

Yep, he was perfect.

So, why had I made a terrible mistake?

Simple. He was too perfect. Perfect hair, perfect teeth, perfect laugh—even his nose was perfect. Not a freckle or a mole or a blackhead in sight.

And with perfect guys came perfect problems. There had to be something buried deep down inside him, waiting to bubble up.

I watched him as he talked.

I wasn't listening.

I was thinking about the way Brantley caught me when I tripped earlier.

About how hot his hands had felt through the relatively thin material of my tank top. About how firm he'd gripped me, how warm his breath had been as it fluttered over my mouth and cheek, how—

"Kali?"

I jerked back to the here and now as Marcie placed the check on the table.

"Are you done with that, honey?" She pointed to my half-eaten dinner.

Crap.

"Oh, yeah, sorry." I offered Declan a sheepish smile. "I'm so sorry. I've been a terrible date."

He smiled, like he didn't mind at all.

Hmm. Maybe he was a psychopath?

"No, it's fine. I've had worse dates. Besides, you said you worked today, right? We probably should have rescheduled so you weren't tired."

Mhmm. Were they thinking about another man on your date, though? Someone they had no place thinking about?

I bet they weren't.

Also: he was responding to me way too positively.

Was I nitpicking for the sake of it now?

Ugh.

"You're right. I'm sorry. Here—I'll pay my half of the check."

He waved his hand at me when I reached for my purse. "Absolutely not. If you must, you can pay for date two." He flashed me a grin and slipped his card in the book without checking the total. "Excuse me—I need the restroom."

I smiled tightly.

Boy, he was presumptuous.

I peeked at the bill, pulled out cash, and slipped it in the book. And ran—right into Marcie.

She winked. "Your dad called. There was a family emergency."

"You're my favorite person in the world," I told her, squeezing her hand.

This time, I managed to escape the restaurant.

It was still hot and sticky outside, but I'd had the foresight to wear a looser dress, and now, I was glad. Declan had picked me up from my house, which now meant I had to walk home.

Not a bad thing.

If only I'd brought flats in my purse.

Oh, well. I couldn't win them all. I'd listen to my feet scream at me all night, but for now, I needed to get away from the restaurant.

I made it onto Main Street, away from the seafront where the Coastal was, and heard a car behind me. My stomach dropped—Declan would have left the restaurant by now, and if this was him, it was about to get real awkward, real fast.

I winced and peered over my shoulder. A familiar, black Range Rover crawled to a stop next to me, and the window on the driver's side wound down.

Brantley poked his head out of the window. "Alone?"

I frowned. "Where are the twins?"

He nodded. "Sleeping in the back. It's easier to shop when it's quieter. What are you doing walking through town by yourself?"

"A not so great date," I replied, tucking hair behind my ear.

Slowly, his bright gaze ran up and down my body, lingering on my bright-red heels for a moment too long. "And you didn't drive?"

"He picked me up, and I, um…"

He half-grinned. "Want a ride home?"

"No, it's fine. It's out of your way."

"It's three blocks over. Not Los Angeles."

"Still, you have to go there and then back."

He rolled his eyes. "Then at least let me drive you to my house. Walk from there."

I paused, running my teeth over my lower lip.

"Get in the damn car, Kali," he said firmly. "It's getting dark and you're by yourself. I can't leave you in the middle of town."

"I—"

He looked at me dead in the eye and repeated, "Get. In. The. Damn. Car."

I checked the road and, after seeing it was clear, got in the damn car.

"Thank you." He smirked at me and quickly looked over his shoulder when one of the kids snort-snored in their sleep.

I peered back at them. Both wearing pajamas with dogs on, they each clutched a stuffed toy—Ellie a monkey, and Eli a blue dinosaur. They both slept soundly, with Eli sucking his thumb.

Brantley reached back and gently pulled it out of his mouth before pulling away from the curb. "Damn thumb sucking," he sighed. He glanced at me. "A bad date, huh?"

"Not so much bad," I said slowly and carefully. "More that he was suspiciously perfect."

"Ah, the decent guy. Terrible bunch of people."

I rolled my eyes. "Stop it. I didn't connect with him, that's all." *Mostly because I kept thinking about you.* "I kinda ran out when he went to the restroom."

"You stiffed him with the bill?"

"No! He'd left his card, but I put the cash for my

half of the bill. What do you think I am, cheap?"

"Well, that escalated quicker than I thought it would." He glanced at me, lips tugging up. "Not at all. I was only wondering."

I wanted to roll my eyes again, but in the interest of not giving myself a headache, I decided against it.

"He thought I was tired from working this morning and apologized for not rescheduling."

"And that's too perfect?"

"Yes. I was being a dreadful date."

"At least you can admit that."

"He assumed we'd get a second. Said as much."

"Ooh." Brantley winced. "Didn't ask?"

I shook my head.

"You've had a bad day, huh? Get woken up early after too much sangria, have to spend the entire morning at my place thanks to an asshole delivery service, witness a dispute over a pony and a superhero, then you have a shitty date and have to be driven home by your client."

Well, when he put it like that…

"And I have blisters on my feet because these shoes are new. So, just a heads up, I'll be painting in flip-flops this week."

"They're great shoes, though."

I looked down. "Yeah, they really are. Shame they're painful. Maybe they're the kind of shoes you wear to watch TV and feel good about yourself."

"Yeah. They're those kinda shoes." His dry tone had me staring at him.

"What does that mean?"

He pulled up into his driveway. The headlights illuminated the side of the house, and he smiled at me.

"Nothing. I was agreeing with you."

I would have called bullshit, but he got out of the car and pulled out his front door key before I had a chance to respond.

Whatever. I'd let it slide, mostly because I should have taken him up on his original offer to take me home. The blister on the back of my foot was now dangerously painful.

Well, like he'd said, I'd had a bit of a shitty day, so what was one more thing to add to the list?

I got out of the car, wincing as I put weight on my right foot and my shoe rubbed the sore blister. "Shit, shit, shit," I whispered.

"Here." Laughing, Brantley walked around the front of the car, holding a small, long, rectangle something. "A Band-Aid. For that blister."

I gasped, taking it from him. "Oh my god, I could kiss you."

He raised his eyebrows.

I froze.

"I mean," I started. "Not—you know. Kiss you. I could kiss you, but I won't kiss you. Oh my god, I have to stop saying kiss you. Crap. Never mind. I'm just going to shut up now."

He said nothing. He simply gave me a way-too-sexy side grin, and his eyes flashed with laughter…and something that looked a little bit like desire.

I looked away, cheeks flaming, and got back in the passenger side so I could apply the Band-Aid.

Me and my big mouth.

Why the hell did I say I could kiss him? Aside from the fact I could—and that was before the Band-Aid.

Ugh. Ten idiot points for me.

I crumpled up the Band-Aid wrapper and gingerly stepped out of the car. It wasn't perfect, but it was sure as hell better than it had been before.

"Sssh," I heard Brantley whisper from the other side of the car. "I'm taking you to bed, El. It's all right."

"Mmk," she groaned.

I turned and peeked over the top of the car just as it rocked when he shut the door. Ellie was draped over his body, her head flopped on his shoulder. Her braids hung down her back, and she had her mouth open like she was catching flies.

Brantley had one arm under her butt, holding her up, and secured her with his other arm. The stuffed monkey hung with its tail wrapped around Brantley's pinky finger.

I smiled as he carried her in. Eli was still fast asleep in the backseat, and I watched him through the window. Although I knew he would be fine, I didn't want to leave him, especially with the front door open and the car unlocked.

So, I hovered awkwardly outside the car, probably looking far creepier than I ever intended to. After all, it wasn't every day you had a nicely dressed woman in heels staring at a four-year-old through a car window.

Not one who wasn't their mom, anyway.

Eli rolled his head to the other side, scrunching his face up. He tried to stretch, but the confines of his child seat didn't allow him to, and apparently, this was the end of the world, because he started to cry.

I stilled. I didn't know how to deal with a crying child. Especially not an exhausted, half-awake, crying child. My gaze flitted between Eli and the open front door, but when he cried louder and Brantley still didn't come back…

I muttered, "Shit," and set my purse down so I could open the door.

"Hey, Eli," I said softly, brushing his crazy hair away from his eyes. "Sssh. Daddy is just putting Ellie to bed. Hey."

His eyes, just a shade darker than his dad's, opened wide and stared at me, glassy with tears. It was almost as if he was looking at me without seeing me, because the tears carried on falling.

"Kawi," he whispered thickly, sleep clouding his voice. "Out." He tugged at the straps that kept him safe in the seat. "Pwease."

Uhhhh.

"Okay," I said, I think more to myself than him.

Like, woohoo, Kali! You got this! It's only a child! Go get 'em, Tiger!

I was a mess.

I leaned into the car and pressed the little clip to undo the straps. Eli wriggled out of them before I had a chance to move, and with a tight grip on his dinosaur, he grabbed hold of me and hung off my neck.

Awesome.

Now what was I meant to do? I was wearing four-inch heels for a start. For a finish, *what did I do?*

See, I really needed a cousin or someone to pop a baby out so I had some idea of how to cope with a child.

I was woefully underprepared for this awkward turn of events.

"Okay." Again, who was I talking to? Me or Eli? We'll never know. One of life's greatest mysteries.

I steadied myself on the sloped driveway and used the momentum with which he was trying to escape the car to pick him up. The second we were clear of the car, he curled himself around me. Arms tight around my neck, legs wrapped around my waist as far as his tiny ones would go.

All I could think as I stepped back was that I was glad he'd evenly balanced his weight. And that I had only drunk one glass of wine with dinner.

Thank god for small mercies.

I nudged the car door shut with my elbow, holding tight to Eli, and carefully made my way up the drive to the front door. Another small mercy I realized: the driveway was clearly better made than the windows in this house, because it was perfectly smooth and there was no way I could trip.

After my day, this was a total silver lining.

I'd just stepped inside the house when Brantley came down the stairs.

"Oh, crap. I'm sorry. She was fussing."

"It's fine," I whispered scratchily. "But I can't breathe."

He dipped his head with a quiet laugh and came to my side. "Hey, buddy. Come here."

Eli shook his head and curled right into me.

Aw, shit.

Now what?

"Come on, let me put you up to bed," Brantley tried again. "Let Kali go home."

Again, he shook his head, this time burying his face in my neck.

I sighed. “Help me.” Leaning against the bottom of the banister, I kicked a leg up. “Take off my shoes.”

He looked at me funny for a moment before grabbing the heel and pulling it off.

“Oop,” I breathed when I put my foot down and shrunk several inches. “Other one.”

Another kick up, another heel grab, another tug.

Barefoot, I padded up the stairs with Brantley behind me.

“He’s in my room,” he said. “Left, the end door.”

Sweet hell. Now I was going to see his bedroom?

I readjusted my grip on Eli when Brantley passed me and opened the door.

Thank God, this room was a lot closer to the rest of the house, just how I’d hoped it’d been. Boxes were piled everywhere, but there was a clear space where his kingsize bed was next to a small, single bed with Batman bedding.

I walked around the large bed with bedding in shades of gray and black to Eli’s. “Here you go, buddy,” I said softly, laying him on the bed.

He released me, finally, and curled up into a ball on his side, hugging the dinosaur close to his chest. I pulled the cover up over him, and he muttered something unintelligible before a tiny snore escaped him.

I covered my mouth with my hand, stifling a tiny giggle at the adorable sound.

Brantley smiled, leading me out of the room and shutting off the light. I went down the stairs before him, breathing out slowly and running a hand through my hair.

“Thank you,” he said softly, joining me at the

bottom of the stairs. "It's been a long time since someone but me put one of those two to bed."

I smiled, sliding my feet into my shoes. At least I didn't wince when the back of the shoe hit my blister… "You're welcome. I'm not used to kids, so let's say that was a first for me."

The smile that stretched across his face was genuine and warm and damn my heart for picking up on that and skipping a beat. "You're a natural."

"In everything but my patience, I'm sure." I grinned. "Ah, crap, I left my purse outside."

He stepped past me and went outside. When I joined him, he was holding it up, staring at it. "It's not really my color," he noted of the scarlet-red clutch. "But it's definitely yours, I think."

I laughed and took it from him. "Thank you." I peeked inside. "Everything is here. Thank god for our almost non-existent crime rate."

"I doubt anyone will be trolling this neighborhood for purses to steal."

"I don't know. Anything's possible. We did have a suspected murder a few years ago."

"Was it murder?"

I pulled out my phone. "No. Not even suicide. The guy wasn't even from here. He just died in his rental apartment."

"How thrilling."

"Hey—you don't move to Rock Bay for the drama. Actually, people just don't move to Rock Bay." I brought up my mom's number and hit dial. "You're an enigma, Brantley Cooper."

He smirked. "Speak for yourself, Ms. Handywoman."

I laughed right as Mom answered.

"Yes?" she said. "Do I need to rescue you?"

"Not exactly. I'm at Brantley Cooper's and have the worst blister on my foot. Can you pick me up?"

Silence, and then, "Why are you at your client's house?"

"Long story," I said. "Please?"

"I want a full run-down of the date and why the hell you're at Brantley Cooper's. Then you've got yourself a deal."

I sighed. "Fine, fine. Deal."

"I'll be there in five minutes." She hung up, killing the line with a click.

Brantley, with four grocery bags in his hands, stared at me. "You just called someone to drive you three blocks?"

"Uh, yes. But that's my mom's job."

"Lord, I hope my kids don't say that in twenty years."

I grinned. "She only wants to know about my date."

He laughed and nodded toward the trunk. "Well? If you're waiting, make yourself useful and carry some of this in."

"Uh." I looked at my shoes. "I'm not exactly equipped for grocery carrying."

Shaking his head as he passed me, he said, "Stand there and look pretty, then. But this is basically the corner of the street, and there's every chance someone might get confused."

"Damn you!" I tucked my clutch inside the truck and grabbed a bag.

That's right. A bag. Just one.

I wasn't going to take this crap sitting down.

When I walked into the kitchen with my one bag, he blinked at me several times. "My God," he muttered, probably to himself. "I don't even know what to say to you."

I put the bag down, smirked, and folded my arms over my chest. "You asked me to help. You never said I had to carry more than one bag."

His lips twitched. He pursed them, but the restrained laughter shone in his eyes. Those goddamn beautiful, bright, expressive eyes.

Shit, what was wrong with me?

"You are something else, Kali. That's for damn sure." He tugged on a bit of my hair as he walked past me.

I followed him outside. "Of course, I'm something else. I wouldn't be nearly as interesting if I was the same as everyone else, would I?"

"I've never met anyone as confident as you," he said honestly. "I don't know if it's arrogant or refreshing."

I shrugged as the familiar rumble of my mom's car sounded around the corner. I grabbed my clutch. "If I don't believe in myself, is anyone else going to?"

"That's a very good point."

Our eyes met, and we shared a smile.

A smile that made a shiver dance its way down my spine.

"Hi!" Mom got out of her car.

Oh, no.

"Hi," Brantley said, turning around. "You must be Kali's mom."

Mom beamed. "Portia Hancock. You have to be

Brantley Cooper." She held out her hand.

"It's a pleasure, Mrs. Hancock." He took her offered hand, but instead of shaking it, kissed it.

Mom raised her eyebrows in an "ooh, hello," kind of way.

"Call me Portia," she replied. "Mrs. Hancock is my mother-in-law."

"And doesn't everyone know it," I muttered.

Mom laughed. "I hope Kali isn't bothering you, Mr. Cooper."

"Brantley, please. Or Brant if you like—I'm not picky. And no, she's not bothering me at all." He slid his gaze to me with a sly smile. "In fact, I think I saved her ass tonight."

I rolled my eyes. "My very own superhero. Why does Eli need Batman when he's got you?"

Mom looked between us questioningly, but Brantley only laughed meeting my gaze fully.

"I don't have a mask or a cape. Or a Batmobile, for that point," he replied. "When you figure that out…"

"I'll keep it in mind," I said dryly, stepping forward. "Mom? Shall we go?"

"Yes," she said slowly, taking her gaze from me to Brantley. "It was lovely to meet you, Brantley. I'm sure I'll see you around soon." She gave him her most dazzling smile, which wasn't hard considering she was one of the most beautiful people I knew, and turned to the car.

"I'll see you on Monday," I said quietly. "Did the twins pick their bedroom colors?"

He nodded. "I'll text you their selections."

"Thank you. I want to get that bought on

Monday."

"No problem. I'll send it tomorrow." He pulled a grocery bag out of the trunk. "I'll see you Monday, Kali."

I bit the inside of my cheek, smiling and nodding. "Oh, and *Brant*?"

He smirked, turning back to look at me. "Yeah?"

"Thanks for saving me tonight."

His laugh was like all the best chocolates—rich and smooth and oh-so-satisfying. "You're more than welcome, ma'am." He finished with a wink, and walked inside.

I sighed, turning around.

Mom sat in the car, windows down, and stared at me. "Get in and tell me everything. Now."

10

Rolling my eyes, I did exactly as she'd said. I recapped the date in record time, and when I got done, she groaned and said all the appropriate things as she pulled into my driveway.

"Well, thanks for the ride! Talk to you tomorrow!" I went to make a swift exit from the car, but she jabbed a button and— "I can't believe you just child-locked me in your car."

She grinned manically. "Oh no, Kali. If you think you're getting away with this without talking to me about Brantley Cooper, you can think again, child."

"I'm twenty-six."

"And? You're still a spotty thirteen-year-old who hates me in my mind sometimes."

"I never hated you. You know that."

"I know." She curved her lips. "But it still works as a guilt-trip, doesn't it?"

I groaned. "Fine, come in, have coffee, question me all you like."

"And you'll answer every one," she clarified.

"Fine!" I rattled the car handle. "Let me go."

Laughing, she turned off the child lock and got out with me. "God, he's handsome, isn't it?"

"Mom!" I laughed as I pulled my keys out of my purse.

"Well, he is!"

"Oh my god." I blushed as I unlocked the door. Why was I blushing? Ugh, I needed a do-over for today.

Mom snorted and followed me inside. "He is very handsome, Kali. Just admit it."

"All right, fine. He's hot as fuck. There. Are you happy now, Mom?"

"Ecstatic."

I turned on the coffee machine and ignored her laughter. I sighed. Sometimes having a mom-figure who was almost closer to a best friend wasn't a good thing.

"Now, tell me more about him. And by more, I mean everything. Is he available? Single? His kids? Their mom?"

"Would you like me to Google his penis size while I'm here?"

"If it would help you, feel free."

I pulled off my shoes. "Well," I said, putting them to the side. "Yes, he's single. Yes, he's available. His kids are hilarious—four-year-old twins. Their mom died of cancer two and a half years ago."

"Oh, dear. I remember you said that now," she said softly. "How terrible."

I nodded in agreement. "He said Rock Bay was a fresh start for him and the kids. He literally left everything behind to come here. No family, no nothing."

"Why Rock Bay?"

I shrugged. "I guess he got a transfer with his work. He's been doing some stuff the past couple days I've been there, and he said his boss was trying to get him to go into the office. They seem pretty flexible with him."

"Are the twins going to Summer, then?"

"Of course, they are. Where else would they go?"

"Good point. Now, back to him being single…"

"Mom."

She sighed and propped her chin up on her hand. "I know, I know. I'm messing with you. He's a client and that's not exactly an ideal situation for any woman to step into, is it?"

I looked down and fidgeted with my bracelet. "You did it."

She held up a finger. "Honey, that was different in a million ways. One, you were thirteen. Two, it had been a lot longer than two years. Three, there was only one of you."

"Would it have made a difference if I had a brother or sister?"

She got up and crossed the kitchen to me. She touched her hands to my face with all the warmth of a woman who deserved to be a mother. The gentleness of her touch made me meet her eyes.

"Kali, never." Her gaze never wavered. "I adore your father—all his idiocies and all. And I love you, honey. It never would have mattered to me." She kissed my forehead then stepped back, lowering her hands with a smile. "If you need to talk, call me. Okay?"

I nodded.

"Turn off that machine. The last thing you need is to spend your Sunday half-dead because you drank coffee way too late." She blew me a kiss as she left. "Talk to you soon, honey."

"Bye, Mom. Love you."

"Love you, too!"

The door clicked behind her.

I let out a deep breath, locked it, and went up to bed.

She was right.

I needed to sleep.

If only to stop thinking about the hot, single dad who had somehow invaded my thoughts to the point of crazy.

Brantley: *I need to ask a favor.*

I frowned at my phone.

Me: …?

Brantley: *Ellie has it in her head that she wants wallpaper. She's demanding we go to the home store to look at it.*

Me: *I thought she wanted pink and purple.*

Brantley: *She does… plus wallpaper. She won't let me talk her out of it.*

Me: *Are you at home?*

Brantley: *No.*

Me: *You're at the store, aren't you?*

Brantley: *Yeah.*

I rubbed my hand across my forehead. I needed to go anyway to get the paint, but there was nothing worse than going to Harvey's Home on a weekend. Mostly because that's when everyone and their damn mother went.

Nobody went at nine a.m. on a Monday.

I sighed and hit reply.

Me: *Be there in 20.*

Thirty minutes later, I pulled up in the parking lot of Harvey's. As I'd suspected it would be, it was packed. I was barely able to get out of my truck without dooring the car next to me.

In my defense, the line was there for a reason, and it wasn't for their fucking tire to go on.

After squeezing my way between my truck and the Honda next to me, I blew out a long breath and hauled my purse up onto my shoulder. Judging by the cars here, I was walking into a level of hell I'd promised myself I'd never experience again.

Harvey's sat just on the brink of town, in the area where nobody could ever truly agree on whether it was in Rock Bay or not. I liked to believe it wasn't, but that never changed the fact that the only two times I'd ventured in here on a weekend, it had taken me three hours to get out, because everyone had a question they wanted me to answer.

Because, apparently, I knew better than the people who worked there.

I did, but that was beside the point.

I yanked a cart from outside the door and put my purse in the child seat, making sure to keep the straps looped around one wrist. I wasn't going to make this trip twice this week, and since Eric had the flooring under control, I only needed the paint.

I pushed the cart into the store and blinked as I

looked around.

Yep.

Packed.

With a sigh, I ducked my head down and made my way through to the small café where I knew Brantley was waiting for me with the twins. Luckily for me, the café was right by the front door, so I made it there without being intercepted by anyone with a hundred questions for the resident builder.

"Kawi!" Ellie beamed up at me as I slipped into the empty seat.

"Hey, you." I smiled and chucked her under the chin. "Hey, Eli."

He sank down in his seat. "Hey," he mumbled, looking away.

Brantley rolled his eyes. "Thank you for this. I don't think I can take another debate about the pros and cons of Disney Princesses or flowers and hearts."

"Well, the entire debate would be rendered void if you simply said no," I said.

"That, I know. I just couldn't be bothered with the argument today. Somebody woke up at four-thirty this morning." His eyes slid to a very sheepish-looking Eli, whose own gaze was now firmly trained on something very interesting on the floor.

I gestured to the giant coffee in Brantley's hand. "That explains the entire carafe you have in that cup."

"If only," he muttered. "I need it." He brought the cup to his mouth and finished whatever was left of it. "Are you ready to get this done?"

I pointed to my cart. "Ready to buy the paint. We need it for the living room, too, right?"

He nodded. "I'm considering new colors. My cart

is just around the corner. Kids, come on."

Ellie got up and tucked her hand into mine. "Can I showed you my bedwoom?"

I raised my eyebrows. "The colors you want?"

She shook her head emphatically. "The paper."

"I don't know," I said slowly. "Paper isn't great. You remember how we peeled it all of the walls before? If you get paper, that might happen to your pretty walls."

Her eyes widened. "Are you sure? I don't wanna had a peewy woom."

"Exactly. Wouldn't you be so sad if that happened?"

She pouted, her bottom lip jutting out really far.

I put my purse back on the child seat and moved her hand from mine to the cart to hold onto.

"Oh, no," she said, pointing at the seat. "I wanna sit dere."

Brantley came up next to me. Eli sat on one side of his half-full cart. "Ellie, come here."

"No, I wanna sit dere," she repeated, pointing at my seat.

He stared back at her. "Do you want the tiara rug?"

Once again, her eyes widened. "Yeah."

He pointed at the seat in his cart.

Ellie sighed and held up her arms. Brantley scooped her up and deposited her in the seat next to her brother.

The look he shot me gave away his exhaustion.

Man, someone needed to introduce him to the wonder of shopping online.

"Okay," I said quietly, meeting Brantley's eyes. "If

anyone tries to stop us, you're here as my client and I'm working. Got it?"

His eyebrows drew together in a frown. "But, you are?"

"No, I mean officially. Last time I came in here on a weekend, it took me two hours to leave because everyone who recognized me wanted my advice."

"Ahh. I see. Don't worry—I don't have the patience for that today. Shall we go to the paint?"

I nodded and pushed my cart.

He followed suit. "I forgot to text you their choices."

"To be honest, it sounds like Ellie doesn't have a clue anyway."

"I wanna pink and purtle woom wif hearts on the curtains," she said confidently.

"You gave up on the wallpaper, then, huh?" Brantley asked wearily.

She nodded. "I no want it to peel."

"Good choice," he said to her, right before he turned to me and mouthed, "Thank you."

I grinned, turning down the paint aisle.

"I want wed," Eli said quietly, playing with Brantley's watch. "Wed and bwoo."

"Red and blue?" I asked him softly.

He nodded.

"You want bright like Superman?"

He looked at me, his entire face lighting up. He nodded enthusiastically before he realized he'd made eye contact and quickly looked away again.

I scratched my cheek, hiding my smile behind my palm. His shyness was so endearing—so unlike the child who, the night before, had latched onto me and refused to let go until he'd been put to bed.

Brantley briefly met my eyes. "Superman blue and red it is."

"That was easy," I said. "Hey, Eli, this red?" I pointed to a scarlet red that stood out.

He peered up toward the can I pointed to and frantically nodded his head.

"Done." I waved Brantley away when he tried to get it. I pulled two cans off the shelf and dumped them in my cart. "Aaaaand, the blue…" I moved backward, running my hand along the shelf. "This one?"

He turned right around, saw it, and nodded.

"Done." Another two cans made their way to the cart. They weren't the biggest, and I'd rather overbuy and know the paint could be used again in the future. I also grabbed a very small can of bright yellow and, ignoring Brantley's questioning raise of his eyebrow, put that with the cans. "Ellie, your turn."

Much more animated than her brother, she turned around almost fully in the cart and looked to the other side of the aisle where the pinks and purples were.

"That one." She pointed to a bubblegum pink color. "And that one." She pointed her other hand to a much softer lilac that would complement the brighter pink to perfection.

"All right, done." I grabbed two of each color and put them with Eli's cans. Turning to Brantley, I held out my hands and said, "Done!"

He muttered something beneath his breath that sounded a lot like, "Damn kids behave for everyone but me."

I laughed, pushing my cart forward so it was level with his. "I'm pretty sure I read on the internet that's something you have to accept as a parent."

He slid his gaze to me. "Yeah? Benjamin Franklin always said you shouldn't believe everything you read on the internet."

Opening my mouth, I paused.

Wait.

"Funny," I said, letting the sarcasm seep into my tone. "I come save your a—butt," I corrected myself, "And here you are, screwing with me."

Brantley grinned, bumping my elbow with his. "You sound surprised."

I narrowed my eyes at him. "Watch yourself, Brantley Cooper. Or I might just leave candy lying around when you least expect it. Exactly where certain tiny humans may find it."

"You play dirty, Kali Hancock."

I pushed up the sleeves of my plaid shirt, one by one, and smiled slowly. "Stop teasing me and nobody gets a sugar overdose."

He skipped in front of me at the register, and with his back to his kids, let an easy smile stretch across his face. "That sounds like a threat."

"Actually, there's every chance I'll forget this conversation tomorrow, but sure. It's a threat."

He burst out laughing, putting a divider on the belt. "Your honesty is so refreshing." He put a rug up on the belt. "But, your warning is duly noted. I'm almost entirely sure that stopping teasing you isn't on the cards right now because it's so damn fun, so I'll take my chances."

I sighed, and was about to reply, when someone

tapped on my shoulder. I jumped and turned, only to look into the familiar eyes of Harvey, the owner.

The corners of his eyes crinkled as he smiled. “Kali. Here on a Sunday?”

“Shh.” I pressed my finger to my mouth. “The People don’t know yet. Can you get me out of here?”

Harvey laughed, taking control of my cart. “Anything for my favorite handywoman. Come over to the customer service desk and I’ll get you sorted out.”

“Thanks, Harvey.” I touched his arm with a smile. Then, turning to Brantley, I grinned. “See you Monday.”

He sighed, but his fight against his smile was so obvious it made me laugh.

I waved goodbye to the twins and followed Harvey to the customer service counter.

“Business or pleasure?” he asked, ringing up the paint.

“Business,” I replied.

“Looks like pleasure to me.”

I rolled my eyes. “You watch too much TV, old man.”

His smile was lopsided as he took both my loyalty card and my debit card. “But I can see the look of a girl with a crush.” He swiped my loyalty card. “He’s handsome, no?”

“You’ve been speaking to Mom, haven’t you?”

“I might have seen her in the grocery store first thing this morning,” he admitted, swiping my debit card. “You seem very comfortable with him.”

I took both cards from his wrinkled hand and shot him the hardest look I was capable of. “No.” I waggled my finger at him the exact same way I had my mom. "Don't go there. It's business, Harvey. All right?"

He grinned, revealing his pearly-white, slightly crooked teeth. "Sure thing, sweet girl. Sure thing."

I put the last can of paint back in the cart and pursed my lips at him. "Stay out of trouble, Harvey."

"Me? Never."

11

If there was one thing I wasn't prepared for on Monday morning, it was Brantley Cooper hustling his children like a boss while wearing a sharp as fuck suit.

That's right.

The first thing I was coherently able to see on Monday morning was a suited and booted guy, herding two tiny humans the way a dog herded sheep.

I stood just inside the front door, blinking at the sight before me.

"Eli! Get your dinosaur. Ellie, I've asked you three times now to put on your shoes."

"I can't find dem!"

"You had them in your hands five minutes ago!"

"Ewi stole dem!"

"Eli, did you take Ellie's shoes?"

"No! I don't want her shoes. I can't find my dinosaur, Daddy."

"It's on your bed. Eleanor, put *down* your juice and find your shoes now!"

"But I'm firstyyyyy!"

"Shoes, Eleanor! Dinosaur, Elijah! Now!" He leaned against the banister, pinching the bridge of his nose. His nostrils flared as he took a deep breath, and with his eyes shut, it was easy to say he was already over this day.

All right, so he wasn't hustling like a boss or herding them like sheep. He was more kinda throwing out instructions and hoping something would stick and that one of them would listen to him.

Huh. Maybe it was kinda like herding sheep…

"Morning," he said, much brighter, dropping his hand from his face. His eyes sparkled a little when they met mine. "Welcome to Hell. At least there's aircon."

I couldn't help it. I burst out laughing. It took all my concentration to cover my mouth with my hand to control it. "You look smart this morning."

Smart. Sexy. Panty-melting. They were interchangeable, right?

He sighed, tugging at the lapel of his suit jacket. "Work won today. I have to go and introduce myself and head up a big meeting. Easier said than done when you have to get kids to daycare first."

"I can't find shoeeeees!" Ellie screamed. "Ewi stole them!"

"I did not!" Eli shouted back. "You won't give me my dinosaur!"

"You can had it when you give me my shoes!"

I slid my eyes toward the living room where World War Three was apparently starting. "Wow. That's fun."

"Don't," Brantley groaned. "Eleanor, give Elijah the dinosaur. Elijah, return your sister's shoes to her right now, or you go without the dinosaur and without shoes! You have two minutes!"

"Shoeless. Pulling out the big guns," I noted.

"Desperate times call for desperate measures. Which is why I'll be buying whiskey on my way home from work for my coffee next time I have to go in to the office," he added, stalking into the front room. "Elijah."

"I don't had her shoes!" Eli yelled. "She put them under the coffee table!"

I bit the inside of my cheek. Ha!

Ellie narrowed her eyes. "No, I didn't!"

Brantley sighed and got on his knees.

Boy, if I thought his ass was good in jeans and sweats…

I cleared my throat and looked away.

"Dinosaur, now." He demanded.

I peeked back in time to see Brantley swap the dinosaur for her shoes.

"Car, Elijah. Now." He pointed toward the door.

Eli muttered something about it not being fair because daycare sucked, but he stomped off, storming right past me.

"You. Shoes." Brantley gave Ellie a death stare.

Wordlessly, she put them on, redoing the Velcro four times before she was happy with it.

"Car, please." Brantley pointed to the door.

Ellie stared at him, her head turning as she walked.

"Sofa!"

She jumped, moving out of the way of the sofa yet still somehow walking into it.

Brantley rubbed his eyes, blowing out a long, slow breath. "I need a nap already."

I laughed as he scooted past me and put both kids in the car. All right, I enjoyed the view as he bent over inside the car, too.

He slammed the door shut. "You hear that? That's silence. It'll last for—"

A muffled scream came from inside the car.

"That long," he sighed. He reached inside and

grabbed the two backpacks on the floor by the door—plus Ellie's monkey. "Okay, uh—"

Another scream.

"God fucking help me," he muttered, then met my eyes with a wry smile. "You'll be done before I get back tonight, but help yourself to coffee or water or what—"

"Go away!"

"Go." I barely managed to keep my laughter inside. "I got it."

He smiled gratefully and headed for the car.

I had no idea how he did it.

I was covered in pink paint. Honestly, I looked like Barbie had thrown up on me. For whatever reason, today had not been my friend, and today was the reason I never put the flooring in before the paint.

It was everywhere. Not only had I accidentally stepped into the roller tray, but sometime around lunch, I'd dropped the paintbrush I was using to edge around the ceiling and it had hit me square in the forehead.

The bristle side of the brush, that is.

So, there was bubblegum-pink paint on my forehead and in my hair. I was pretty sure it'd managed to drip down beneath my shirt at some point, so my boobs had gotten a makeover, too.

I hadn't dared touch Eli's room. Not that I'd had time with The Great Monday Battle of the Paint.

Driving home barefoot had been a joy, too. The

boots I always wore to work had become my most comfortable shoes, and I'd never actually driven barefoot in my life.

I never wanted to do it again, either.

I slammed my front door shut behind me and instantly went upstairs to my bathroom. The only thing I wanted was a shower—I needed it, too, since I was supposed to go to my parents' to see how Dad was getting on with the twins' beds.

The hot water was amazing as it beat down on me. I scrubbed and scrubbed until I was red all over and there wasn't so much as a drop of paint on me.

It felt so damn good to be clean.

I stepped out of the shower and wrapped myself in towels. I secured a towel turban on top of my head and killed the water. With the rush of silence as the water shut off came the distant sound of my phone ringing.

"Shit!" I jumped from the bath rug to the carpeted hallway, only just making it. The last thing I needed right now was to slip and fall on my ass and break a bone.

I darted down the stairs to where I'd dumped my phone on the hallway side table with my keys. It'd stopped ringing, but I grabbed it anyway and checked the call list.

Three missed calls: Brantley.

I frowned.

That was…overkill.

I was still staring at my phone when it buzzed violently, following up with a shrieking ring.

Jesus. I had to turn that volume down.

Brantley's name was on the screen, and I

swallowed down the mild panic at the number of times he'd tried to call me. Had I done something wrong? Trodden paint through his house?

I wasn't sure, but…

"Hello?" I answered on the fifth ring, only just getting it before it would go over to voicemail.

"Thank God. Kali?" He was rushed—his tone tight, frustrated, helpless.

"Yeah. Is something wrong? I have a bunch of missed calls from you."

"Yes. No. I need your help—do you know anyone who would be able to get the twins for me?" he said quickly, almost too quickly.

I clutched my towel at my chest. "Whoa, whoa. Slow down. Why do you need someone to get the twins?"

The line crackled as he exhaled heavily. "My meeting got pushed back. The other company was flying in from out of state, and their flight got delayed. We're almost done, but it's rush hour and I'll never get back to town on time to get them."

Crap.

"Can't Summer keep them a little longer?"

"No. Something about her grandparents coming to town for her parents' anniversary dinner or she would."

Double crap.

"You're the only other person I know. Can you think of anyone?"

I nibbled the inside of my lip. It stung slightly, and I thought of how I'd have to explain this one to my parents without my mom getting ideas…

"I can get them," I said before I could change my

mind. "They know me, right? I know where the spare key is. I can take them home."

"Are you sure? Fuck, no, Kali. I can't ask you to do this."

"You're not asking me. I'm offering. You'll be what, an hour? Two?"

"Two if I'm lucky." He paused. "How soon can you be there?"

"Uhh…" I pulled my phone away from my ear and checked the time. "At least half an hour. I was in the shower when you called."

Silence for a moment.

"Brantley?"

"Sorry. Someone yelled at me."

Hmm. I smelled bullshit.

"Half an hour should be fine. Jesus, Kali. Thank you so much."

"It's not a problem," I replied. "I'll head over there as soon as I can, okay?"

"Thank you. Hey—there's ground beef in the fridge. I was going to make them spaghetti…" He trailed off.

"Stop panicking. Aside from the fact Eli barely speaks to me, I'm sure I can manage for two hours."

He laughed, albeit a bit nervously. "Keep that confidence. You'll need it."

"Reassuring," I said dryly, heading upstairs. "Call Summer. Don't panic. I got this."

"Brave woman." Then, he clicked off the line.

I stopped at the top of the stairs.

What the hell was I doing?

Brantley: *Summer has spare car seats and she'll fit them. I'm trying to get out of here.*

Me: *I told you. I got this.*

And I did. Summer was fitting those seats in the back of my truck as I texted him back. I tried not to put his panic into a box that said he didn't trust me, because he had to know they'd be safe with me.

Whether I'd be safe with them was another matter entirely.

No, he wasn't panicking because he didn't trust me. He was panicking because he didn't want to be that person who imposed on another.

Hell, I'd already lied to my parents.

No, it's fine, I'd said. Just something in work that I have to deal with. I'll come by tomorrow, I'd promised.

Something else I would do tomorrow would be to get back to basics. Just do their rooms. Not help him. Show up after he'd left and leave before he got home where I could.

I had to put some distance between myself and this family, because as I watched the twins grin as Summer ushered them over to my truck, my heart softened.

I was getting a little attached to these adorable kids, and it was no wonder. They fought like cat and dog, but they were the sweetest things.

Yeah, shit. I needed distance. Soon.

"Kawi! Where's Daddy?" Ellie bounded up to me

and hugged my legs.

Awkwardly, I patted her shoulder. "Daddy's stuck at work, so I'd said I'd take you home and make you spaghetti. Is that okay?"

She nodded enthusiastically, eyes sparkling with a larger than life grin on her face. "Yes! Are we going in your big car?"

"Sure are. Miss Summer put seats in the back for you. See?" I pointed. "Climb up and over."

Ellie examined the height of the truck for a moment. Then, she cocked a leg, put her foot on the door, and tried to heave herself up.

Summer burst into laughter. "Come here, chickee. You're never getting yourself in there." She left Eli standing on the edge of the grass and helped give Ellie a foot-up into my truck. "Eli?" she said, turning back to him. "Come on, sweetie. I'll help you into Kali's truck."

Silently, he walked over and waited for Summer to lift him up and into his seat. She did the straps that went over his arms, clipped him in, then shut the door and went to do Ellie's seat, too.

I swallowed hard.

The gravity of the situation weighed down on me quickly and heavily.

I have no idea how to look after two children.

I mean, I'd known that before I'd agreed, but it seemed like a good idea until they were in my car. Now, I was actually in charge of them, and Jesus—I couldn't keep a house plant alive!

How did I keep children alive?

Two hours, but still.

A lot could happen in two hours.

Like regret.

Summer half-smiled as she came back around to my side of the car. "You're regretting this already, aren't you?"

"Let's say I agreed before I'd thought it through and leave it at that," I said warily. "I don't have the tiniest clue how to look after kids."

She laughed, a tiny, tinkly giggle that made me jealous of the fact I tended to snort more often than not when I laughed. "Don't worry," she said, tucking her bright, blond hair behind her ears. "You'll be fine. They know you, right? Ellie's done nothing but talk about you all day long."

Oh, boy.

"She has?"

"You sound alarmed."

"I am." I laughed nervously, glancing in my truck. Ellie bobbed her head from side to side, singing something I couldn't make out. Eli sat quietly, poking the spots on his dinosaur one-by-one. His lips moved, but if he was counting out loud, I couldn't hear it over his sister's noise.

Summer's smile became a wide grin. "He's a cutie, isn't he? Shy as anything, though. They're total opposites to say they're twins."

I nodded in agreement. "If he says anything above a whisper to me today, I'll count it as a win."

More laughter. She touched my arm. "You'll be fine. Honestly, have a little faith in yourself, Kali. You'll do perfectly."

"Have fun at dinner tonight."

She beamed. "Thanks! Have fun with those sweethearts!"

I smiled.

Honestly, I think it came out more alarmed than anything else. If she was referring to them as sweethearts, they'd obviously snapped out of this mornings' dreadful mood.

I got into the truck and started the engine. "Right. Ready to go?"

"Woohoo!" Ellie threw her arms in the air. "Yes! Wet's go!"

Eli nodded, a move I saw in my rearview mirror.

I took a deep breath and pulled away.

And said a little prayer we'd all make it to bedtime without anyone getting hurt.

12

"Okay, no." I waved my arms. Literally waved them. I imagined I looked like a baby bird trying to fly for the first time. "We're not fighting over the remote control."

They both swiveled their heads toward me. Their expressions were identical—wide eyes, parted mouths, red cheeks.

God, it was so weird.

"It's been twenty minutes. We're not fighting already. I'm trying to cook. So, here's what we'll do. We'll pick a show everybody likes, and then I'll look after the remote." I plucked the controller from their hands.

Or…I tried to.

What really happened was that I wrestled it.

I'm not proud of that.

Several tugs and gentle chops on their wrists later, I managed to extract the remote from their surprisingly-tight grips and held it up high.

"Okay," I said slowly, going to the TV guide and finding the 'Kids' section. "What are we watching?"

"Sofia!" Ellie shouted.

"No, Twansformers!" Eli yelled at her.

"No, Sofia!"

"No, Twansformers!"

Help. Someone help.

"Well, you can't both watch different shows," I talked over them. "You have sixty seconds to agree on a show I'll read out to you before I make a choice for you. Deal?"

They both grumbled about it.

"Okay. There is Sofia the First, Peppa Pig, Calliou—"

"We're not awowed to watch Cawiou," Eli said softly. "Daddy said he's naughty."

Ellie nodded enthusiastically. "Daddy said Cawiou is a little shit."

I froze.

Did she just—

I choked back a mixture of shock and laugh. "Well, Daddy is very naughty, too. That's a bad word, Ellie, and you shouldn't repeat that."

"It is?"

"Yes. It's only for grown-ups."

"Can I say it when I'm firteen?"

"You can say it when you touch the ceiling without climbing on furniture or going on your tippy-toes," I said to her.

Eli looked at me and then the ceiling. "Can you touch the seewing, Kawi?"

Hey. He wasn't whispering!

I glanced upward. "Uh, I don't know."

"Twy!" They both said, clapping their hands three times in unison.

I hesitated, but the expectant way they both grinned at me broke me down. "Okay. I'll try." I reached up as far as I could, stretching right out, but my fingers came an inch or two short of the ceiling.

Damn it.

"You're not awowed to say the naughty words!" Ellie exclaimed, climbing up onto the sofa and getting a closer look at the gap between my fingertips and the ceiling.

"You're too small," Eli said. "You gotta grow some more."

I was screwed, then.

"Looks like it," I agreed. "How about the TV? No to Calliou. There's Spongebob Squarepants—" Hey, a show I knew! "—Or…Paw Patrol."

"Paw Patrol!" they shouted, scrambling to sit together on the sofa. "Paw Patrol!"

Thank God.

I hit that channel, and when an incredibly annoying theme tune filled the air, I left the room, taking the controller with me.

I wasn't going to cope with anymore fighting. Not this soon into my babysitting session. Nope.

The ground beef on the base of the pan had burned slightly. No wonder—their fighting had overridden my ability to make the choice to turn the damn heat down before I'd gone in there.

With a sigh, I scraped the burned meat the best I could and drained it all of oil over the sink. I threw the jar of sauce into the pan, then replaced the meat, and stirred.

The spaghetti bubbled over, so I turned it down so it didn't splash everywhere. There was still silence in the front room which was both welcomed and slightly worrying. I dashed quickly to peek.

They were cuddled together, Eli sucking his thumb as they watched.

I knew Brantley didn't really like him sucking his thumb, but I was picking my battles, and this was not one of the ones I wanted to fight.

I just wanted to feed them.

If I could do that without another argument between them, I'd be okay.

Right?

Right.

I stirred the Bolognese mix. It smelled good, and I mentally patted myself on the back.

Until there was a scream from the front room.

I dropped the spoon, splattering sauce everywhere, including on myself, and ran.

Ellie and Eli were pushing and shoving at each other, and he had hold of a fistful of Ellie's hair.

"Hey! Whoa! No!" I rushed to them and removed Eli's clawed hand from Ellie's hair. "What's that all about?"

"He pinched me!" Ellie shouted at the same time Eli said, "She hit me!"

I covered my face with my hands. "Okay, come into the kitchen. Opposite ends of the table. Your dinner is done."

"But I wanna watch Paw Patrol," Ellie whined.

"Nope. We tried that, but you fought. Kitchen for dinner, please."

They both sloped off the sofa and sulked their way to the table. They did as they were told, taking their seats at the opposite ends of the sofa. I blew out a long breath and searched for their plates.

"Next to the fwidge," Ellie said.

"Huh?"

"Our pwates." She smiled.

"Oh, thanks." I crossed the kitchen for the plates and pulled two out.

Minutes later, they were both eating silently,

slurping spaghetti up. The sauce went everywhere except in their mouths. Over their cheeks, on their noses, down their necks…Right down their shirts.

"Good?" I asked.

They both turned, grinning at me with half-orange faces.

It was like Willy Wonka had let his Oompaloompas free in Rock Bay.

Ellie even managed to get it in her hair.

Oh, dear.

They were going to need a bath.

In hindsight, what I should have done was cleaned them up with a wet cloth and waited until Brantley got home from work.

In hindsight, I was a fucking idiot.

I was a fucking soaking wet idiot, to be precise.

Who knew that saying, "Please stop splashing!" meant, "Hey, splash some more!"

Not me. Nobody ever told me that.

Even reverse psychology didn't work. I pretended I didn't care they splashed more, and so they splashed more.

It was pretty inconvenient, actually, given that I was wearing a white shirt. I should have known better than to do that, because it was decidedly less white than it had been when I'd put it on.

Spaghetti sauce and bathtub water were not friends of white shirts.

Or my sanity.

So, here I sat, on the toilet—with the seat down—watching them as they splashed each other and caused the Great Flood of Monday. They didn't care a bit, of course.

Me? Well, I kept creeping looks at my phone. The time? Was Brantley home yet? Would he retrieve his demons from me?

Time passed.

So did the twins' ability to keep water in the tub.

Until, finally, through their shrieks of delight, a door sounded downstairs.

It opened.

It closed.

I stared at the wall.

"Daddyyyyy!" Ellie screamed.

"Daddy!" Eli followed suit with.

"Help," I whispered.

They splashed each other extra loud.

"Oh, hell," Brantley said, storming up the stairs.

Slowly, I turned my face to his. I was soaking wet, from my little socks to my hair and everything in between. "I made a bad choice."

He rubbed his hand over his mouth. His eyes flitted across the bathroom, from the soaking twins to the dripping wall and the miniature swimming pool that was now forming on the bathroom floor.

Who was I kidding? It'd been forming for the past ten minutes.

Several emotions flitted across his face, but the one I wasn't expecting was the one he hit me with.

Amusement.

Pure, raw, silent laughter.

"How's that confidence working out for ya,

sweetcheeks?" He grinned, leaning against the doorframe.

I glared at him.

"Daddy!" Ellie shouted. "Kawi gave us sketti and a baff, look!"

"I clean!" Eli shouted. "So shiny!"

"So wet," Brantley said, pushing off the frame and shrugging off his suit jacket. He tugged at his tie. "You ready to get out now? Clean hair, clean tummies?"

They both looked at their stomachs. "Clean," they said. "Clean hair," Ellie added.

Brantley looked at me.

"Clean hair," I echoed.

He laughed. "All right. Ellie, Eli, one, two, out." He turned, opened a door, and brandished two towels from a cupboard. "Let's get warm and dry and into bed."

"But—" they both said.

"No." Brantley wiggled a towel. "Out."

Ellie was the first to get out. Her tiny body was tinted pink with the warmth of the water despite knowing it wasn't too hot, and her hair hung down her back in stringy, lightly curled strands.

Brantley wrapped her in a towel, and I averted my eyes as Eli climbed out after his sister.

"Bedroom," Brantley said. "Underwear and pajamas. Give me five seconds to change, okay?"

Both twins nodded. Ellie disappeared into what I knew would be the spare room, Eli into Brantley's room.

Brantley left me alone in the bathroom. I pulled the plug in the bathroom and slowly made my way across the hall. I needed another shower, that much was for sure.

"Kali."

I stopped at the top of the stairs and looked over my shoulder. "Yeah?"

"Here." Brantley threw a light-gray t-shirt in my direction. "Don't stay in a wet shirt."

Um, that was his shirt.

"I can't." I held it out to him. "This is yours."

He closed his hand over mine, eyes on mine, and said, "They'll be in bed in fifteen minutes. You wanna wait fifteen minutes in a wet shirt?"

"No. I intended on leaving right now."

"Don't." Deep, husky, raw. "Wait. Okay?"

I swallowed hard, looking down at the shirt in my hands.

"Kali?"

"Okay," I replied, clutching it tight to me. "I'll wait."

"Eli!" Brantley ushered him out of his room. "Into your sister's room. Let's get changed real quick." He winked at me and pointed to his room when Eli had left it.

I smiled. I was grateful for the offer, but it felt a little wrong to wear a shirt that clearly belonged to him. A lot wrong. He was my client, not my boyfriend.

Why was I agreeing to this?

Still, the sensation of wet fabric against my skin was gross, so I shut myself in his room and changed from my tank top into his looser t-shirt. It was huge on me, so I tied the side into a knot at my hip. It made me feel better, and also had me staring down at myself a little longer than a normal.

Soft gray, the shirt hugged my tits before loosening around my stomach and tightening at the self-crafted hip knot. The material met my shorts at the most flattering point, and I swallowed as I pushed my wet bangs away from my forehead.

Tonight had shown me exactly why I didn't want children.

I opened the door and almost collided with Brantley in the hall. We both stilled, each of us half-gasping as we almost touched.

"I need to put Eli to bed," he said softly.

"Right. Sure." I slipped to the side. "Goodnight, Eli."

He peered out from behind Brantley with a shy smile. "Night, Kali."

I smiled a little wider and gripped the banister. His golden-brown hair was still damp, but Brantley ushered him into the room all the same. He wore nothing but fitted, navy pants and a white shirt. He'd unbuttoned the shirt and rolled the sleeves up to his elbows.

Awkwardly, I hovered halfway down the stairs.

Did I stay? Did I go? I was wearing my client's t-shirt. So many things were wrong with this situation.

"Daddy?" Ellie shuffled out of her room. "I need a bwaid."

Brantley poked his head out of the door. "Can you give me a couple minutes, princess?"

She pouted.

"You want a braid?" the words left my mouth without warning.

Ellie nodded at me.

"I can do your hair," I said softly.

Ellie's eyes widened and she looked at Brantley.

He shrugged. "If Kali can do it, then sure."

I nodded and smiled. "Come on, Ellie. Grab me a hairbrush and tie and I'll do it for you."

I followed her into her room and sat on the edge of her bed with my legs parted. She stood between my legs like she'd done it a thousand times, handing me the brush and tie without moving her head.

Gently, I brushed her wet hair. It moved in thick streaks until all knots had gone, and I separated it into three to braid it. Left, right, left, right, left right, left, right. Lock by lock, I braided her hair until the perfect braid lay down the center of her back.

I tied the end of it, ending the braid with a few swift twists of the band.

"All right," Brantley said softly. "Into bed, princess, okay?"

Ellie nodded, turning briefly to smile at me. I fought my smile as I stood and headed back toward the stairs.

She ran her hand down the one, long braid that now hung over her shoulder. "Fanks, Kawi."

"You're welcome." I smiled and ducked out of the room, heading downstairs so he could put them to bed in peace.

I tugged at the hem of the shirt. It was soft and comfortable, a million times better than the wet tank top, there was no doubt about it.

Reaching the bottom of the stairs, I sighed, hovering at the bottom, gripping onto the banister. I didn't want to leave, but I also knew I couldn't stay. What did I say, though? Did I offer to wash the shirt and bring it back the next day?

God, why did I accept that idea?

I wandered into the kitchen. Floorboards creaked above my head as Brantley moved around, and I leaned against the counter, picking my phone up and checking it. I had a hundred and one notifications, including emails from clients and potential ones and texts from my mom demanding to know the real reason I bailed tonight.

Fucking awesome.

The woman could see right through me.

I ignored the message and replied to an email requesting a quote for a custom-made bookshelf. That was Dad's territory, but I didn't think my mom would appreciate me ignoring her and texting him, so that would go on tomorrow's to-do list.

"Hey." Brantley appeared in the kitchen.

I jumped, almost dropping my phone. My heart thundered with the shock of his arrival.

He fought a laugh. "Sorry. I didn't mean to scare you."

I pressed my hand to my chest and waved my phone in a dismissive way. "Working. I have emails out my ass."

"That's an interesting analogy." He paused right in front of me. "I have to admit, that's the first time I've seen a shirt of mine worn that way."

I glanced at the knot at my hip. "Oh—sorry. I didn't mean to stretch it. I didn't think."

I moved to undo it, but he grabbed my hand, laughing.

"Don't worry about it, Kali. It's an old shirt. Wear it however you want."

My skin tingled where his hand had hold of mine.

Up and down my arm, across my palm, across my knuckles…I practically buzzed with the sensation of his hot skin against mine.

I pulled my hand from his and took a tiny step back. "Thanks. I'll wash it and return it, I promise."

"Don't worry." His lips tugged to the side. Once again, his eyes roved over me, flicking down to the faded image on the front of the shirt for a second. "I wanted to say thank you for helping me out tonight. You have no idea how much I appreciate it."

My cheeks heated slightly. "It's okay. I mean, I have to be honest and say I probably won't rush to do it again…"

His laughter cut me off. "Don't worry—I told them that if they do this again, they'll have to reschedule."

"And they didn't care?"

"They're not allowed to care. I'm the head of the department. They have to do what I say." He grinned, pushing off the counter and heading for the fridge.

"Ah, well, I can see how that would be useful."

"You could say that." He paused. "Hey…I didn't get a chance to eat yet. I was going to order in. Do you want to join me?"

For dinner?

That's not in my "distance" plan.

"I…I really should be going home." I swallowed. "But, thank you for asking. That's sweet."

He smirked, pulling a beer bottle from the fridge. "Okay, I'll rephrase. I'm ordering pizza because there isn't a single bone in my body that wants to fucking cook, and you should tell me what pizza you like, because I'm buying you dinner."

"Oh, boy, that's the most romantic proposal I've had all month."

"I'm guessing you're a pepperoni girl."

"That's presumptuous."

"Am I wrong?"

I hesitated. "Yes."

Turquoise eyes flicked across my face. "You're a terrible liar."

"I try." I pushed my still-damp hair behind my ear. *Kids*. "Honestly, it's fine."

He pushed the fridge door shut and used a magnet in the shape of Colorado state to uncap his beer. He replaced it on the door with a click. "Did you eat tonight?"

I went to answer, but nothing came out.

Brantley raised an eyebrow. "I'll take that as a no."

"It's fine," I insisted. "I can go home and heat something real quick. You might not be surprised to know that my stepmom regularly hands me Tupperware tubs of food."

He paused. "Your stepmom?"

Crap. He didn't know Portia wasn't my real mom. I forgot that not everybody knew that.

"Um, yeah." I set my phone down and my hands instantly went to fidget with the hem of my shirt. "My mom isn't my real mom."

He blinked at me. "Now, I'm definitely ordering pizza."

"No, you—"

He left the room before I could finish my sentence. I chased after him, but by the time I joined him in the living room, I was greeted by the sound of

"Hi, yes, I'd like to place an order for two pizzas, please."

I'd lost this round.

Fine.

I was a red-blooded, human woman.

I wasn't going to turn down free pizza.

My ass wouldn't thank me for it, but you could bet *yours* that my soul would throw a fucking party.

Brantley smirked as he placed the order and handed over his card details. Honestly, he was lucky I had a terrible memory. If I had a better one, I'd be able to buy more than just pizza on his dime.

As it was, I couldn't even remember my own phone number. Never mind any card details.

He hung up and put his phone on the coffee table. "Do me a favor?"

"I already let you buy me dinner without causing a fuss."

"Sit down and let me get you wine."

"That sounds more than an order than a favor."

"Favor…Order…Interchangeable."

I stared at him. No, no, they weren't. "Actually, they're completely different. A favor is something agreed upon between two people. An order is something given by one person and followed by the other."

"Interchangeable," he replied."

"No. The person on the receiving end of the order doesn't have to agree."

"Are you always this pedantic?"

I paused. "Only if the person telling me things is incorrect."

"By incorrect, you mean 'idiotic,' right?"

"Ah, look—you understand me more than you thought."

Laughter filled the room. That deep, raw, rough sound that forced goosebumps onto my arms made the hairs on the back of my neck stand on end.

Slow, easy steps closed the distance between us.

"Kali." Brantley said my name slowly, sexily, temptingly. He set his hands on my shoulders, pulling me forward as if my feet were nothing more than his slaves, until I stood in front of the sofa. "Sit," he said, pushing me down.

I sat.

He left me there, sitting in silence while he went to the kitchen and into the fridge. A cupboard, a clink, the swish of a fridge closing.

Returning to the front room, Brantley put a glass of white wine in front of me. He dropped himself on the sofa, his beer dripping with condensation as he put it on the table.

"Just one," he said. "I know you drove. It's the least I can do after you looked after my hellions."

"They're weren't too bad," I said honestly. "But, shit. I feel like I could referee an international soccer tournament after this."

"Don't. They dive a lot."

"They're on grass. How can they dive?

He stared at me. "You don't watch soccer, do you?"

"No. Baseball is where the tight pants are at."

He leaned back on the sofa and laughed at me. "Of course. All right—never mind. Tell me about your mom. Stepmom?"

I shifted uneasily. I never really talked about

Portia or my mom. Everyone here knew about my family, so it was never an issue.

"Yeah," I said slowly. "But she's just my mom, really."

13

He looked at me. Not judgingly. Not even expectantly. Patiently. Waiting for me to elaborate.

I was ready to respond when there was a knock at the door. I knew that was the pizza—there was only one pizza place in Rock Bay and they prided themselves on super-fast delivery.

Freaky-fast delivery, actually.

Brantley got up and took the boxes from the young guy who was responsible for it. The door clicked shut, and I tucked my legs beneath my butt as he set the boxes on the coffee table in front of us.

"Eat it," he said. "It's my thank you for helping me. I know you're hungry."

I glanced between the box and him. I was hungry, no doubt about it, but there was something about him buying me food that didn't sit right. Nothing nefarious, but it felt…weird.

Still, I slid the box from the table to the sofa in front of me.

Silently, I picked off a slice of pepperoni, watching as the hot, stringy cheese desperately tried to keep its prisoner safe on the slice.

We ate. Both of us. Questions faded in the silence we shared.

Or, so I thought.

"Portia. Your stepmom?" Brantley's question came again after three slices.

Man, he wasn't going to let it lie, was he?

I shut the lid of my box and out it back on the table. "Yep."

"You don't want to talk about it, do you?"

"I never have to," I admitted. "Everyone here knows everything about me. That's what living in a small town does to you."

"I don't know," he said softly. "But I'd like to."

I cast my gaze over him. Over that dark hair and those full lips and that stubble and those strong shoulders.

Those compellingly bright eyes.

"My mom died when I was five." I pulled my wine glass onto my lap.

Brantley took a deep breath. "I'm sorry."

I drained the rest of the wine and looked at the empty glass. Words danced on the end of my tongue, teasing and playing. In the time they'd done that, Brantley had gotten up and returned with the bottle.

He filled my glass. "I didn't know."

"Why would you?" I cradled the now-full glass in my hands. "You just moved here."

"True."

I looked away from him, sipping slowly, focusing on anything but him. Anything but his gray sweats and white tees and muscles that wanted to distract me from reality.

"When did you meet her? Your stepmom?" Brantley asked, voice soft like silk. "How old were you?"

I didn't even glance at him when I said, "Thirteen."

"Really?"

I nodded. Once. "I kinda hated her for three months, then she became my best friend. She's been my mom ever since."

"You call her Mom?"

Side-eyeing him, I smiled. "Of course. I was so young when my mom died. Me and Dad were alone for years. Portia came along when I needed her most, and it's just how we are. She's my mom, but she's a different kind of mom. She'll never replace my mother."

Brantley tilted his head to the side. "Interesting. I love your perspective on it. It's very…open and honest."

I brought my glass to my lips and sipped. "I don't think it's my perspective. It's just how it is."

"You say it like it's nothing."

"On the contrary, it's everything." I pulled both legs up onto the sofa and crossed them, Indian-style. The base of my glass rested on my ankles, and I stared into the swirling mass of my wine. "Portia was there when nobody else was. She guided me when I was alone. She was the friend and support I needed when my father was lost. Our relationship isn't perfect, but she's the best friend I've ever known."

Brantley nodded slowly. He tipped his beer bottle up, draining what was inside it. Wordlessly, he got up, retreating to the kitchen. I cradled my glass and stared at where he'd left until he appeared again.

He handed me the bottle of wine.

Against my better judgement, I poured.

I set the half-empty bottle back on the table.

He popped the cap of another beer. Settled back. Sipped. Sighed. Breathed easy. "Moving on is hard," he said quietly, staring into the brown-tinted neck of the Budweiser bottle. "Sometimes it seems impossible. You just made me feel like, one day, my kids will feel some kind of happiness."

"You think they aren't happy?"

"I know they aren't."

"You're wrong."

He hit me with his bright gaze. "You think?"

"I know." I glanced into my glass before our eyes met again. "Look at them, Brantley. They love you."

"Sure, they do. But happiness is something else."

"They're happy with you. Anyone with a brain cell can see that."

He stared at me.

Really stared at me.

Moved closer to me, closing the distance between us.

"You're a great dad," I said softly, cradling my wine glass. "You have to know that."

"I do," he replied. "But I have no choice. I'm a great dad because I have to be. Because without me they have nobody."

"You don't believe in yourself enough." I turned my head and finished what was in my glass. It clinked against the coffee table. "You're an amazing father because you love them beyond anything I could ever understand."

He met my eyes. "You know love, Kali. I watched you braid my daughter's hair earlier."

"Out of kindness." I swallowed hard and put my glass down. "You were busy. She wanted her hair braided. It was easy."

Weird, to be precise.

But easy, sure.

Brantley swigged his barely-touched beer and put it down. His sigh echoed off the walls.

I shouldn't be here.

I put my glass on the table, closing my barely-touched pizza. I had to go home. His intentions had been good in buying me dinner, but this was wrong. Mostly because I didn't really want to leave at all.

I looked down as I shuffled toward the edge of the sofa. "I should go. I—"

"Kali." He reached for me as he said my name. His fingers brushed my lower arm, and I took a deep breath in.

Brantley's hand raised then fell, hovering close to my hair almost as if he was going to push it behind my ear.

I took a deep breath in.

I wanted him to kiss me, but at the same time, I knew that if he did, I'd probably never be able to look him in the eye again.

"Don't," he said softly. "You don't have to leave."

"I do, I—" The words caught in my throat.

He glanced at my lips, and my tongue flicked out across my lower one. His jaw twitched as he brought his gaze back up to mine.

My heart thundered against my ribs.

Yeah. I needed to leave. But I couldn't. I was basically frozen in place, eyes focused firmly on the mesmerizing blue of Brantley's.

Then—he did it.

Touched his lips to mine.

Kissed me.

His hands framed my face, holding me in place. Not that he needed to. I couldn't move away even if I wanted to, because here I was, leaning into him, into the kiss, into his touch.

He pulled back. His lips hovered inches from mine. I drew in a sharp breath. His hands were still on my cheeks, and there was no way he couldn't feel the way they heated beneath his touch.

Brantley met my eyes for a split second, then he kissed me again. This time, one hand slipped around the back of my neck. My scalp tingled as he wound his fingers in my hair.

This kiss was harder, needier, more insistent than the last.

Like he'd tested the water, and now, he was ready to drown.

I leaned right into him. My fingers found his shirt and rested on his stomach, fisting the soft cotton of his tee.

Closer and closer we became. His other hand trained down my body, sliding around my back, pulling me against him. His tongue flicked at the seam of my mouth, and I let him kiss me deeper.

Let him drag me further into the regret I knew I'd feel the second this stopped.

I didn't care.

My whole body was alive. Skin tingled, my chest burned, my heart beat so crazily fast my pulse thundered in my ears.

Everything else had melted away, just as long as his lips were on mine.

I slid my hands up his body, cupping his neck. I barely swallowed a whimper as he dragged my lower lip between his teeth, leaning back on the cushions and pulling me with him.

His hands went lower. His thumb brushed the bare strip of skin at the base of my back where the t-shirt didn't quite meet the waistband of my shorts. I shivered at the fleeting touch, and—

A scream ripped through the air.

A gut-wrenching, ear-splitting scream that had, quite possibly, just woken the occupants of the nearest graveyard.

The other thing it'd done?

Brought both me and Brantley crashing back down to Earth with one hell of a fucking thump.

"Fuck," we both said.

But, I bet it was for different reasons.

I shuffled up the sofa as he stood and ran out of the room. My heart was still thumping against my ribs, and I buried my face in my hands as the reality of what had just happened fell down onto me.

Shit, shit, *shit*!

I'd just kissed my client.

Oh.

My.

God.

I'd just fucking *kissed* my client, and Lord above, my body damn well knew it, too. Swollen lips, a struggle to catch my breath—an aching fucking clitoris that throbbed inside my little lacy panties.

What the hell had I done?

I grabbed my phone and stood up. I couldn't see my shirt, not that I could wear it. At least I hadn't drunk so much wine I couldn't drive.

God, I wish I'd had more wine. That might have

made the fact *I just kissed my client* easier to bare. Blame it on the wine and not my inner slut.

Yup.

Shit.

I clutched my phone to my chest and went to the hallway to grab my keys from the bowl where I'd thrown them in my effort to hustle the kids inside without losing one of them. They clinked and scraped against the glass bowl.

The stairs creaked.

I hesitated, hand on the door handle, and turned my head back toward the stairs.

Brantley stood halfway down, leaning against the wall. His hand gripped the banister, making his knuckles white. His hair probably looked in better shape than mine, and his shirt was stupidly crinkled where I'd grabbed it.

"Everything okay?" I asked lamely.

He nodded. "Ellie. Thought there was a crocodile under the bed."

My lips still tingled where he'd kissed me.

Four-year-olds: taking you from kissing to crocodiles in under a second.

"Right. Glad she's fine. I, um…" I paused, glancing away briefly. "I thought I should go. It's getting late and stuff, so…"

Christ, Kali. Just say goodbye and be done with it.

He didn't reply. Just stared at me with his unnaturally turquoise eyes—eyes that, if I stood there for much longer, would probably be able to see right through me.

So, I left.

I walked through the door as quickly as I possibly

could without running, got in my truck, and got the hell out of there before I did anything else stupid.

14

Jayda blinked at me. "Well, you're an idiot."

I groaned and wrapped my hands around the coffee cup. "I know that. I told you that like five times."

She leaned back against my kitchen counter, picking up her own mug. "I can't believe I'm here at seven a.m. in my pajamas because you can't keep your mouth to yourself."

I dropped my head so my chin touched my chest and closed my eyes. "I didn't kiss him deliberately."

"No, no. I'm sure you slipped on a banana peel and your mouth landed on his."

"He kissed me."

"That makes the world of difference."

"I know it does. Thank you."

She stared at me. "Kali…That's called sarcasm."

"I know." I propped my chin up on my hand. "I'm pretending it wasn't so I feel better about my monumental fuck up."

Jayda pushed off the counter and joined me at the table. "Is it really that bad? So, you kissed the guy. He's handsome, he's single—you're single. Who are you hurting?"

"Well, nobody, but—"

"Suck it up, buttercup. If you don't want it to be awkward, put your mouth back in its cage."

"It's the number one rule," I said before she could carry on with her speech that would ultimately end with telling me to pull up my big girl panties. "Don't mix business with kissing."

"You're not very good at following the rules."

"No shit. Sherlock better watch out, or your ability to state the obvious is going to put him out of a job."

She waved her hand. "Cumberbatch will take one look at me and not mind at all."

I rolled my eyes. "Still, the point remains. Don't get involved with clients. It always ends in disaster."

"Um, didn't your dad meet Portia on a job?"

I paused.

She raised an eyebrow.

"Yes," I said slowly. "But they didn't get involved until after he was done." Another pause. "I'm pretty sure."

"You believe that if it makes you feel better, honey."

"Don't honey me. The only person who does that is my mom, and she's not a sarcastic bitch like you."

Jayda grinned, her make-up free eyes crinkling at the edges. "Your compliment is heard and accepted."

I flipped her the bird. "What am I supposed to do now? I have to show up today and start painting and he's going to be there. What am I supposed to say to him?"

She tapped a blood-red nail against the table. "I'd start with good morning."

Oh my god. She was so fucking sarcastic. I was going to pin her down and force some genuine shit out of her soon.

"Thanks for the advice, Dr. Phil. I hadn't thought of that," I said dryly. "But after that? "Sorry I let you kiss me last night? It won't happen again? How dare you kiss me you bastard?'""

She toyed with a lock of her hair. "In the interest of keeping this job, nix the last idea."

"At least you finally answered sensibly."

She rolled her eyes, planted her forearms on the table, and leaned forward. "Kali. You kissed him. So what? You'd done him a favor, he thanked you with pizza, and you both got carried away. It's never going to happen again because you're too professional for that. You weren't working when you kissed, so you didn't break the rules, technically speaking."

"I like how you've laid that out."

"You're welcome." She nodded with a solemn look on her face. "Now, you get over it. Show up like nothing happened and do your job. If he's at work, problem solved. If not, he has kids to look after and will leave you alone."

Yeah, no. She didn't know Ellie and Eli.

"Just deal with it. You're both adults, you're unattached, and you're free to kiss whoever you like in your personal time. End of freak out."

That was easy for her to say.

I took a deep breath and slowly let it go. "All right. What you're saying is, show up, act like it didn't happen, and pray like fuck he's working in the office today."

She was silent for a moment. Then, she pursed her lips and nodded. "That's the gist of it, yeah."

"Ugh."

"Hey, it could be worse," she said, swiping the screen on her phone to unlock it. "Check this message I got from a wannabe Casanova last night."

I slid her phone toward me and swiveled it so I could read. """Hey, saw your profile. You're hot,""" I read. """Wanna have dinner? Don't wear underwear, you won't need them where we're going.""" I finished in a slower tone. "He wanted you to go commando on a date?

"Right." She took her phone back. "When I messaged him back—"

"Why did you do that?"

"Curiosity. Why didn't I need underwear? Were we seeing a gyno? That's the only reason I think underwear is useless," she said. "Duh. So, I message him back, and he tells me he has a leather sofa perfect for fucking on."

I frowned. "He wanted you panty-less on his leather sofa?"

"Basically."

"Doesn't he know our vaginas clean themselves? There's nothing remotely comfortable about not wearing panties. And you sure as hell don't need to be panty-less on a leather sofa. Nobody wants to clean that up."

Jayda made a gun with her thumb and two fingers and pointed it at me. "Boom. There's my reply. Thanks."

I blinked. "He's not going to date you after you say that."

"Oh, I know. That's a good thing. But, hey—at least you're not freaking out about Hot Dad anymore."

Famous last words.

***

Oh my god, I was going to be sick.

I was a dreadful adult. I was a terrible businesswoman, a dreadful adult, and an inconsiderate human being.

All right, no, I wasn't. But I felt like it.

I was definitely going to be sick, though.

No doubt about it.

That was dramatic. And untrue. Oh my god, what was wrong with me? Jayda was right. We were adults who kissed. I was there today to do a job and I had to do that.

I wish doing things were as easy as saying them.

Then again, if that happened, I would have given up Twizzlers years ago.

I pulled up next to Brantley's car on the drive. The fact the car was there wasn't even remotely reassuring to my hope that he'd be at the office again today.

Mind you, him going to the office had led to the kiss…

Man, I was between a rock and a hard place. And the only hard place I liked being up against was a penis.

I took a deep breath and got out of the car. I wore my usual uniform of denim shorts, a white tank, and a plaid shirt. I had to own more plaid shirts than the guys in Outlander did kilts, but I liked them. For work, that was.

I remembered to grab Brantley's shirt—that I'd washed and dried overnight—from the passenger seat. Folding it up smaller, I held it against my stomach as I locked the truck and headed toward the front door.

Knock, knock, knock.

"Come in, Kali!" Brantley shouted from somewhere inside.

I stared at the door handle like it wanted to eat me.

The door swung open of its own accord.

And, standing there, in front of me, was Eli. Wearing nothing but striped underwear, rain boots, and a superhero cape. A red mask the exact color of the cape covered his eyes.

I blinked at him.

"Kawi!" he said enthusiastically. "Come in!"

"Um, thank you?" I stepped inside. "Nice…outfit?"

He beamed at me like I'd paid him the greatest compliment ever. Then, he pulled some ninja-moves, slicing his arms through the air before he lifted his leg and kicked the door shut. "Kachow! I'm Ninja-Man!"

"Eli!" Brantley groaned. "What have I told you about kicking doors shut?"

Eli sped into the front room and held his hands before him in a ready-to-attack position. "Ninja-Man doesn't have rules! Zoom! Zoom! Zoom!" He ran around the room in circles.

Ellie sat in the armchair, wearing a glittery tutu and a crown. Satiny-looking gloves covered her hands and arms up to her elbows, and both wrists and several fingers were adorned with plastic jewelry.

Ah.

They were playing dress-up.

Why Eli was wearing underwear and rain boots was something I was interested in, though.

"Hi." Brantley shot me a weary and awkward smile.

"Hi. Should I ask?"

"As a rule…no."

"Hi, Kawi! I'm a pwincess! You has to curt-saw to me."

Brantley clapped his hand against his forehead. "Curtsey, Ellie. See, not saw."

She frowned and looked at him. "Curt-sawing is more fun. Look see." She jumped up and bent her knees, then rocked side to side. "See? That's a curt-saw."

I blinked at her.

She had a point.

Brantley clearly felt similarly to me. "Awesome. Would Her Highness enjoy a fruit snack?"

"A candy snack," Ellie countered.

"Zoom, zoom, zoom!" Eli held his arms out wide, gripping his cape, and ran right between where Ellie was standing and Brantley was kneeling on the floor.

Brantley eyed him. "Someone already found the candy, so it's fruit or nothing, I'm afraid."

Ahh.

That made so much more sense.

"All right. Well, then. I'm going to head on upstairs and get started." I cocked my thumb over my shoulder in the general direction of the stairs. "I'll leave you to…this."

Brantley coughed to cover a laugh and shot me a thumb up. "Thanks. Your support is noted."

I shrugged, smirked, and disappeared upstairs.

Thank god for that.

There was only so much I could take of looking him in the eye. Especially when he was particularly exasperated with the twins—and there was no way he wasn't given Ellie's curt-saws and Eli's apparently intense sugar high.

Hell, I could still hear him zoom-zooming around the room and Brantley asking him to "Please stop zooming for a moment."

I had a little chuckle at that. He was a different person when he was over their games—funny yet serious, and totally adorable in his frustration.

Shit.

Wait.

No.

Abort that line of thinking, Kali. That's not going to lead anywhere. Nowhere good, anyway.

I retrieved my brushes, roller, and tray from the bathtub and went into Ellie's room. The paint was, obviously, completely dry, but not as even as I'd have liked. The walls had been in such bad condition from bad papering and peeling paper that it was going to take more effort than I'd planned to paint it properly.

Still, I got started.

My tools and things were in a pile in the middle of the room. I opened my toolbox and pulled out a flat screwdriver to open the can of paint. I slipped it beneath the lid and pushed down, popping it open.

The bubblegum-pink was almost painful to look out, even for someone like me who liked pink, but I poured it into the tray and grabbed a roller.

I glanced at the door. There was some kind of a ruckus downstairs about who was better, princesses or superheroes.

Hmm.

That sounded like it was only a matter of time

before a princess infiltrated my work.

Roller firmly in hand, I crossed the room and shut the door. Then shifted my toolbox in front of it.

There—it was now child and Brantley-proof.

Hopefully.

Knock, knock.

"Kawi?"

I rolled paint onto the wall.

"Kaaaawwwwiiiii?"

I gritted my teeth.

More knocks.

Quicker, endless knocks that went on until I felt like my brain was ready to explode.

"Yes?" I called. "I'm busy, Ellie."

"I wanna see my woom."

"It's not done." It had been two hours. I haven't even done the two biggest walls yet.

"Pwease."

Judging by the muffled huff and bang against the door, she'd slumped against it.

"Where's your dad?"

"Making me a chocwat sammich," she replied. "I wanna see."

"You should go check on lunch," I replied.

"I'm a pwincess, you know. You had to do what I say."

Last time I checked, this was a republic, but whatever…

I set the roller in the tray, pushed my tools to the

side, and opened the door.

She stood there, pouting for all it was worth, arms folded across her chest. Her tutu stuck out almost at a ninety-degree angle, and she had now adopted some plastic, backless, dress-up shoes that, in the color blue, were at odds with her pink outfit.

"Ellie," I said softly. "I have to get my work done, okay?"

"Painting isn't wort. It's fun."

"If you're four." I tapped her nose. "But painting rooms is part of my job. So, it's work. Can you let me do it?"

She leaned to the side, her tiny hand gripping the doorframe. "Okay, but I don't wanna." She pouted and stalked off, sulking.

I dropped my head. I felt guilty, but there was no way I could have her in here. Turning back to my roller, I coated it in paint, and picked it up.

"Ellie," I heard myself say. "Come here."

Damn it, self.

She appeared as if by magic, a huge, hopeful grin stretched across her face. "Yeah?"

I sighed. "You can stay, but you sit quietly, and you must put on some proper clothes."

Frowning, she stared down at herself. "Oh."

She looked so sad, I was pretty sure she was going to change her mind about wanting to be in here with me.

"Okay," she said after a moment of silence. "I get changed."

I blinked, watching her as she disappeared.

A glob of paint fell off the end of my roller and hit my bare foot.

And that was reason number one why I didn't want Ellie in the room.

I couldn't focus for the life of me.

Another sigh escaped my lips as I turned and wiped it off my foot with my fingers. I awkwardly flicked it back into the tray, before wiping my fingers on my thigh awkwardly.

I could have gone to wash my hands in the sink, but…Actually, I had no reason for why I didn't. Other than the risk of Ellie being in this room, alone, with paint, I was just being lazy.

"Hey—did you say Ellie could come up here with you?"

I squealed, dropping the roller. It landed smack on top of both of my feet before flipping onto the floor and coating the old wood in the teeth-gratingly sweet pink paint.

"Shit!" I turned. "Oh, crap! Is she up here?"

Brantley surveyed my feet, then the floor, then ran his eyes up my body. They lingered a little on my thighs, and I was going to believe it was because of the random pink stripes on them.

I mean, it probably was. Why was I even thinking that it wouldn't be?

His lips pulled to one side. "No, she's not up here. You're all good."

"Thank God." I bent over and put the roller back in its tray so it could think about the mess it'd made of my feet—twice. "Yes, I did say she could come up here with me. I swear she has some freaky voodoo that sends me on a guilt trip every time she doesn't get what she wants."

He nodded solemnly. "Yeah. That's something

they should really mention before you have kids. That you'll spend the rest of your life feeling guilty for anything from, "No, you can't have a puppy," to "You cannot eat the moldy cookie you hid behind the sofa six months ago.""

"Why would you feel guilty about that?"

"The eyes. They get you every time. Which is why they're not allowed a puppy. I can't have three people to guilt me into stuff."

"The puppy would probably eat the cookie, though. It'd solve that problem."

"There is that," he agreed.

We shared a smile.

It was a little too intimate.

I coughed and broke the eye contact, getting my roller once again.

"Do you want a towel, or…" He paused, and I peered over at him. "The paint. It's, um… You're covered in it."

I glanced at my feet and my legs. "It happens. Today more than usual."

"You know you don't have to have Ellie up here, don't you? You can tell her no. I'll even tell her no and take the guilt-trip for you."

I laughed and started painting again. "It's fine. She'll probably get bored of watching me and disappear without me knowing it."

He met my eyes and held my gaze for a long, hard second. "Your optimism. It kills me." Then, he turned and left.

"What does that mean?" I shouted over my shoulder.

His answer? A barking laugh that made me shiver.

At least I wasn't too awkward in that conversation. That was a win.

15

"Annen I told Daddy that if he won't buy me the Cindewewa castle for my birssday I cry and ask Santa but Santa is before my birssday but I don't wanna wait for Santa or my birssday I weally want it now." Ellie paused to take a deep breath, and before I could interject some bullshit comment about patience, she started again. "Ewi got his superhewo cave and the twiceratops. It's not fair."

I stared at her, paintbrush dripping into the tray.

Now, I had two options here. I could resume my original attempt at talking to her about patience, but I had the feeling it would be falling on deaf ears.

Maybe because she'd started talking again, while I stood here and blinked at her.

My second option was to make soothing noises of sympathy and agreement and nod my head along with her that it wasn't fair.

Or, a third one, I could turn around and do my job and let her whine.

That last one seemed right. After all, I'd already tuned her out. Aside from a dull buzzing, I was watching her lips moving at the speed of light, but I wasn't hearing what she was saying.

Now, that was a skill I was interested in developing further.

I turned back to the wall, faking a nod, and finished my edging around the doorframe. She talked the entire time. Momentary flashes of paying attention said she'd gone from complaining to talking about how real unicorns were or the validity of fairies.

It was a long-ass half an hour.

"Done!" I said, stepping away from the door with a flourish.

Ellie stopped talking.

Oops.

"Can I sweep here now?" She turned her head side to side, staring out over the room.

"Uh…Not yet. You need a new floor, and curtains, and a bed…"

She huffed from her seat in the middle of the floor. "Can Ewi sweep in his?"

"Nope. I'm going to paint it now." I put the brush in the tray and picked it up. Then, I paused. "Do you want to help me clean up?"

She pursed her lips. "Cwean up?"

"Yeah. I have to wash the pink paint off of this stuff." I gave the tray a slight shake. "Do you want to do the brushes in the sink for me?"

She clambered up to her feet, rushed to me, and peered into the tray. "Aww fwee?"

"Not the roller. That's hard. But sure, you can do the brushes."

She hesitated for only a second before she nodded her head and ran. I'd barely stepped foot outside her bedroom when I heard her shout, "Ewi! Get off the toiwet!"

Okay.

Maybe I wasn't going into the bathroom right now.

"No! I'm pooping!" Eli shouted back.

That was too much information.

"Well, stop pooping!" came Ellie's response. "You smell bad!"

Still too much information.

"I can't just stop pooping, Ewwie. There's still poo in my tummy!"

"Okay!" Brantley came up the stairs, taking them two at a time. "That's your weekly quota of the 'p' word used in about ten seconds. Eleanor, let your brother use the toilet. Elijah…Please stop telling the entire neighborhood what you're doing in the bathroom."

I snorted, dipping my head since I was still holding the tray.

Brantley turned to look at me. "Oh, Jesus. I'm sorry you had to hear that."

"So am I," I replied.

"Here, let me take this. I'll clean it downstairs." He grabbed the other end of the tray.

"I can do it." I gently tugged.

His eyebrows shot up. "You just heard that conversation. Let me do it. Honestly. Think of it as my apology for it."

"It's fine, honestly. It'll take me about five seconds to do, and I—"

He gave the tray a good yank and pulled it right out of my hands. "Thank you."

My jaw dropped. "I didn't—hey!"

He ignored me completely as he went down the stairs. I stared at his retreating back until I couldn't see it anymore. I was frozen at the top of the stairs, and while a part of me wanted to chase him down and force him to let me clean the stuff, the rest of me didn't want to be alone with him.

Was it any wonder why?

I left it. Turned and headed into Eli's room where the blue and red cans of paint and a fresh set of brushes and a roller were waiting for me. After all, I didn't need the dirty rollers, but I just liked to clean them while they were wet.

I poured the red paint into the tray. Eli had been very clear he wanted the bigger walls red and the smaller ones blue, so I lumped a ton of paint into the tray, ready to get started.

I touched the roller to the wall. The squelching noise it made as it transferred the paint to the wall always made me cringe at first. But not quite as much as the sound of Ellie shouting at Eli to wash his "poopy hands."

Yep.

That was definitely the worst thing I'd hear all day.

I shuddered and carried on with the painting. I'd pushed the door almost closed, and the boards outside in the hall creaked. There was muffled whispering, and I braced myself for the onslaught of two tiny people, but then…

"Ellie. Eli. Downstairs!"

"But—"

"Down. Stairs!"

There was a pause, then there was the unmistakable sound of two people going downstairs.

I breathed a sigh of relief.

Thank you, Brantley.

***

The door creaked open.

Kneeling on the floor with my brush dipped in the tray full of red paint, I peeked over my shoulder. Eli hovered in the doorway, his eyes wide with delight as he looked at the two bright-blue walls.

"Hi," I said slowly.

He jerked his attention to me and held out a bottle of water. "Daddy said you might want some water."

Actually, I did.

I set down the brush and motioned him to come in. "I'd love one. Thank you. That's so nice of you to bring me it."

He blushed. Quickly, he handed me the bottle and shuffled back. His eyes flitted side to side again, never really making eye contact with me.

He was looking at the walls again.

"Do you like the blue?" I asked softly, tracing my gaze over his face.

He nodded. "Wots," he whispered.

His shyness sucker-punched me in the gut. Never had I known twins so polar-opposite in their personalities.

Then again, Ellie spoke so he didn't have to.

"Do you want to see the red, too?"

He nodded again, stuffing his hands in the pockets of his shorts.

"Come here." I capped the water bottle, set it down, and shifted over for him to see. "There's not a lot, because I just started doing the edges."

He bent forward at the waist, looking at the bottom corner and where I'd started to edge the corner of the wall. "Why are you doing that?"

"Just at the edges?"

More nodding.

"Well, it's quite tricky. It's to stop me getting a lot of paint on the other wall or the ceiling or baseboards with the roller. Look—watch." I removed excess paint from the brush and gently painted a little, getting the bristles in at the corner. "Sometimes I use tape to help me, but this blue might still be a little wet."

"Is that the tape?" He pointed at the taped baseboards.

"It is. I don't like to take it off until the paint is dry. I think the other wall might be done. Want to see?"

Nodding again. "How does it work?"

I dropped the brush and shuffled across the room on my knees. "It helps me get the lines right. I don't have to be as careful, because if I get paint on the tape, it doesn't matter." I pinched the edge of the tape and slowly pulled it. "See?"

He basically leaned right on top of me and watched as I gently peeled the tape from the baseboard. He moved with me as I crawled across the floor.

"You see? It's a perfect, straight line." Near enough.

"Wow," he breathed, awe filling his tone with lightness. "That's 'mazin'."

"It is. My daddy taught me that trick."

Eli turned to me, eyes wide with delight, cheeks flushed with excitement. "Do you think my daddy knows the tape twick?"

"Maybe. I think a lot of daddies know it."

"Wow," he repeated. "Is the udder one ready?"

"The tape on the other wall?"

He nodded.

"Not quite. Did you want to help peel it off?"

Another nod. How did he not have a headache?

"How about I come and get you when I think it's ready?" I offered. "It'll be before bedtime tonight."

I'd have to re-tape these boards tomorrow, but oh well.

Eli gazed out at all the boards. "Okay," he said quietly. "Deal?" He stuck out his tiny hand.

I took it and shook. "Deal."

"Can I watch you paint?"

I hesitated. I couldn't say no, could I? I'd let Ellie. "Sure," I said. "As long as you don't touch anything."

Nodding his agreement, he dropped to sit exactly where he was in the middle of the room. He crossed his legs and put his hands in his lap, staring at me expectantly.

My lips twitched at his interest in my work.

I remembered when I was a couple years older than him, sitting like that, and watching my dad do exactly what I was doing right now.

I was six. My mom had died nine months before. It'd been the first week of summer and Dad couldn't get a sitter. I'd been brought to work under the rules I wouldn't touch anything, I wouldn't go anywhere without him, and if I was really bored, I could pass him tools.

That was the day I grew a real interest in everything he did. The day I was first amazed that two hands could change a house so much with nothing more than love and dedication.

I glanced back at Eli and picked up my brush

with a smile. He sat silently as I painted. I didn't even hear him cough—not even a creak of the floorboards. If I didn't turn and check on him every now and then, I wouldn't have guessed he was there—or moving to get a better view of what I was doing.

It was peaceful. And fun, almost.

Until Tornado Ellie blew in.

"Whatcha dooooooooooing?" she sang, hovering in the doorway.

Eli sighed.

"Painting," I replied.

"Can I watch?"

"No," Eli said. "You watched your woom."

"I wanna watch yours, too."

"No."

"Kawi!"

I shrugged, rolling the paint on. "Sorry, Ellie. It's up to Eli. I think he's having fun watching me."

"I had fun watching you, too!"

"You awready watched," Eli said quietly. "I wanna watch now."

Ellie stomped her foot on the floor.

"Ellie!" Brantley shouted from downstairs. "You better not be upstairs!"

"I'm not," she shouted back.

"Go away, Ewwie," Eli said.

I shook my head as she stomped her head again. I was focused on a patch of wall by the ceiling and, in my attempt not to get red on the white ceiling, I didn't know until it was too late.

"Nooo! Ewwie! Nooooo!" Eli shrieked, stomping and thumping as he got up.

I turned.

And, fuck.

"Ellie!" I didn't mean to shout, I really didn't. But seeing her deliberately and spitefully plant her red-paint-covered hands all over the blue wall because Eli said no made me.

Eli cried as he pulled her away from the wall and pushed her over. They both went down, kicking into the tray of blue paint.

It happened in slow motion.

They hit the ground.

The tray flicked up and over.

The paint splattered over the floor and the wall I intended to be red.

I stood there, covered in pink and blue and red paint, on the opposite side of the room, roller in hand, dripping paint on the floor, and stared at the twins.

They were still struggling. Ellie was screaming. Eli was shouting. And they were both covered in paint.

"What the—" Brantley stopped in the doorway, cheeks red. Slowly, he swung his gaze from the fighting twins to me. "What the hell happened?"

"Are you sure you want that answer?" I replied.

He took a deep breath. Picking his way between the paint splatters, he separated the twins. Holding them both by the arm, one in his left hand and the other in his right, he knelt down and stared at them both.

Ellie's face was bright red from screaming. Eli was still crying, and as a number of emotions danced over Brantley's expression, I could see he was torn on how to react.

"I just wanted to watch Kawi paint," Eli sobbed, hiccupping halfway through the sentence.

"What happened?" Brantley demanded, turning to Ellie.

My eyes widened a bit.

Boy, that was hard.

Even I wanted to tell him what happened and he wasn't talking to me.

"Ewi hit me first!"

"No, he didn't," I interjected. I put the roller in my tray, folded my arms over my chest, and raised an eyebrow at her. "Did he, Ellie?"

She sniffed. "He pushed me over."

"And why did he push you over?" Brantley asked. "It wouldn't have anything to do with the red handprints on the wall now, would it? The wall Kali has spent all day painting."

"It was Eli!"

Brantley turned over her hands. "Really," he said flatly.

Ellie shrunk back.

"You have ten seconds to tell me the truth before *I* go and put blue handprints on *your* walls and see how you like it, young lady." He dropped her arm and pulled Eli into his side. He'd almost stopped crying now, but he looked like he'd gotten in a fight with a Smurf.

Ellie glanced across the room at me.

I didn't move or change my expression. She had to know I'd tell the truth even if she didn't.

"I wanted to watch Kawi paint, too," she finally started. "But Ewi wouldn't wet me. So, I painted, too. But then he pushed me over and frew paint on me."

"Did not!"

"Let me get this straight," a now-paint-covered

Brantley said. "You disobeyed me in coming upstairs, you lied to me, and you deliberately ruined your brother's wall because you didn't get your own way, although you already spent the morning upstairs with Kali while he helped me in the kitchen."

Ellie looked, for a second, as if she was going to deny it. Instead, her bottom lip trembled, she dropped her chin, and she nodded.

Brantley put a finger under her chin and met her eyes. "Don't fake cry. It's not going to work this time, Eleanor. What you did was very cruel. I suggest you go and sit in the corner of the bathroom and think about what you've done while I put Eli under the shower. You can have one when he's clean." He pointed in the direction of the bathroom.

She sniffed, but she went, trudging across the hall to the bathroom.

Eli tugged on Brantley's shirt. "Daddy, are you mad I pushed her over?"

He took a deep breath. "I'm not angry about it, Eli, but I'm not happy. You shouldn't do it again. I know she upset you, but you could have really hurt her, okay? Plus, now there's paint everywhere. Maybe next time you shout for me instead of hurting her, okay?"

He hesitated for a moment before nodding his head. "Can I had a shower now?"

"Yep."

"Oh." He stopped and looked at me. "Kawi, are you mad at the walls?"

Much like Brantley had done, I inhaled deeply, and looked at the walls. I was frustrated, annoyed, feeling helpless, but not angry. The extra few hours I'd now need to cover it up, not to mention repaint the baseboards, were totting up in my head, but I was more resigned to it than anything.

"We need to get you in the shower, buddy." Brantley stood and, taking hold of Eli's shoulders, directed him toward the bathroom.

"I sowwy, Kawi," I heard Eli say before Brantley shut the bedroom door behind him.

I let go of a long, shaky breath, slumping down as I was able to fully take in the sight of the mess that had been created by Ellie's tantrum.

Then, I turned, and forgetting—or maybe just not caring—that the red paint was still wet, pressed my forehead against the wall.

Ground rules.

No. More. Kids. Near. Paint.

16

Five p.m. rolled around before I knew it. I was pretty sure I still had paint on my head. I sure as hell had it just about everywhere else. I was all dry and crusty and gross.

I'd barely been able to fix the mess caused by the kids when they fought. I'd managed to wipe the surplus paint off, but other than that… Let's just say I had a couple more coats of white paint to do tomorrow.

I finished cleaning the rollers and trays off in the bathtub. The mix of blue and red as it swirled through the water before draining away was almost headache-inducing. It was much brighter wet, and mixed with water… Ugh.

I turned and caught a glimpse of myself in the mirror. I looked like a complete mess. Red paint in my hair and over my forehead. There were streaks of blue and pink across my neck and chest. The same happened when I looked down. I was a walking art exhibition.

One day, I would be able to paint a wall and not cover myself in it.

It was amazing. I could install a kitchen without getting a splinter, but painting a wall without getting covered in paint?

Not a chance in hell.

I glanced around for a cloth to wipe my face with. I didn't see one, so I switched on the tap and did the best I could with my fingers. It wasn't great, but I managed to get the majority of it off, and a scrub with a towel did the rest. There wasn't much I could do about my hair.

I gripped the edge of the sink and took a deep breath. I was exhausted. I could feel it as it snaked its way through the body. The last few hours of today had been hell, and Ellie had essentially wiped out everything I'd done in Eli's room.

For that, I wanted to do Eli's room first. To make her wait. But that was spiteful, too, and it didn't make me, as a twenty-six-year-old adult any better than her at four-years-old.

I huffed and straightened up, then grabbed my stuff from the tub. Shaking off the excess water, I put one tray inside the other, then stacked the rollers and the brushes inside to pick up easily.

And walked right into Brantley.

Everything I'd just picked up clattered to the floor.

"Shit," I whispered.

"I got it." He got on his knees and picked it all up as I ran my hand over my face. Standing, he flicked her eyes over me. "You look exhausted."

"Damn. I should have left the paint on my face if it's that obvious."

He smirked. "Should I pretend that the paint on the rest of you hides it?"

"Could you? Thanks."

"In Eli's room?" He lifted the tray slightly.

"Oh, er, yeah. Thanks." I fidgeted with the hem of my shirt. "Hey, I wanted to talk to you about something—"

He held his hands up. "Don't worry. They won't bug you anymore, I promise. I called Summer. They're going to her every day until the walls and floors are done so you can work in peace. At the very least."

I opened and closed my mouth like a fish.

"I'm sorry." He met my eyes. "They never should have been with you in the first place. I was working with Ellie watching a movie, then the next thing I knew, she was upstairs. I was on my way up when…"

"When the gates of Hell opened up and swallowed my afternoon whole?"

"When the gates of Hell opened up and swallowed your afternoon whole."

I grinned. "It happened. There's no point in dwelling on it right now. I can't change it, but I can fix it."

"You're very optimistic about this."

"Hey—fixing things is what I do. If I got annoyed every time something went wrong, I'd never get my job done."

He folded his arms across his chest, smiling. "You really are a regular little Miss Fix-It, aren't you?"

I mock-curtseyed. "That's what you're paying me for."

He laughed. "True. Thank you for, well, your bright outlook on the bullshit my children brought to your day."

"You're welcome." I skirted around him and slowly made my way down the stairs. "I'll see you at eight tomorrow."

"Kali?"

My name on his lips sent a tingle down my spine.

I stopped, gripping the banister.

"I, er… I made a bit too much pasta tonight. Would you…wanna stay and help me eat it? The kids are ready for bed, and it just needs reheating…"

Dinner? Again?

Did we not establish last night that was not a good idea?

"I don't think it's a good idea," I said slowly. "I mean…"

Brantley's lipped thinned, his eyes flashing with something I couldn't recognize. "Right. Forgive me. I'll see you tomorrow."

I raised my hand in an awkward wave. Willpower made me walk, not run, down the stairs, but the second my feet hit the hallway, I was off. I left the house before either of the kids saw me or I changed my mind.

I pulled my keys from my ass pocket and got into my truck. My phone was in the glovebox, and I retrieved it, sticking my keys into the ignition at the same time. Then, I pulled up my messages and texted Jayda.

Me: *He just asked me to stay for dinner*
Jayda: *Call me right now*

I sighed and, still sitting in his driveway, did just that.

"He asked you to stay for dinner?" she rambled the second I answered my phone. "Why are you messaging me and not eating?"

"Because I said it wasn't a good idea."

"Of course, it's a terrible idea! But, first, free food. Second, he's hot."

"You think the fact he's hot and giving me food negates the fact it's a bad idea?"

Silence. "Yeah, pretty much. Is it home-cooked food?"

"Does that make a difference?"

"It's home-cooked." She sighed heavily, the line crackling at her exhale. "Damn it, Kali. Just have dinner with the guy. What harm will it do?"

"What good will it do?" My voice raised a few decibels.

"With any luck, it'll take you a little closer to getting laid. You're basically a virgin."

"I'm done with this conversation."

"Wait! Maybe he needs a friend!" She quickly spat out. "Have you thought about that? Does he know anyone else in town? He spends all his time with pint-sized, puny humans. You're, like, a unicorn."

I paused. She had a point. And if Jayda had a point, we were all doomed. "You think that's it? He needs a friend?"

"I think you should see if that's what it is."

"What if he kisses me again?"

"Kiss him back and hope you get laid."

"Bye now." I hung up before she could continue on any further down that track. But, damn. She'd planted the seed of an idea in my mind, and now I couldn't shake it.

As far as I knew, he didn't know anyone in town. Certainly not anyone on anything more than an acquaintance level. We were practically friends, I guess. If you considered we knew stuff about each other and talked every day…

And kissed once.

Sadness.

That had been what passed through his eyes when I'd said no.

A flicker. The barest hint of sadness, and loneliness, too.

I turned my phone over and tapped his name in the contacts.

Me: *Just how much is 'a bit extra pasta?'*
Brantley: *Are you texting me from the driveway?*
Me: *…yes. Is this not normal?*

I stared at my phone, waiting for the response. When I didn't get one, I hopped out of the truck to go knock.

The front door opened as my feet hit the floor. He walked out and to my truck, eyebrow quirked in amusement.

I blushed, shutting the door and leaning against it. "Not normal, huh?"

His lips twitched, and he stood next to me, elbow on the wing mirror. "Definitely not normal. Why are you asking?"

"A 'bit extra pasta' is relative. You either did enough for one person or enough to feed another family. I didn't consider that when I said no."

"Enough to take it to the town hall in an hour and feed everyone at Bingo," he admitted. "And, you didn't say no. You said it was a bad idea." His eyes met mine. "And I'm hard-pressed to disagree with you, which is why I don't understand why you're still here."

"Let's just say I'm very good at making bad decisions."

Eyes.

Dropped to my mouth.

"You and me both," he muttered.

I cleared my throat and glanced away briefly. "If you can give me half an hour to shower and change, I'd love to help you finish that pasta," I said quietly.

"Half an hour. Really?"

"Forty-five minutes."

"Shall I have it ready in an hour?"

I nodded. "That's a good idea."

He grinned, pulling back from the truck. "All right then."

"I…Hold on. Did you…shower…after all hell broke loose?"

"No. I cleaned up, but I didn't have a chance yet. Why?"

"You've got…" I stopped, biting the inside of my lower lip as I smiled, eyes following the giant, blue streak that colored his dark hair.

He blinked at me. "Got what? Why are you grinning at me like that?"

I stepped forward. "Paint." Lifting my hand to his face, I ran my finger along the side of his head, from a spot just above his ear, through his hair, and down to the soft spot just beneath his air. "Right along there."

His gaze shifted from the inside of my arm. Our eyes met, and I took a deep breath. I was still touching him, my fingers just barely ghosting down the side of his neck.

A short breath juddered out of me. Stutter-like and harsh, I forced myself to take another deep breath in or I knew I'd lose control.

Especially when he raised his hand to mine and

curled his fingers around my wrist.

Hot little bursts of desire danced up my arm where his fingertips pressed against the tender skin there. It almost tickled as they trailed up the inside of my arm when it lowered.

"Good to know." His voice was deep and low, almost *rough*. "I'll go fix that now. You'll be back in an hour?"

I nodded, pressing my hands flat against the hot door of my truck. "An hour," I said scratchily. I swallowed, then cleared my throat again, pretending not to see how his eyes dropped when my throat bobbed. "Right. An hour. See you then."

Brantley took a few steps back, lips twitching as he backed away. "See you, Kali."

I dressed as casually as I could. Yoga pants, a loose shirt, and an old, zip-up sweatshirt. My hair was still-damp and in its natural state of loose curls, all pulled up into a ponytail on top of my head. I barely even wore make-up. A light layer of foundation and some mascara was all I'd put on.

I wanted to believe that the nugget of bullshit Jayda planted in my mind was real.

A part of me did. I couldn't begin to imagine how lonely Brantley actually was. My whole life had been lived here in Rock Bay. He'd uprooted his entire life in favor of a new one—of one better than the one he'd been existing through before.

He wanted, maybe even needed, a friend. Sure.

But there was more there.

I'd felt it when he'd kissed me, and I'd felt it an hour ago when I'd made the mistake of touching his paint-covered hair.

I was an idiot, that much was true. I don't know what had possessed me to do that. I could have just said and pointed, but no. I practically ran my fingers through his hair and down the side of his neck.

What was wrong with me? I'd spent the entire morning berating myself for kissing him, and I'd allowed my best friend to guilt me into having dinner with him.

I was an idiot, but here I was, ready to get free pasta.

The door swung open before I could knock. "Come in. Sorry. It's burning."

My eyebrows shot up, and I stifled a giggle as I closed the door behind me. Sure enough, as I joined him in the kitchen, I could smell the faint yet distinct scent of something burning.

"Fuck it, fuck it!" Brantley swept a huge pan over the sink and ditched the contents in a drainer. "Goddamn stove!"

I leaned against the table, taking a moment to notice that it was set. Plates, cutlery—the half-full bottle of wine I hadn't finished the night before.

Um.

"Having problems?" I grinned at his back.

"I know you're smiling, so stop it," he said without looking at me.

I smiled wider.

"And, yes. Problems. This damn thing drives me crazy." He waved his hand in the direction of the stove-top. "It heats up quicker than I can turn it down, and now I can't turn it off."

I leaned over. "The child-lock is on."

He froze, looking over his shoulder at me. "It has a child-lock?"

Closing the distance between me and the stove, I pressed the key-shaped pad on the top until it beeped, then turned it off.

"Well, fuck me," Brantley muttered.

Okay.

Wait, no.

I shook my head and took a seat at the table. He chuckled, and… Oh my god.

Oh. My. God.

I shook my head. It looked like I was answering his question.

This. This was why I shouldn't be here. I couldn't even plan a goddamn headshake that was the equivalent of an eyeroll.

He poured the spaghetti back into the pan and mixed in some sauce, this time, operating the stove-top very carefully. I stifled a laugh as he jabbed frantically at the flat buttons hoping they'd register his touch.

"Motherfucker," he muttered.

Biting the inside of my cheek, I got up and nudged him out the way. "Gently is the key," I said, wiping off the touch pad with the bottom of my shirt to clear his prints. I hit the power button, then the back circle. "What number power?"

"Uh…"

"Five it is." I pressed the 'down' key until it was on the middle heat. "You're jabbing at it too hard. Just touch it, like your phone."

"My phone doesn't beep at me angrily every time I touch it."

"Yours is better behaved than mine."

He laughed, pulling a spoon out of the utensil pot. "Thank you. I don't think I'll ever get used to this kitchen."

"Well, if it comes to it, I know someone who can fit you another."

His gaze slid to me. "Pimping yourself out?"

"No. I actually know someone who can fix this." I circled my finger in the area of the stove. "But, if you want new cabinets…" I clicked my tongue and pointed to myself. "I'm your girl."

"Good to know." He held my gaze, spoon stilled in the center of the pot.

I blushed.

"Did you know that you blush a lot?"

I blushed harder. "Did you know that you didn't put the sauce in that pasta and you're burning it again?"

"Shit!"

I didn't try to hide my laughter this time. I laughed out loud, pressing my hand to my stomach as I gripped the edge of the counter. This was the very first imperfection I'd seen in Brantley Cooper, and it was both wonderful and curious.

Wonderful because he'd been almost too perfect until now.

Curious, because how had he kept himself and two other people alive if he was burning pasta?

"Stop laughing at me." He poured the sauce from the other pan into the pasta. "I swear, I'm not a culinary idiot."

"You can't work your stove!"

"That's a simple matter of electronic semantics."

"Electronic semantics, my ass! It's a simple matter of male impatience. And you're still burning the pasta!"

"Fucking hell!"

"Oh god, move." I shoved him out of the way, literally plucking the spoon from his hand and shifting in front of him. I pulled the pan off the burner and stirred it then, scraping the pasta off the bottom of the pan. "Sauce."

Brantley slid past me, his hand brushing my lower back as he went. I ignored it the best I could, if we considered the fact I was biting the inside of my cheek and avoiding his eyes.

He put the sauce into the pan, his chest brushing against my arm as I put it back onto the burner. I cleared my throat and stirred, mixing it all into the pasta and chicken carefully. The creamy, white sauce splattered as I lost my hold on the spoon, and I winced, screwing my face up as it spat at me.

Brantley laughed. "Painting…cooking…it's all relative for you, isn't it?"

"Shut up," I muttered, wiping my forehead.

He leaned over and swiped his thumb along my cheekbone. "There. Now it's all gone."

I blushed and turned off the burner. "It's done." I stepped back from the stove and went back to the table.

He side-eyed me with a half-smile as he took over, pulling two plates from the cupboard closest to him.

I turned away, looking out of the window as he served it up. This was exactly why I hadn't wanted to have dinner with him—this attraction.

It was undeniable. For us both. It was the elephant in the room every time our eyes met, and it was getting harder and harder to hide my reactions whenever we touched.

The problem was, I'd screwed all my own attempts at putting distance between us. I was sitting on the wall that divided professional and personal, one leg on each side, staring down the line until it disappeared.

I had no idea what I was doing with my life.

Brantley set a plate in front of me, and I murmured a "thank you" as he took his seat.

What were we going to talk about?

Did we have anything in common? I doubted he enjoyed *Friends* re-runs as enthusiastically as I did, and there wasn't a chance in hell I'd be drawn into a conversation about sports. The last sports I watched was when I was a senior in high school, and that was only because I had a crush on the running back on our team.

Sidenote: showing up in short-shorts totally worked.

All that said, relief flooded through me when Brantley began to eat in silence. I followed suit, digging into the delicious, creamy, cheesy pasta dish in front of me.

Amazing. He burned pasta, yet cooked the sauce.

My mind boggled.

The minutes ticked by. Had Jayda been right? Was it just company he wanted? If so… I mean, this was better than anything I had the patience to cook. I'd be his dinner friend any day if he'd feed me like this.

I was almost done eating when he put down his fork and sipped at his wine.

"I'm sorry if I made things awkward when I kissed you yesterday."

17

I almost choked on my food. I grabbed my wine and washed it down, thankfully without giving into the urge to spit it everywhere.

That came out of nowhere.

"I'm sorry if I made it awkward apologizing for making it awkward," he added, lips twitching as he gazed over at me.

"Nope. You're good. Just surprised me, that's all." I took another mouthful of wine, swilling it around before I swallowed it. "Not awkward. I mean, a little, but mostly because it's against the rules. No company-client relations. You know?"

He nodded. "Like I said, I'm sorry. It was a spur-of-the-moment thing. It won't happen again."

Oh.

Why did that suck?

Goddamn it, it didn't suck. That was absolutely the right choice. It couldn't happen again. No way.

"Right. Of course. You know you didn't have to invite me for dinner just to say that, right?"

"I know. It happened to work in my favor. I'll never get the hang of cooking the right amount of pasta." He frowned. "I don't know how people do it."

"My mom is one of those weirdos. Like, she just knows how much pasta to cook. I generally cook enough for a small army."

Brantley waved his hand. "Speak for yourself. I think I have enough for lunch tomorrow, too."

I laughed, resting my forearm on the table. I nudged my plate aside so I had room to cup my wine glass in front of me. "Just let the twins eat it."

"They're at daycare tomorrow. Do you have any idea how amazing it'll be to have a day to myself?"

"Really? You mean I can paint without chaos?"

His smile reached his eyes. "You can paint without chaos," he confirmed. "I might bug you if I get bored, but I promise not to screw up the walls."

"If you come and bug me, I'll be handing you a roller and telling you to start painting."

"I can do that." He tapped his fingers against the table. "After I've been to the store and had my ankles ripped to shreds."

"I don't know why we still shop there. There's a Target half an hour away."

"That's the problem. Target is half an hour away. Irma's is five minutes for anyone in town."

Sighing, I propped my chin up on my hand. "And you won't get the local gossip at Target."

"Small towns," he muttered. "So in each other's business."

I nodded. "Everyone will assume we're dating tomorrow. Just so you know."

His eyebrows shot up, and he stood, grabbing both our plates. "That's a bit of a jump, isn't it?"

"Not really. They're simply putting two and two together and getting five, as they generally do. It's not much of a jump when you consider that I'm single and you're single and hot."

He glanced over his shoulder at me, amusement curling his lips.

"I…Um…I wasn't supposed to say that out

loud," I said slowly.

Crap.

"You think I'm hot," he said. He didn't ask, he just said it.

"I, well, I, er…"

He quirked a brow at me.

I took a deep breath. "Yes. You don't?"

"I have to admit I've never really looked at myself that way." His restrained laughter made his shoulders shake. "I'll consider it next time I look in the mirror."

"There's no need to be sarcastic about it." I finished my wine and got up. The chair squeaked against the floor. "And now I'm the one who's made it awkward, soooo, I think I'm going to make like a banana and split." I put the wine glass on the side by the sink and turned. "Thank you for dinner. It was great. Let's pretend this conversation never happened."

He stood in front of me, blocking my way. His biceps clenched with how he had his arms folded across his chest, and the white material of his t-shirt stretched over his shoulders in a way that was more than a little distracting.

But it was his eyes that made me stop. The way a darkness that hinted at desire tickled the edges of his gaze. The way they shone bright with laughter at the same time they revealed how he was feeling in that very second.

I swallowed.

"We could pretend it never happened," he said in a low voice. "Or we could just admit that we're attracted to each other and deal with it from there."

"I don't—I mean, I'm not… Attracted to you," I

finished stupidly.

"You mean you're not very good at lying."

"Yeah. That, too."

He dropped his arms and approached me. I backed up until my back hit the edge of the counter.

Shit. Idiot. Now, you're trapped.

I gripped the edge of the marble counter and took a deep breath.

He stood in front of me, towering over me by a few inches, and rested his hands either side of my body. His thumbs brushed my pinky fingers, settling where I could just feel the tickle of them through the air.

"Deal with it," I echoed, my mouth dry. "What exactly do you mean by that?"

He glanced at my mouth.

Dear god, how was he able to answer my question without speaking?

"Okay, but, um, here's the thing." I couldn't breathe. I sounded like a panting idiot trying to get the words out between each short, sharp breath I took. "This," I motioned between us, "is bad."

"Bad." His lips tugged to the side.

"Yes. Because,"—help. Someone help—"because this isn't allowed. Company rules. No cavorting with clients."

"No cavorting with clients." That half-smile turned into a full-blown grin. "That's very…proper."

"Well, I can't exactly put, "No fucking the clients" now, can I?"

"You could have, but it would have been unfortunately precise."

"I should change that."

"I disagree."

I licked my lips. "You should agree. Because this is—"

"Bad. You said." More lip twitching.

"I thought you were sorry you made it awkward by kissing me."

"That was before I found out you were attracted to me. Now, I'm a lot less sorry I kissed you."

Oh. Well. Fair enough.

"Should I take back my acceptance of your apology?" I asked.

"You should stop talking and see how you feel when I've kissed you again."

"Kissed me—"

He silenced me with his lips on mine. A huge shiver wracked my body, and he smiled against my mouth, hands slowly sliding up my arms. He grazed his teeth over my lower lip as he pulled away, and my heart pounded against my chest.

There was only a breath of air between our lips. I could taste him, and although I knew I'd hate myself, I couldn't help it.

I placed my hands either side of his neck and kissed him right back. Firmly. I kissed him the way he had me the night before, with force and unfightable desire. As he wound one hand into my hair, I pushed up on tiptoes, my ass now digging into the edge of the counter as he leaned against me.

My head spun. It felt so fucking good, probably because I knew it was wrong. But, I couldn't stop. I couldn't stop my heart from pounding or my body from reacting to him the way it was. The skin tingles, the chest tightening, the lust that pooled between my legs and made my clit ache…

None of it.

It was out of control, and all because of him.

His body was hard against mine—and so was his cock. It pressed, fighting against the confines of his jeans, against my lower stomach. This only turned me on more, sent more desire running at a fast pace through my blood.

I wanted him to fuck me right here, right now, up against the kitchen counter, and I no longer fucking cared about it.

I just wanted more—more touching, more kissing, more of him.

His lips moved over mine so smoothly. His fingers toyed with my hair just enough that tiny stings radiated over my scalp, and his tongue fought with mine as the kiss got deeper and deeper.

Rougher. More desperate. More—

The floorboards above us creaked.

I pulled back with a half-gasp and looked at the ceiling.

Brantley stayed where he was, perfectly still, until there was another creak. It was followed by the sound of hollow footsteps on the top stairs.

"Fuck it," he muttered, briefly pressing his forehead against mine. With a deep breath, he released me and pushed away. I dropped my eyes to his crotch where his erection was completely visible, and he adjusted his jeans in an effort to hide it.

I buried my face in my hands. I'd done that a lot lately, but I could feel the tingles across my lips as the heels of my hands pressed against them.

Brantley's voice was muffled at the bottom of the

stairs, and I heard the distinct, sleepy tone of Eli muttering something in response. There was a shuffle, then the sound of the stairs creaking as they went upstairs.

I dropped my hands and blew out a long breath. There was no denying that this time, I'd been the one who'd crossed the line. I could have said no, kept up denial, but I didn't. I'd given in, and, one again, been saved by one of the twins.

Who knows what would have happened if Eli hadn't woken up just now?

I wouldn't have stopped. That much I did know.

I had nothing with me but my car keys which were still in the pocket of my sweater. I patted it just to make sure, and they answered with a reassuring jingle.

The urge to leave overcame me, but it wouldn't solve anything. It would just put off another conversation about the fact we'd kissed.

A conversation that had, ultimately, led to us kissing again.

That and the fact me and my big mouth had let slip that I think he's hot.

Really, I only had myself to blame. I was such an idiot.

My mouth was dry. I grabbed a glass from the cupboard and filled it using the dispenser from the fridge. I drank it in one, the coolness of the water soothing as it slid down my through.

Setting it by the side of the sink next to my empty wine glass, I took yet another deep breath, except this one was a steeling one. One that straightened my spine and grew me a pair of balls for the conversation I was about to have.

Brantley stood in the doorway, arms crossed, leaning against the doorframe. His eyes ran up and down my body, and though I shouldn't have, I glanced at his crotch again.

Yep. Still noticeable.

I looked back up and met his eyes. He had one eyebrow cocked in amusement, and I bit the inside of my cheek so I didn't justify the fact I'd just blatantly looked at his erection.

I mean…there was no justifying it, was there? Not really. I wasn't going to apologize or anything.

"I half-expected you to be running out the door," he commented.

"I decided to be an adult about it tonight," I replied, fidgeting with my zipper.

"Is that why you can't stand still like a toddler?"

"Pretty much."

He laughed and pushed off the doorframe, dropping his arms to his sides. "Are you still here so we don't have another awkward conversation with semi-sincere apologies tomorrow?

That was about right, yeah. "Basically."

"Don't worry, Kali. I didn't intend to apologize again. You certainly don't seem to want one."

I opened my mouth, then paused. He was right. I didn't want one. He didn't need to apologize. "You don't have to apologize again," I said quietly. "But, this is against my company rules. I can't get involved in any way with clients. So, this…" I waved my hand between us. "No matter how attracted we might be to each other, it can't happen again. Okay?"

He leaned back against the counter, once again

folding his arms. "Okay."

"Okay? You're...okay?" I blinked at him.

"What else do you want me to say? No, I insist you continue to break your rules?" He smirked. "I'm sorry I made you break a rule you obviously stand by...Most of the time."

"Uh, all of the time, except for yesterday. And just now." And probably the next time he decided to kiss me.

"Of course." The smirk didn't leave his face. "So, I'll see you tomorrow?"

This conversation had done a one-eighty.

I decided to take it and run with it. "Tomorrow. Right. Bye." I slipped past him, but he shot an arm out, stopping me.

His eyes searched mine, almost as if he were asking permission to say what he wanted to next. Something I didn't know if I'd like when it left his mouth.

"I'm not sorry I kissed you, Kali. And I won't apologize for the fact I want you."

Boom. Boom. Boom. My pulse echoed in my ears, and I knew then, staying was a mistake. I should have gone when he was upstairs.

Because those words changed a lot.

I said nothing as he released my arm. I held his gaze for a moment too long—a moment that said he wasn't lying about wanting me—and left.

And as I got in my truck and drove home, as I pulled up in my drive and let myself into my house...As I locked the door and ran upstairs to my bedroom and slumped onto the end of my bed, his words echoed around my mind.

I want you.

18

Jayda: *You have got to learn to keep your tongue in your own mouth.*

Me: *You're the one who made me have dinner with him.*

Jayda: *I didn't make you do anything. I dangled a guilt bait in front of you and you took it.*

Jayda: *Besides, I didn't make you shove your tongue down his throat, did I?*

Me: *It just happened.*

Jayda: *You know what just happens, Kali? Dropping a glass. Kicking the remote off your table. Forgetting about the peppers in the bottom drawer of your fridge. Those things just happen. Kissing someone does not just happen.*

Seriously. You forget about peppers one time. One. Time. And you're victimized over it for years. Pfft.

Me: *It does just happen and it did just happen. Now I have to paint his house all day when his kids are at daycare.*

Jayda: *Kiss him again and finish the job when you won't be interrupted.*

Me: *Against company rules!*

Jayda: …*Which you've done a stellar job of following so far.*

Me: *Fuck off.*

Jayda: *Get fucked.*

Jayda: *No, literally. Literally get fucked.*

Me: *We're done here.*

While I didn't disagree with Jayda's recommendation of getting fucked, it was inappropriate. We'd already crossed that line, but I wasn't sure crossing it even further was a wise thing to do.

For now, I was going to focus on my job. Nothing else but my job. That was my plan, and I was going to stick with it, no matter how hard it seemed at times.

After a quick call with my dad to check on the progress of the kids' beds, I got stuck in to painting. I'd called Eric and had him delay the floors by another twenty-four hours. It was annoying, and he hadn't sounded too impressed.

Until I'd explained why.

Then he'd laughed for a good five minutes before telling me he'd waive the extra delivery fee.

Gee, thanks, friend.

I told him if he really wanted to make it better, to get his ass over here and paint. Naturally, he refused, so here I was, by myself, painting.

In silence.

It was, actually, quite nice. Aside from the first few days, I hadn't been in the house alone to get work done. There had always been the undercurrent of noise from the kids downstairs—if they weren't up here.

In an odd way, though, I missed that same noise. It was almost eerie to be alone in the empty house, so

I set my phone on the windowsill in Eli's room and opened Spotify. The quiet hum of music made it a little easier to cope with.

I painted and painted and painted, going over and over the spots that had been…affected…yesterday. That was the nicest way I could put it in my mind.

While the white paint dried on those bits in Eli's room, I washed my hands and, with my phone between my teeth, moved into Ellie's. Her paint had dried evenly—more so than I'd thought it would—so I knew that with one more coat, her walls would be done.

I pulled my phone from my mouth and texted Eric quickly to confirm he could get the flooring in at least Ellie's room tomorrow. Without hanging around for his response, I cracked open a paint can using a screwdriver and poured it into a tray.

I would be glad to see the end of this pink paint.

Shamelessly, I sang along to Justin Bieber as I painted. It cycled through my favorite, big playlist on shuffle, taking me from the country twangs of Luke Bryan to the latest Maroon 5.

I hummed along, not knowing the words, until it flipped over to Sam Hunt. Trading my roller for a paintbrush, I dipped it in the paint and sang along to *Body Like a Back Road.* Between dips, the paintbrush acted as my microphone.

Oh my god, I'd never had so much fun painting in my life.

I stood, wiped paint from the brush, and continued my personal concert. The music flipped over from Sam to Demi Lovato's *Instruction*, and, well, I got into it a little too much.

The brush was my mic; the window my adoring fans. I slid left and right and back just like the song demanded. My braid swung around my shoulders as I danced.

I spun.

And froze.

Open-mouthed, mid-chorus, I stopped on the balls of my feet, staring at Brantley in the doorway.

Oh, shit.

The grin that stretched across his handsome face was disarming, and it was clear to see that he'd been quietly laughing his ass off as he watched me.

I took a step to the side, my bare foot kicking the paint tray. "Ouch!" I grabbed my ankle and hopped to the side, leaning against the dry wall. "Um…Hi. I didn't see you there."

He just grinned at me.

"How long have you, um, been there?"

"Long enough." His eyes sparkled.

Oh god.

"Oh goddddd," I moaned.

"If this building thing doesn't work out for you, can I suggest the X-Factor?" He rubbed his hand over his mouth.

I blushed furiously, my cheeks burning right red.

"I have to be honest. If I knew I'd be getting a show, I'd have come home half an hour ago."

"I was just taking a break. Stretching, you know." I let go of my ankle and gingerly put my foot down. "Getting rid of some cramp."

"Is dancing to Demi Lovato conductive to getting rid of cramp, then?"

"How do you know it's Demi Lovato?"

"I listen to the radio in the car, you know."

"Right. 'Course." I turned and paused the music, taking a second to realize why I didn't know he was coming: I'd turned the volume right up. "I'll just…" I waved my brush. "Get back to work."

"Are you sure you don't have the Macarena on that list?"

"One song!" I threw my arms out. "One song. God. Everyone does it."

"Generally, not with paintbrushes."

"I improvised. Sue me."

He laughed, pressing his hand against his stomach. "Come on. It's lunchtime. I stopped in to the Coastal. I got lunch and an interrogation."

I narrowed my eyes at him. "Did you accidentally buy too much, or…?"

"No, I deliberately bought you a sandwich. Marcie told me your favorite, then proceeded to interrogate me about dinner last night."

"Oh no." That meant my mother knew and I could expect a visit tonight. "What, um…What did you say?"

"I told her I couldn't tell her anything because a gentleman doesn't kiss and tell, but that you left later than she'd been told." He winked and ran out of the room.

My eyes widened. "No, no, no! You did not say that!" I ran after him. "Brantley! Brant! No! Tell me you didn't say it!"

He had his hands flattened on the kitchen table. He leaned forward, laughing.

I pointed my paintbrush at him. "Tell me you're messing with me!"

"Nope. Sorry. That's what I told her."

"No! Oh my god! My mom is going to kill me!"

He laughed even harder.

I darted around the side of the table.

"Oh, shit!" escaped his lips as he ran around it.

I stopped where he'd just been. "I swear, I will paint you with this brush if you don't tell me you're messing with me. I cannot cope with this."

"I gave them something to gossip about!" He held his hands up.

My heart skipped a beat. Oh no, no, no. "You have no idea what you've just done!" I ran back to my side of the table, and he went back to his. I was still waving the paintbrush menacingly in his direction. "I'm going to kill you!"

He waggled his eyebrows. "You'll have to catch me first."

I glared at him.

Clearly, he had no idea how determined I could be.

Three times. I chased him around the table three damn times to the sound of his laughter and my frustrated shouts.

"Stop it! Come here so I can paint you!"

"That," he wheezed, gripping a chair to catch his breath, "would be so much sexier if you weren't chasing me around my kitchen table."

"Urrrrr!" I half-growled, half-groaned.

I feinted to the right—but went left. The exact same direction Brantley went in.

"Ha!" I grabbed his arm and slapped it with the paint-coated brush bristles.

"Damn it, Kali!" He reached for the brush, and

before I knew it, he was chasing me around the table.

There wasn't a chance in hell I was going to give him the brush. Who knew what mess he'd make in an effort to get me back for that measly mark on his arm?

Judging by the mess the twins were capable of…He'd make me regret ever pointing my paintbrush at him.

"Give me the brush. Now." He dad-voiced me, holding his hand out expectantly.

I folded my arms, carefully keeping the brush close to my body without getting paint on myself. "No. That voice won't work of me. I have twenty-six-years of practice of resistance against the Dad-Voice."

"Worth a try. But, still… Give me the brush."

I shook my head. "I'm not giving you the brush, because I know exactly why you want it."

"All right. I gave you a chance." He darted forward.

A scream left my mouth. I ran around the table once, before making a grave error—I ran out of the kitchen. Into the living room and around the coffee table before running into the hallway.

And running smack into Brantley, who'd apparently been waiting for me.

"No! Nooo!" I wrestled to keep control of the brush, but he had me. One strong arm clamped around my back, and his other hand fought for the brush. I wriggled and tugged with all my might, both hands on the brush handle while I laughed.

I wasn't giving up, but neither was he.

A fact I realized as he angled the brush and swiped it down my face.

"Oh my god!" I released the brush with one hand

and wiped it over the paint.

He laughed harder than I'd ever heard him laugh, and my whole body vibrated with the sound. Even through the annoyance that I was, once again, covered in paint, I couldn't deny the attraction that pooled deep in my tummy.

"I told you to give me the brush!"

"Never!" I fought back, just missing getting a mouthful of paint. I managed to get the brush across his jaw, turning his stubble pink before he regained control and wiped it over my cheek.

Honestly, I had to wonder what someone would think if they could see us. Two grown-ass adults fighting over a paintbrush, both covered in pink paint.

"Oh my god, stop!" I giggled as he tickled the brush down my neck. Wriggling away, he clamped his arm tighter around me and held me against him. I managed to turn away from him, almost twisting my wrist as I kept my iron-clad grip on the brush. "Let me go!"

"No. I warned you, and you didn't listen to me. This is your punishment."

"Being covered in paint isn't a punishment. It's a daily occurrence."

"You're right. This is backfiring. Can you stop wriggling?"

My mouth formed a tiny 'o' as realization struck. My ass was snuggled carefully against his crotch, and I wasn't the only person strangely turned on by this paint fight. Then… "Let me go."

"That's not how this works."

"You're right. It's not." I deliberately wriggled my ass against him. "Now, let me go."

He gritted his teeth and slid the brush down my cheek.

"Ahhh!"

"Stop moving!"

"Let me go!"

He sighed. "We're at a stalemate, aren't we?"

"No." I wriggled again, poking my ass out a little further.

"Stop it." He painted my cheek again.

I wiped my hand on my shirt and covered my eyes. I would keep this up as long as he kept up his painting. It was already going to end badly, and there was no way I'd be able to look him in the eye after having his cock rub against my ass, so what did it matter?

"Kali…" His voice was lower, almost dangerous in its roughness. "If you don't stop moving, I'm not going to be responsible for how hard I shove you against the wall and kiss you."

That almost sounded like a challenge.

"Against the rules. I'm working," I breathed.

"Given that my cock is twitching against your ass, and it's your fault, I don't think you can use that as an excuse."

"If you'd just let me go…" I dropped my hand from my eyes since he seemed to have given up painting my face for now.

"You wouldn't be covered in paint."

"You wouldn't have a raging hard-on."

"A raging hard-on, eh?"

"I should stop talking right now."

He released the paintbrush, finally, and walked around. His hand slid across my stomach as he moved so he was standing in front of me.

"I agree," he murmured, brushing two fingertips across my temple.

My scalp tingled when he softly pushed hair behind my ear, his eyes following the movement of his hand. I shivered as the pads of his fingers brushed my earlobe, and that movement brought his gaze back to mine.

Indecision. It warred in his eyes, as I was sure it did in mine.

I wanted him to kiss me again. I wanted to feel that bliss, that escape from reality for just a few seconds.

At the very same time, I wanted him to let me go. To stop making it hard for me to resist him. To be the aloof guy he was the first couple times we met.

He leaned in.

I did the only thing I could think of doing.

I swiped my paintbrush down his cheek.

"Fuck it!"

I laughed and ducked under his arm as he raised it to wipe the paint. I ran into the kitchen and grabbed the brown paper bag with the Coastal's logo on it.

"No." He pointed at me. "You don't hold food hostage."

"I do hold food hostage." I carefully considered my next words. "You can have it back if you promise not to kiss me again."

He blinked at me. Looked at the bag. Met my eyes. Shrugged. "I guess I'm skipping lunch."

My jaw dropped. "Seriously?"

"What? You want me to make a promise I can't keep?" He raised an eyebrow. "The only reason you just got away with the shit you just pulled is because it's during work hours."

"Chasing me around your kitchen table doesn't exactly equal work hours, now, does it?"

"Careful, Kali. You might talk yourself into something you can't get out of."

"Oh, I'm pretty sure I already did that," I muttered to myself. "Fine. Here you go. But, I can't promise I won't kick you in the balls if you try again."

"No, you won't."

"Try me."

He smirked, taking the bag from me.

Crap. There was me talking myself into something I couldn't get out of…

19

"I heard you stayed late at Brantley's house," Mom said, turning on my coffee machine.

She had, very helpfully, let herself in before I'd gotten home from work. After way too many questions about the state of me, still covered in paint, I'd convinced her to let me shower before she went down her line of questioning.

I really needed that spare key back.

I chewed on the end of a Twizzler. "I can't imagine who told you that."

She peered at me over her shoulder. "Marcie. I stopped in to get some pastries."

"Why didn't you go the bakery?"

"I did. She was there."

Well, that was clear. "Right. Well, it's not true. Sorry to disappoint you."

She pulled her mug from the machine with a roll of her eyes. "Why does she think that if it isn't true?"

"Because he's a little shit who's about to learn that small town rumors will come back to bite him on his very fine ass," I huffed, still chewing down the Twizzler.

"So, is there truth to it or not? And how does Marcie know?"

I sighed heavily, putting the candy down. "I had dinner with him last night—as a friend," I added pointedly. "And I guess the Bay-vine got hold of that information. He got us lunch from the Coastal, Marcie asked, and he elaborated to give everyone something to talk about."

Mom's lips twisted to the side. "Is that how you ended up covered in pink paint?"

"Long story short, yes. I wasn't happy with him."

"No kidding. You looked like you got in a fight with the paint aisle in the home store. Or Barbie."

"Definitely Barbie." I went back to chewing on my Twizzler.

"It was just dinner, then?"

She was fishing. Honestly, she may as well have pulled out a damn fishing rod, attached a Twizzler to the end, and baited me into telling her.

Well, she was the moron who gave me the Twizzlers first. So, ha.

"Just dinner," I said breezily.

"Kali." She met my eyes with a look that make me bristle. "Do you think I'm stupid?"

"It was just dinner!" I insisted, finishing the candy. I was an animal, eating with my mouth full, but I didn't care.

"You're being defensive, and you're a godawful liar."

"I've heard that a lot this week."

"Start telling the truth."

"Can't." I paused. "The truth is against company policy."

Her eyes widened, and she grinned like she'd hit the jackpot. "I promise not to tell your dad."

Sighing, I took the Twizzler packet and went into the living room. Mom was hot on my heels like a puppy begging for scraps. I threw myself onto the sofa, tugged up my shirt, and yanked another bit of candy from the packet.

"Talk. Now." She wiggled her fingers at me.

"I don't wanna," I mumbled.

"Kali."

"We kissed. Twice," I admitted, looking down. "Almost three times, but I attacked him with my paintbrush."

Mom snorted. "There's something you don't hear every day."

I peered up at her through my lashes. "It doesn't matter. I told him it can't happen again."

"Because it's against company policy?"

"Exactly. I was part of making that rule with Dad. I mean, I know you guys met when you hired him, but still. He told me nothing happened until after, and him meeting you made him realize how important that rule was."

She blinked at me. "He told you nothing happened until after he was done working for me?"

"Yes," I said slowly. "That was the reason we made the rule."

"Oh boy." She exhaled slowly and put her mug on the coffee table. "Honey, I'm not sure how to tell you this, but your father and I were fucking like rabbits before he was ever done working for me."

I froze. I didn't even fucking breathe. That was way more information than I'd ever wanted to know about them.

I smacked my lips together. "And now I'm going to be sick."

Mom laughed, tapping her fingers against my knee. "That was a little blunt. My point is, he only added that rule because he realized that one day, you'd run the company, and he didn't want you mixing business and pleasure."

I frowned. That changed everything I knew. "But…isn't that my choice?"

"I think he wanted you to stay on schedule. He…lost some time when we met."

Holding up my hands, I shook my head. "Nope. Enough on that, thank you."

Her laughter filled the room. "Point taken, honey. So…Can I ask about Brantley?"

"You're going to whether I want you to or not."

"True." She grinned, picking up her coffee again. "Do you like him?"

"That's a very high school question. I mean, I'm not scribbling "Mrs. Kali Cooper" in a notebook or anything."

"Kali Cooper sounds good."

"So does Kali Hancock," I retorted. "Stop taking this places it isn't meant to go, Mom. I'm attracted to him, but I'm also attracted to Tom Hardy. That doesn't mean I'm going to marry him and have his babies."

"You and every other woman in the country." She sipped. "You know what I mean when I ask if you like him."

"Mom." I held my hands up. "It's not…easy. You know exactly how it is to have feelings for someone who already has a family. I'm in the exact same position you were, except my mom's death wasn't as raw for me and dad as the twins' is for Brantley. Two and a half years isn't that long. Even if I did have strong feelings for him, I couldn't waltz in there like he belonged to me. His heart belonged to someone else.

Enough that they had a family." I sank back into the sofa. "That isn't what I want. I don't want to be second best to a memory."

"Do you think I'm second best to a memory?"

"That's not what I meant."

"I know. I'm asking you a real question, Kali. Is that how you think I feel?"

I met her eyes. They were soft and gentle. They were honest. She really was asking.

"You're not to me," I answered after a moment. "Do you feel like you are?"

"I never have, no. She's your mom, but I am, too. We're just your moms at different times in your life. Your dad still loves her, but it's a different love. I accepted that a long time ago. You can't erase the memory of someone, but that doesn't mean you have to be second best to them. And anyone who makes you feel that way doesn't deserve you in the first place."

I smiled sadly. "Thanks. That makes me feel better. But, still, you're a stronger person than I am. Does it make me a bad person if I say I don't know if I want the baggage of someone else's kids?"

"Not at all. That makes you human." She finished her coffee and put the mug down. "For the record, I felt the same. Sometimes you don't get a choice." She stood and kissed the top of my head. "I'll see you for dinner, honey."

I smiled, and just before she left, turned around and said, "Hey, Mom?"

"Hmm?"

"I'm really glad you didn't get a choice."

She winked. "Me, too, Kali."

Lunchtime passed in peace. The crazy started when Eric showed up, armed with floorboards and anything else you could imagine. Together, we cleared Ellie's room of all my crap and got started. The delay in my schedule meant he was by himself, and that meant I had to get my hands dirty.

We went through the motions. One by one, we laid the boards and nailed them in, cutting them to size where we needed to. After about an hour, it started to take shape.

I was glad we were doing this together, in the end. It took my mind of the monotony of the painting I'd spend the last forever doing, and being with Eric was always fun. His humor made the time pass a little bit quicker.

His constant requests for a date… Not so much.

"Gonna date me yet, Kali?"

I looked at him as I hammered a nail into place with one swift whack. "That's what I think of your offer."

"You wound me." He shot me a lopsided grin.

I rolled my eyes and got back to work.

Half an hour passed before he spoke again, and when he did, it was because Brantley had shown up and poked his head through the door.

"Hey," he said. "Everything okay?"

I couldn't help my blush as I looked up and our eyes met. "Fine. We should be done in here soon, then we can get Eli's done."

He held my gaze for a moment with a smile, then looked around. "It looks amazing. Ellie's going to freak out when she gets home."

"Lord, I hope I'm gone by then," Eric muttered.

I shot my leg out and kicked him. "Only because you can probably remember the epic tantrums you threw as a kid."

"I did not throw epic tantrums as a kid!"

"Oh, really?" I slid off my knees to sit properly and look at him. "When we were seven, your mom made you get out of the pool to eat at your birthday party. You tantrummed so hard you almost drowned."

"She's lying," Eric told Brantley. "It's not true. That was her."

I kicked him again and grabbed my hammer.

Brantley gave him a tight smile. "Oh, I believe it."

"Hey!" I pointed my hammer at him. "What does that mean?"

He held his hands up. "The hammer is way more terrifying than the paintbrush."

I waved it.

He laughed, all the tension from his smile at Eric disappearing. "All right, all right. Put it down. Do you need anything before I work?"

I glanced at Eric. When he shook his head, I did the same. "Thanks, but we're good. How long until the twins are home?"

He checked his watch. "You've got about three hours."

Eric looked at me. "We're not gonna get it all done today, Kali."

Aw, shit.

"Can't you get one of your guys in? I can't be

anymore off schedule."

"I can try."

"Please." I shot him the sweetest smile and held my hands together. "I'll pay you extra."

He paused. "I'll waive that fee if you go out with me."

"I'll pay you extra," I repeated.

He sighed, putting down his hammer. "I'll see what I can do."

"So, you're good?" Brantley reiterated. His eyes swung from Eric to me, softening in the process.

Hmm.

"We're good. Thanks." I smiled, and he returned it, something that seemed completely at odds with the look in his eyes.

He disappeared, and Eric stood up. He stared at the empty doorway for a moment before looking at me.

"Somethin' going on with you two?" he asked, eyebrows drawn together.

"No," I answered a little too quickly, turning away to line a nail up to bang in. "Why?"

"Dunno. I get the feeling he doesn't like me."

"That's 'cause you're an asshole," I said cheerily. I hit the nail.

He nudged me with his foot. "Shut up."

I grinned at him until he'd turned and left the room. Then, I let the smile fall away and sighed.

If Eric, the guy who was about as observant as snow in a landslide, noticed that Brantley and I had… a thing… then I really needed to sort this out.

Soon.

Ellie gasped, clapping her hands against her cheeks, her mouth wide open. "It's 'mazin'!"

"It's…a floor, Ellie," I said, bringing her back down to Earth. "Just a floor."

"I know, but I can put my wug on it!"

"Not quite yet. I'm not ready for you to do that."

"Why not?" She jutted out her bottom lip and put her hands on her hips.

I knelt down so I was at her level. Gently, I tugged her hands from her hips and poked her lower lip, making her giggle instead. "Because I have a list of things to do. I have some shelves to put up, your curtains need to go up, plus I have to build all your furniture and hang pictures. If you put your rug in there now, it'll get all dusty."

"Oh." She tilted her head to the side. "That's okay, I suppose. Is Eli's fwoor done, too?"

Eli looked at me expectantly.

"Almost. You wanna see it so far?"

He nodded and took hold of my hand. I led him toward the door, opened it, and let him take a look at his three-quarter-done-floor. If Eric's employee hadn't taken an hour to get here, it would have been done. Even with all three of us working on it, we hadn't quite managed to get it done.

Eric promised to show up at eight-thirty the next day to do it, and I was taking him at his word.

"Wow," Eli breathed, ever the child of few words.

"You like it?" I asked him, bending down.

He nodded enthusiastically, his default way of answering in the affirmative.

I smiled and ruffled his hair.

"Kids? Dinner's ready!" Brantley called from downstairs.

Ellie sniffed the air. "I smell pizza!"

That was all it took. Both of them went running down the stairs at a speed that made me cringe and almost tell them to slow down. I shut both their doors with a shake of my head and followed them down—at a normal speed.

I poked my head in the kitchen and waved. "I'll see you tomorrow."

Ellie looked at me with horror. "Don't you want pizza?"

I smiled. "I'm good. It's time for me to go home now." And at least I wasn't covered in paint today.

Brantley set two plates with a big slice each down in front of the twins. "You can stay. There's plenty."

I'd heard that before. "And how much, exactly, is plenty?"

"He bought one for you, too!" Ellie shouted.

"Ellie! Hush!"

"No, you didn't," I said to him. "He didn't?" I asked Ellie.

Eyes wide, she nodded slowly, reaching for her juice box.

I glared at Brantley.

"I didn't buy it for you," he started. "There was an offer, so I took advantage of it."

"Oh, am I not worth full price?"

"Don't even go there." He shook his head. "I'm not falling for that."

I smirked.

"So? Stay? Or do you have other plans?" His voice took on an edge I'd never heard before, and my eyebrows twitched together in a frown.

"Other plans? No. I was going to watch *Friends* re-runs without pants on. I'd hardly call that a plan."

"Can I watch TV widdout pants, Daddy?" Eli asked.

"You never wear pants." Ellie rolled her eyes, poking the hot cheese on her pizza.

"Neither do you," Brantley pointed out. "Are you or are you both not pantsless right now?"

On cue, they both looked down at their legs.

"No pants," they said at the same time.

"Right. So, this conversation is pointless."

Imagine that. A pointless conversation with a four-year-old. What a novelty.

"Pweeease had some pizza," Ellie asked, pulling some of the stringy cheese off the pizza. She placed it on her tongue. "Pwease."

I glanced at Eli who gave me a shy smile. "Fine. But I'm going home after, and there's nothing you can say to make me change my mind. You got that?"

They both nodded, sipping juice at the same time.

Seriously. So weird.

Brantley handed me a plate and opened a pepperoni pizza with a grin.

I side-eyed him, gave him back the plate, and grabbed the box.

He laughed.

My stomach flipped.

I was an idiot. Again.

20

"I don't understand. How am I losing at Snap to a four-year-old?" I looked at Brantley.

"It's one of life's greatest mysteries," he said, frowning at his own pile of 'won' cards.

My plans to leave after dinner had been thwarted by eyes bigger than my belly, swiftly followed up with two pairs of puppy dog eyes and a beg that if I stay to play games they'll never ask again.

Right. I believed that like I believed it'd snow in Rock Bay this winter. On the SoCal coast, that was about as likely as what the twins were promising me.

"I don't get it," I said, staring at the cards in my hand. "How can I lose at Snap?"

Ellie and Eli giggled.

"You don't shout 'snap' kick enough," Ellie explained. "I faster than you."

Yeah, no kidding. I'd figured that much out.

I hmphed and put another card down. Ellie slapped one on top of mine. I did another, the picture matching, and before I'd even opened my mouth, Ellie hollered, "Snap!"

With a sly grin, she whacked her hand on top of the pile and slid the two matching cards toward her.

I stared at Brantley with my mouth open in a "What the fuck?" look.

He glanced at Ellie. "Are you cheating?"

"Nope." She jutted her chin out and up. "I just weal good at Snap."

No kidding. If there was such a thing as a Snap World Tournament, she had a positive future.

Eli put a card on the pile he had between him and his dad. They exchanged cards for a moment before two matched and Eli screamed, "Snap!"

"Oh my god!" Brantley threw his cards down. "This is ridiculous. You're four! I'm almost thirty! How are you beating me, dude?"

"Oh dear, Daddy. Are you hading a tantwum?" Ellie looked at him with her eyebrows raised.

"Do you need a time out?" Eli asked, eyes wide.

I bit the inside of my cheek and looked away.

I was pretty sure I'd heard Brantley say that at some point during the time I'd known them, which just reaffirmed that kids really were tiny sponges in human bodies.

"I need a beer," Brantley muttered, sweeping all the cards into a neat pile. "Come on, you two. It's time for bed."

"Awwww," they whined in chorus. "But we not tired!"

I glanced between them.

"Of course, you're not," Brantley agreed. "But it's still time for bed."

"That's not faaaair," they continued together.

Well, neither was life. Better they learned that early.

"Bedtime," he said again, putting both sets of cards back in their boxes.

"Aw, Daddyyyyy."

"No." He got up and crooked fingers at them. "Let's go."

"Is Kawi staying?"

"No," I said, standing up. "I have a lot of work to do tomorrow, and I already stayed and lost at Snap. I really do have to go."

"Ohhh, but that's not fair," Eli muttered.

Brantley flapped his hands at them. "Go. Upstairs. Find your pajamas. It doesn't matter if Kali stays or not, because you'll be asleep." He herded them out into the hallway, and I followed, clutching my phone and keys.

"But, Daddy," Ellie said, turning halfway up the stairs. "If Kawi goes, then you'll be alone."

He paused. "Yes?"

"Doesn't dat make you sad?"

No. I wasn't going to do it. Not tonight. Not this time. I'd spent more than enough time with him lately, and something had to give. I was not going to be guilted into staying by her.

Nope.

Absolutely not.

I pulled away from the stairs, toward the door.

"No," Brantley said slowly. "I'm used to it. Kali is right—she has a lot of work tomorrow, and you need to get some sleep because you're at Summer's again."

"Again?" Her eyes bugged.

"She bakes nice cookies," Eli said quietly. "I like it there."

My lips twitched up.

Goddamn it, no, they couldn't be doing that.

Every time I smiled at those kids, they stole a little piece of my heart.

"Let's go." Brantley waved his hands, ushering them up the stairs.

"Night, Kawi," Eli shouted over his shoulder.

"Night, kids." I smiled and edged toward the door.

Ellie caught my eyes, a sad look in hers, and waved a tiny hand in goodbye. She dipped her head as Brantley's hand touched her back and pushed her up.

I took a deep breath and sighed it back out. That right there was the epitome of a guilt trip. The sadness in her eyes at the idea of me leaving—

No.

I wasn't going to fall for it. I wasn't going to let it work. I couldn't let it. We'd already crossed too many times and if I stayed…

I leaned against the front door and stared through the door into the kitchen. The smell of pizza still lingered, and I knew there was at least an entire pizza in the box on the side that was probably the reason for it lingering.

I hugged my phone to my stomach, then pulled it out in front of me and texted Jayda.

Me: *At Hot Dad's. Do I stay or do I go?*

Her response was immediate. She needed a life.

Jayda: *Stay.*

In hindsight, she wasn't the best person to ask that question to.

"Jesus, you scared the crap out of me." Brantley laughed, hand on his stomach.

I looked at him wide-eyed.

"I thought you'd left," he said through his laughter. "Is something wrong?"

"No, I…" I paused, narrowing my eyes. "I think I'm falling for Ellie's guilt trip."

"Oooh." He winced. "My apologies. But, that explains why you're still here."

"Yeah, I can't decide if I feel bad for leaving and you being lonely or worse that I'm staying and I probably shouldn't," I said slowly.

"You're staying?" He quirked a brow. "You're welcome to."

"I guess I am. I mean, I was only going to go home, put on *Friends*, and take off my pants."

"You don't need to go home to do that. I'm not the biggest *Friends* fan in the world, but I'd watch it if it meant you weren't wearing pants." A wolfish grin spread across his face.

I rolled my eyes and pushed off the door. "No. I'm not going to take off my pants."

"You wound me." He laughed. "It's a nice evening. Wanna sit outside?"

"Sure." As I followed him out, I realized I'd only ever looked at the yard from Ellie's bedroom window.

Brantley pushed open the back door onto a wooden porch. A large, rattan sofa took up one corner of the porch, and a few half-burned candles sat on the glass table in front of it. The porch looked out over a lush, green yard dotted with kids' toys, everything from a soccer ball to a swing set with a slide.

He took a seat on one end of the sofa, and I dropped myself into the corner, kicking off my shoes. I tucked my feet up and sighed, leaning against the squishy back cushions.

It was basically silent. Aside from the gentle hum of the TV inside, there was nothing. It was incredible, because I'm not sure I realized how loud the twins were until right now.

"Do you feel like this every day when they go to bed?"

Brantley quirked a brow. "Like what?"

"Like, wow, shit, they're really loud."

He stared at me for a moment before bursting into laughter. I blinked at him, watching as his shoulders shook with each deep chuckle that escaped his lips.

"Am I funnier than I think I am?"

He shook his head, still laughing. "No. I'm laughing because I've never put that feeling into words before, but you just nailed it. It really is exactly that."

"They are really loud," I said again, frowning. "Are all kids like that or is it just because there's two of them?"

"You have no idea about kids, do you?"

"Not really. I'm pretty ignorant about them," I admitted with a shoulder shrug. "I've never been around them. The closest I've ever been is in the grocery store with Janie Green's son who screamed the entire trip. I wanted to punch him in the face." I frowned. "That makes me sound like a horrible person."

"Nah, I'm pretty sure we've all felt like that once or twice." He winked with a smirk. "It's pretty amazing, though. You're so good with the twins."

A blush rose up my cheeks. "I'm just nice to them."

"You're more than nice. You're weirdly patient. Like, with the paint. Kali, anyone else would have lost their minds and been so fucking angry, but you just brushed it off."

"I was annoyed." I tucked hair behind my ear. "But me showing them that wouldn't have achieved anything. You handled it. I'm just the builder. My anger has no place here."

"Just the builder." He smiled, meeting my eyes.

"Are you sure I'm not being really funny today?"

He shook his head again, rubbing his hand over his forehead. "I think it's funny that you refer to yourself like that. I think you're more than just the builder."

"You do?"

"Do you have any idea how much fun you are to be around?"

"No, but if you're about to give me some compliments, I'll happily listen."

He laughed. "I just…Hell. You're just fun, Kali. I don't even think you realize how much of an amazing person you are. Moving here was so hard, and until you showed up on my doorstep, I was sure I'd change my mind. You make me laugh more than anyone ever has."

"That's because I'm an idiot," I pointed out. "Like the paintbrush mic thing. Idiocy."

"You're an adorable idiot. It works."

"Aw, you think I'm adorable." I grinned.

"You are when you smile like that."

Another blush heated my cheeks. I cleared my throat and looked down.

Brantley laughed again. "See? Still adorable."

"All right, stop it. You're just saying it to make me blush now."

"Pretty much. Is it working?"

I clapped my hands over my cheeks. "No."

He reached over, grabbed my wrists, and tugged my hands away, revealing the red-hot blush that was coating my cheeks. A disarmingly sexy grin stretched across his face, and I pouted as his gaze flashed across my face.

"Stop it." I wriggled my hands out of his grip. "I swear, messing with me is your new favorite hobby."

"It is," he admitted, eyes sparkling. "You're so easy to fuck with, I don't even have to try."

I rolled my eyes. "And to think—I let myself be guilt-tripped into this."

"More fool you. I warned you about her, and you obviously didn't listen."

"That's so not fair. I did listen, I just don't have freaky skills to avoid the guilt like you do."

"I don't avoid the guilt. I pretend."

"Would you have pretended if you were me, knowing you'd leave a poor guy to be lonely?"

He raised his eyebrows. "I wouldn't have been lonely. I'd have watched TV with my pants off."

"You don't get to use my plans as an excuse," I scoffed. "And unless your daughter is a master manipulator, you would have been lonely."

"She's four. All four-year-old's are master manipulators. If kids came with manuals, that would be the title of the chapter that talks about age four," he said.

"There are technically manuals. They're these wonderful, futuristic things called *books*."

"None of which are geared toward a single dad," he pointed out. "The last time I Googled something, I diagnosed Eli with a rare, deadly disease, learned that there are way too many styles of braid for any human being to master, and also found out how to get the kids out of the door by eight and have time to do my make-up."

I paused. "I can see how that last one would be of use to you. Your mascara looks wonderful today."

He dipped his head and laughed, his shoulders shaking.

I looked out over the trees at the end of the yard. The sun was beginning to set, and bright flecks broke in through the leaves.

"Can I ask you a question?"

Brantley shifted. "You mean another question, right? Since you just did."

I quickly flipped him the bird, which did nothing but make him laugh again.

"Yes. I have a question."

He nodded his head toward me, resting his arm along the back of the sofa. "Shoot."

"Was it Ellie being Ellie, or do you get lonely by yourself?"

He opened his mouth, then stopped. Closing it again, his eyebrows drew together in a frown that made deep furrows across his forehead. "I don't know. I used to, right after Katie died. Now, I think I'm so used to being alone, that even if I were lonely, I wouldn't be able to tell the difference."

I looked down, playing with a loose bit of thread on my shirt. "Is it hard? Like…Do you ever think that one day you'll wake up and it was all in your head? That she's actually alive?"

"It's hard, but she's gone. There's no changing it. I knew she was going to die, and I made peace with it before." He tapped his fingers against the cushion. "But, no, I don't ever wonder if it wasn't real. Too much changed for it to never be real."

Slowly, I nodded. "It's weird. I used to dream that when I was a kid. That my mom hadn't died, and one day I'd come home from school and she'd be baking cookies. I think I convinced myself she was a spy once and that's why she wasn't around."

He smiled. "Grief is weird. When Katie died, I didn't cry. I was numb, but I couldn't show any pain. Everyone thought I was weird, and I swear, if she hadn't been so sick, I would have been questioned over her murder."

That made me laugh. "So, you're a psychopath. Good to know."

"Don't tell anyone. I think I'm starting to make friends and I don't want to scare everyone off."

"Your secret is safe with me. Don't worry."

"Thank God. I might still have to kill you, though." He smirked. "Do you…This is probably a really dumb question, but do you miss your mom? Like really miss her."

"I miss her every day," I answered softly. "It doesn't hurt to miss her anymore, it just kinda is, you know? It's more like it's become a part of me and is as natural as the delight I feel when I find an extra Twizzler in the packet."

"A Twizzler."

"Ah, you haven't been introduced to my obsession yet. Everyone who comes to my house has to bring me Twizzlers. You'd be surprised how steady that candy stream is."

"Good to know." He paused. "And thanks. For

answering the question. It gives me hope that when the twins understand, maybe one day they'll be able to cope with it."

"Do you miss her?"

He blew out a long breath. "I don't know, honestly. It's a bit like the loneliness. I think if I do, I miss what she would do. Like, Ellie's hair, or cutting their nails, or sewing up the knees of Eli's jeans. Does that sound bad?"

"I think it makes sense." I bent my knee and hugged it to my chest. "You miss the fact that they don't have a mom. You miss what she represents instead of her as a person."

He rubbed his hand down his face slowly. "God, that sounds bad."

"I don't think so." I glanced away before meeting his eyes. "That's what my dad missed, too, I think. Our lives changed so suddenly, and he had to learn to do all this stuff he'd never done. I don't think he'd ever threaded a needle in his life until after Mom died. Over time, he reached a point where he missed what she was more than who she was. He had to learn to be a parent all over again."

"Learn to be a parent all over again," Brantley echoed. "That's exactly what it is. I never imagined myself braiding hair or putting softener in Barbie's hair because she got dragged through a bush backwards. There's just so much…stuff. And that's all it is. Stuff. And I can't thread a needle for the life of me. I just buy new jeans."

"It's really not hard. Especially if you patch the knees."

"What part of "I can't thread a needle" is

confusing to you?"

I glared at him. "I'm giving you advice. Take it."

"I still can't thread a needle. It really doesn't matter if patches work or not. I won't be able to apply them."

"Honestly, you're making it sound like threading a needle is like running an army."

"I run an army every day. The problem is, I created them."

"They're not an army." I rolled my eyes. "And I'll teach you how to thread a needle."

"Can't you thread it for me?"

"If I hear the word 'thread' one more time, I'm literally going to punch myself in the face."

Brantley leaned forward. "Thread."

I punched myself in the face, then winced.

"That hurt, didn't it?" He grinned.

"Lil' bit," I replied, rubbing the side of my nose. "Thanks for hurting me."

"I didn't do a damn thing to you."

"You said the word and made me punch myself."

He shrugged. "You're the one who said you'd punch yourself in the face. I was merely conducting an experiment on your ability to follow through with your promises."

"Great. It was a social experiment in trust." I rubbed my nose again. "That really did quite hurt."

He laughed, then leaned forward. Two fingers brushed my jaw, and he turned my face to the side. "There's nothing there. I don't know why you hit yourself so hard."

"Because I'm an idiot. We established this earlier." I turned my head back.

"An adorable idiot."

"Still an idiot."

"The best kind of idiot," he corrected me, a small smile teasing at his lips. "My favorite kind of idiot."

I side-eyed him. "I can't decide if you're still complimenting me."

"Don't take it too highly," he replied. "I have Ellie in the 'adorable idiot' camp, too."

I leaned forward and smacked his shoulder. "Just when I was starting to like you."

"Starting to like me?" He snatched my hand, wrapping his fingers around my wrist. His fingertips pressed on the inside, and he rubbed his thumb along the sensitive skin, sending a tingle up my arm that made me shiver. Eyebrows raised, he continued, "I think you like me a lot more than you're letting on."

Then, like the—adorable—idiot I was, I said, "Prove it."

He blinked and tugged me toward him. I didn't move at first, but he grinned wolfishly and pulled harder. My resistance was useless, and I knew exactly what he was doing. I should have stopped him, but at this point, I couldn't.

I knew what he was doing, and I was so fucked, because I wanted him to do it.

21

Brantley pulled me right over to him, grinning the whole time. My stomach flipped as he literally dragged me on top of him so I straddled him. My knees dug into the cushions either side of his hips, and he slid his hands up my thighs, gripping my hips, and pulling me right against him.

My crotch was nestled against his, and I swallowed hard. This was probably the most intimate position we'd ever been in. My heart beat so fast my chest ached. I didn't know what to do with my hands or where to look—nothing.

"You're blushing again," he muttered, eyes finding mine. "You're so damn cute when you blush."

"First adorable, now cute. You're dishing out the compliments today. Anything else you wanna call me?" My hands finally came to rest on his stomach.

"Plenty," he said in that same, low voice.

I waited for him to elaborate, and when he didn't, I said, "Well?"

He tilted his head to the side. "No."

"Come on!" I tapped his chest. "You can't say that and then stop talking. It's going to drive me crazy."

He smirked. "Welcome to my world."

Ignoring that. "One. Give me one word that you think I am."

"Well, like you said, idiot is well established…"

"I'm done." I pushed myself off him.

Laughing, he pulled me back into him. "You asked."

"Yes. I'm regretting it now," I said dryly. "Are you going to be serious or not? It's bugging me. Come on. Give me one word you think describes me."

"Okay, all right. Fine." He thought for a moment, meeting my eyes, then reached up and pushed my hair behind my ear in strikingly tender moment. "I think you are remarkable."

Whoa.

That was a weighted word. And not at all what I'd expected him to say.

I wet my lips with my tongue. "Remarkable?"

"Yes." He nodded once, his gaze never wavering from mine.

"Why?"

"You make me feel alive."

I took a deep breath in. What was I supposed to say to that? What I wanted to ask was how—how did I do that? I didn't do anything special. I was just me. How did I make him feel alive?

"You make me laugh," he said softly, as if he could read my mind. "Sometimes, it feels like I'm nothing more than Dad. But, with you…When you're around…You make me feel like I'm me again. The person, not just the parent. Almost…Happy."

I made him feel alive.

Like himself.

Happy.

That was crazy. There was no way I had that effect on someone.

I was just me. Just Kali. Crazy and idiotic.

Not all the things he was saying.

"Stop," I said softly, sliding my hands up his chest. "That's not me—that's you. That's you living again."

He cupped my jaw, his fingers curling over my skin. Our gazes collided, and there was no controlling the rapid-fire of my heart as my dark eyes met the turquoise perfection of his.

"Maybe it is," he replied, tilting his head in acknowledgement of my words. "But I'd be remiss if I didn't admit you had an awful lot to do with it."

I swallowed hard. My thumb stroked across the soft material of his t-shirt, eliciting a shiver from him. The reaction was so unexpected my breath hitched, because realization fell at the same time.

How many times had I shivered at *his* touch?

I affected him the same way he affected me.

I slid my hands up his chest, and without hesitation, cupped the sides of his neck and kissed him.

I knew I shouldn't do it, but I didn't care. There was something deep and…*jarring*…about knowing that I made a difference in his life. Something that hit me hard, that made me not care anymore.

That make me want to break all the rules, even if it only lasted for right now.

My lips worked across his even as the thoughts sped through my mind. I didn't want to stop—I couldn't stop. In that moment, I wanted him more than I ever knew I could want a person.

I wanted to feel him, breathe him in, suffocate myself with his touch.

I didn't care about anything other than kissing

him.

And the foreign feeling took over me. Grabbed hold of every cell in my body, pushing its way through my veins until I felt it from the top of my head to the tips of my toes.

Consumed.

I was consumed with the taste of him—consumed with the way I felt when we kissed. Kissing him made me feel like all my nerve endings were fireworks, and every kiss was a fuse burning down until, finally, everything exploded, blinding me with the intensity.

Brantley flipped me over onto my back. His hard body covered mine, and I welcomed his weight as he settled over me. Our lips met again, and I sighed as his tongue found mine.

My fingers combed through his soft hair. His hand slid down my body and down my thigh, pulling my leg up as his fingers probed my thigh. A shiver ran through me when he shifted and his hardening cock pressed against my clit through my shorts. The pressure was intense, making me gasp into his mouth, and his lips twitched into a shadow of a smile.

It lasted only a second.

The amusement was quickly replaced with a raw need that tingled through my veins. The kiss moved from deep to desperate quicker than I could keep up with it, and before I knew it, my hands had slipped out of his hair and was tugging at the material of his shirt.

Up, up, up. I tugged it up his body until it was scooped under his armpits. He finally got the message, sitting up. It slid down, and he grabbed the hem and tore the shirt over his head.

My gaze flitted up and down his torso, over the hard pecs of his chest to the shadows that lined the packs of muscle on his stomach.

Steadying himself with one foot on the floor, he pinched the collar of my shirt, tugging with a half-grin on his face. His fingertips tucked beneath it, brushing my collarbones, before he sat fully upright, grabbed my arms, and pulled me up, too.

He wasted no time in sliding the shirt over my shoulders and down my arms. He threw it to the other side of the soda, then grabbed at my tank top and pulled it up. I raised my arms so he could pull it over my head.

I bit the inside of my cheek as his gaze swept over the white, lacy bra that cupped my boobs. I glanced up, and, just like that, our eyes met.

He kissed me again.

Hungrier. Harder.

Together, we sank down into the soft cushions of the sofa. His hot skin rubbed against mine, and I cupped his neck, stroked his hair, explored the muscles over his shoulders.

I wanted to touch every inch of him—map out the dips and curves of his body and commit him to memory. Revel in touching him and feeling the sensation of my fingertips across his skin.

The hair that dotted the lower half of his stomach and trailed off beneath his waistband.

The gentle bump of his shoulder muscles as they connected his neck and his shoulders.

The roughness of his stubble against my chin.

The softness of his hair between my fingertips.

The pressure of his cock between my legs…

"Daddy?" The call came from somewhere inside the house, snapping us both out of it.

"Here. I'm coming." Brantley stood quickly and, after adjusting his pants, quickly walked into the house.

I clapped my hands over my face. My cheeks burned red-hot, and my stomach dropped with the realization I was basically half-naked, and once again, we'd been interrupted from going further by a kid.

Sitting up, I grabbed my shirts and stood, covering my chest with them as I made my way inside. Footsteps sounded from upstairs, and I moved into the front room to put my clothes back on. I had no idea where my keys or phone were, because my mind was spinning.

Spinning with the implications of what we almost did. Of what I wanted to do—of what I never would have stopped.

My entire body buzzed with the after-effects of our make-out session. There wasn't even enough left to regret it. I think I was past that. I think I'd long accepted that as long as I worked here, I'd have to fight with the irresistible attraction I felt for him, even though he was everything I didn't want.

Everything I thought I never wanted, that was.

I ran my fingers through my mussed-up hair and sighed heavily. What was I doing? Had I no self-control?

No, wait. I knew the answer to that. I had none. None whatsoever.

I grabbed my tank top and put it the right way around before rolling it up and shoving over my head.

I was just about to put one arm in the right hole

when I paused, catching sight of a still-shirtless Brantley in the doorway.

He quirked a brow at me. "Going somewhere?"

I cleared my throat. "Um, well…"

Slowly, he walked toward me. Step, step, step…Closing the distance between us until he was a breath away. "Going somewhere?" he repeated.

I moved back. Glancing over my shoulder to make sure I never tripped on anything, I was apparently unable to judge the distance between me and the wall and slammed back into it.

"Oh, shit," I muttered, flattening my hands against it. I could only imagine what I looked like with my white tank hanging around my neck.

An idiot.

An idiot was the answer.

"Yes," I replied, sinking against the wall. "Can't you see I'm busy trapping myself against the wall like an idiot?"

Brant reached forward. His fingers curled around my shirt, and he looped it over my head, then threw it behind him to the sofa.

There was a predatory glint in his eye, one that made me shudder with anticipation. My whole body shivered with it. I was on fire where his fingertips had brushed across my collarbones.

"We're not done," he murmured, stepping ever closer to me, closing the distance between us completely. "They're asleep and, right now…" he trailed off, saying nothing.

"Right now, what?" I asked.

Hesitation hitched his breath, making his chest heave, but his turquoise eyes never left mine. "Right now, you're mine."

"For—for what?" I stuttered. My heart thundered against my chest, because I knew exactly what for.

Brant pressed against me, cupping my face, his large hands ignoring the blistering heat of my cheeks entirely as he took control of my face. "I want you, Kali. I want you so badly that I'm on the brink right now. And I know you feel the same way—I can feel it."

"And what do you want me to do about that?"

"Give in," he breathed, holding himself against me. "Give in to what you know you want. You want me."

"Maybe so, but—"

Lips.

Mine.

"I can't," I whispered.

"You can," he whispered right back. "Once, Kali. Just once. Be mine. Right now. Tonight. Stop fighting it."

He was right. I wanted him. I wanted this.

I wrapped my fingers around his neck and pulled him into me. It didn't mean I'd be his, but for tonight, maybe he could be mine.

Pushed against the wall, he held me solid, flat, stable. I melded against the surface. He leaned into me, hands riding down, and pressed his mouth to mine.

"Trust me," was all he whispered.

Trust him was all I could do.

His hands slid down my body. He explored my body from my head to the waistbands of my shorts. He tugged them down and let them pool at my feet. Pulling his lips away, his expectant gaze met mine, and

I chewed the inside of my lip as I stepped out of them and flicked them to the side with my toe.

He trailed his gaze up and down my body a few times. I squirmed back against the wall under his scrutiny—until I looked right back at him and the bulge in his pants.

He cupped my face and kissed me, pressing his hips right against me. The kiss was deep and hungry, and as desire throbbed through my veins, I reached between us and undid the button of his jeans.

He was right.

I wanted him.

And there was nothing I could do about it.

I shoved his jeans down over his ass. He laughed against my lips as the jeans fell down to his feet. He stepped out of them and kicked them away the same way I'd done with my shorts.

With both of us in our underwear, this was the point of no return.

Fuck it.

I cupped his hard cock. My fingers brushed over his balls, and he jerked his hips into my hand. He basically pushed my hand away from him and trailed his fingertips up the inside of my thigh.

I shivered.

His fingers got closer and closer to my aching clit. I clenched, squeezing my thighs together, but with one swift movement, he slipped his fingers between my legs and brushed the pad of his thumb over my lacy thong.

Another shiver ran through me.

I took a deep breath as he toyed with the material.

"Open your legs," he murmured, slipping my

panties to the side.

I obeyed. Shuffled my feet a couple inches apart, although what I really wanted to do was clamp my legs shut.

He peered down, brushing the backs of his fingers across the mound of skin above my clit. Then, slowly, carefully, he ran one finger across my pussy.

I gasped, flinching at the contact.

"You're so wet." He dipped his head, kissing my neck, his finger just pushing inside me. "And you were going to leave." Another finger joined the first inside me. Slowly, he moved his hand, his fingers pumping in and out of my wetness.

I arched my back, eyes closed.

He gripped my chin, pulling my head back down. "Open your eyes. I want you to look at me when you come."

I couldn't speak. But, I did as he said. Opened my eyes and met his gaze as he worked his fingers inside me.

He pulled them out, moving now to my clit. I ached so bad, and never mind that staring into his eyes while he circled his fingertips over my clit was the most awkward thing I think I'd ever done, I wanted to come.

I needed to come.

I was turned on beyond belief.

Never had I wanted something—someone—as much as I wanted this. Brantley.

I clenched and clenched as he rubbed my clit. My legs shook, and he wrapped an arm around my waist as if he knew they were ready to give out. I pressed further and further against the wall, as if I could sink into it.

Tiny moans escaped me, mingling with his harsh, heavy breaths. It was the only sound, and it took everything I had to stay as quiet as I was.

"Come," he whispered, lips close to mine. "Come, and I'll fuck you."

I held on for all of thirty seconds before I gave in.

The orgasm flooded through me with a sweetness I didn't know possible. Every part of my body was touched by it, from the hairs on the back of my neck to my aching thigh muscles. It felt so fucking good—I was both exhausted and exhilarated by it.

He held me for a moment, then he kissed me and released me. "Give me a minute. Take off the rest of your clothes while I'm gone."

I did a double-take. "Where are you going?"

He motioned to his cock. "To get a condom."

"Oh. I, um." What was I doing? I'd never had sex without a condom. "You don't...I mean..."

Spit it out, Kali.

Awkwardly, I held up my arm and pointed to the tiny scar where my contraceptive implant was. "I'm good," I finally said. "And...I mean, I trust you."

He raised his eyebrows. "You don't want me to wear a condom?"

"If you want to. I'm not stopping you. I'm just saying. I'm good."

"You're so awkward." He came back to me, cupping my face. He kissed me deeply, then hooked two fingers in the sides of my thong and pushed it down my legs.

By the time I'd stepped out of them, I'd unhooked my bra and taken it off, too.

He kicked it to the side and kissed me. Deeper…harder…more desperately than before. With one hand on the back of my neck, he fidgeted. Dropped both hands. Grabbed my legs—

Heaved me up, wrapping my legs around his waist. His now-free cock brushed against my wet pussy, and I circled my arms around his neck as he grabbed my ass, using the wall as leverage.

He reached down and positioned himself to enter me. In one slow, easy thrust, he did just that.

I half-moaned, half-gasped.

God, he felt so good inside me.

Both hands now on my ass and gripping it so tight it bordered on painful, he moved, in and out, and soon enough, I adjusted to him, and it was easy.

He kissed me.

Moved faster.

Really *fucked* me. Like he meant it, like he needed it, like he was desperate to. Whatever it was he was feeling, he channeled it into his movements and fucked me harder and harder, his grip on my ass holding me in place.

My back arched, and I moaned, my nails dragging across his shoulders. Whether I was trying to hold onto him or push him away, I didn't know. I was hot all over, my heart thundering, and all I wanted was to feel the release I knew was building up.

Desperation.

That's what his kiss tasted like.

That's what he fucked me like.

And I loved it.

I couldn't get enough. I wanted more. More of the ass grip, of the lip bite, of the deep satisfaction I felt when he buried himself fully inside me and pressed against my clit at the same time.

More of his deep, guttural grunts of pleasure when I squeezed.

More of the hard-hitting orgasm that had me burying my face in his shoulder, my nails digging deep into his skin. Of the pleasure that wracked my body, head to toe, sending my heartbeat skyrocketing as I came hard all over him.

He thrusted faster, then, deep inside me, stilled, moaning into my shoulder. I swear, I felt it as he came.

It shouldn't have turned me on, but it did.

He held me there against the wall until we'd both regained our breath. Leaning back, he pulled out of me and gently lowered my legs to the ground. My toes touched down tentatively, and although I was shaking, I nodded to tell him I was fine.

Brantley curled one hand around the back of my neck and kissed me. At odds with the way he'd fucked me, it was gentle and sweet, and seemed to say so many things I couldn't figure out.

"Oh no," I whispered when he pulled away.

"What?" Alarm tinged his tone, and he met my eyes.

I sighed. "Now, it's going to be awkward when I leave. And I have to leave, or everyone and their mother will be discussing the fact I didn't."

He blinked at me, then burst out laughing. "Is that it?"

"That and I have a healthy amount of come dripping down my leg right now."

He tilted his head, lips twitching. "Let me get you a towel for that."

"That would be great, thanks," I deadpanned. And squeezed my legs shut.

God, that doesn't happen in porn, does it?

Never mind porn giving men unrealistic ideas about a pair of tits—it'd given me an unrealistic expectation of how clean wall sex was.

Which was not at all.

"Here." Brantley handed me a black towel, and I stuffed it between my legs in the most unladylike way possible. He laughed at me again. "Now, for the second problem… Since you like to run, would it help if I used the bathroom and be in there just long enough for you to get dressed and leave? No awkward goodbyes, no nothing that you tend to avoid."

Huh.

That wasn't a bad idea.

I nodded. "Let's go with that. It'll save me doing something stupid like thank you for the orgasm on my way out."

He pressed his lips together, shoulders shaking. "Right. Well, I'm going to use the bathroom."

I nodded again, casting my gaze around for my clothes. Bra…shirt…shorts…

"Oh, and, Kali? You're welcome for the orgasm*s*."

I grimaced. Ah, well. He knew I was awkward anyway.

The sound of his laughter accompanied his exit, and I quickly wiped my legs and between my thighs. God, sex was gross. They really needed to teach that in sex ed.

I gathered my clothes, shoving my bra and shirt on quickly. My plaid shirt was a crumpled mess on the back of the sofa, but whatever. The only thing I couldn't find was my panties.

Where the hell had he put them?

Another quick look, and I had to cringe and throw on my shorts without them. There was only so long Brantley could pretend to be in.the bathroom.

I grabbed the rest of my things and paused at the front door.

Did I shout goodbye? That I'd see him tomorrow at ten?

Shit.

I opened the door and ran before I really made a fool out of myself.

22

I stared at the ceiling. My alarm had gone off an hour ago, but I'd barely moved from bed since. Not that it mattered, because I didn't have any work to do first thing this morning.

What I did have was a healthy dose of regret for the decision I made last night. Except this time the regret wasn't because of what I'd done, it was because I didn't feel bad about it at all.

No. For the first time since I'd met Brantley I was…happy. It felt right. The guilt was there because it shouldn't have, but no amount of staring at the plain white ceiling would make me feel any differently about what we'd done.

I sighed and rubbed my hand over my face. If I thought it had been awkward after we kissed, I didn't know what I was gonna say to him today.

More to the point, I didn't know how I was going to cope with the realization that I had feelings for this man. It was weird that it had taken sex for me to realize that I had genuine feelings for him, but hey, my life was weird, and so I didn't expect this to be any different.

The next issue, of course, was what I was going to do about the feelings. Which was, at this point, not a damn lot. What was I supposed to do? After all, he'd moved her to escape the death of his wife. I couldn't exactly try to convince him to have a relationship.

Not that I wanted a relationship.

Besides, even if I did want a relationship, falling for a man with children was never in my plan. Except, of course, these weren't just any kids. Eli and Ellie were different—and, dammit. I wasn't just falling for their dad, I was falling for them, too.

And that was the biggest problem.

Avery time I looked at them, I saw myself. I saw myself as the five-year-old girl who lost her mother. Granted, they lost their mother a lot younger age than I had, but it didn't change the fact I knew how it felt to grow up without one.

Not that it meant that it was my job to take over as their mom.

Not that I thought I could. You didn't just take over a job like that, after all.

See? This was exactly why I didn't want to fall for somebody who had kids. There were too many questions, almost a strange kind of etiquette that came of this situation. And I didn't know how to handle it. I was too flighty to handle it.

But…was there a way to handle it? I knew my stepmother had. Portia had never had an issue, at least that's not what it seemed. To me, she'd stepped smoothly into the role of being a parent although she never had any kids of her own. Maybe that was why she was able to. Her maternal instincts had been there after all and it had never been her choice not to have children but one that the universe is decided for her.

The difference was, I'd never wanted to have children.

It had never even been in my plans. Never considered, never been anything I'd ever particularly wanted.

Well, until now.

At least, I thought I wanted that.

Maybe, I just wanted Ellie and Eli.

It was a strange feeling. I never thought I'd find myself falling in love with somebody else's children. The problem was, Ellie and Eli were so very easy to fall in love with. Sure, they fought, but what kids didn't?

No, the best part of their relationship was the way they loved each other even when they were screaming at each other. Not to mention they were both just so adorable it would be hard not to love them anyway.

With a sigh, I pushed the bed sheets to the side and climbed out of bed. I'd laid still long enough, and it was time to get up and do something. Even if that thing was only walking to the coffee machine.

Not that walking to the coffee machine didn't achieve anything, and, honestly, it felt like the only thing I could do right now.

Because I still hadn't figured out what I was going to say to Brantley when I saw him this morning.

I couldn't exactly be like, "Oh, hey, thanks for the sex last night, I'm going to build your kids wardrobe now."

No. Ugh.

What was I saying about not regretting last night?

Stupid me. I'd spoken too soon.

I walked into the bathroom to a doubletake in the mirror. There were dark bags beneath my eyes and my hair was messed up beyond belief.

Honestly, I looked like I'd been in a fight with a bush and lost.

I turned on the shower, and stared at myself in

the mirror while the water ran behind me. I looked like shit. My make-up was smudged, giving me dark circles under my eyes. My dry lips still held hints of my red lipstick where I hadn't bothered to wash my face before going to sleep last night.

And I didn't even include the zip that was coming up on the side of my nose. Great. Just great.

I took a deep breath and grabbed my face cloth. I dipped it under the flow of water coming from the shower and wiped my face until all traces of yesterday's make-up had gone.

I sighed heavily, stripped off, and got into the shower.

Letting the water rush over me, I tried to relax. It wasn't working. So many horror theories about what would happen when I saw Brantley were swirling around in my head. I didn't know why I was so nervous. Was it because I knew he wasn't really in a position to have a relationship? Or was it because I knew no matter how much I liked him this wasn't the kind of relationship I wanted?

Was it just because he was a closet dirty talker?

I shivered as the memory of last night washed over me. Everything is thought about him had been proven different. I'd only ever seen as this funny, sexy guy, who was a great dad.

But, last night sent me a different side of him. It'd shown me this alpha male who wasn't afraid to take charge, and make me do something that had made me blush as hard as I'd come. I certainly hadn't expected him to get me off and looked me in the eye while I came.

Yeah.

Dear God. How was I supposed to look him in the eye, knowing that he knew exactly what I looked like when I came?

Jesus, I was a mess.

I quickly washed my hair and soaked off before I got myself into even more of a mess than I was already in. By the time I turned off the shower water, I'd gone over fifty different scenarios about what was going to happen when I finally got to the Cooper house.

All of them involved me blushing like crazy and him smirking at me. Which, to be honest, was exactly what was going to happen.

With any luck he'd be taking the kids out, and I'd be able to just walk in, go upstairs, and get on with it.

I dressed in my usual uniform and towel dried my hair before putting the damp locks into a braid that hung over my shoulder.

The best thing to do was get there and get this over and done with.

Even if it sucked.

Unfortunately for me, when I pulled up outside the house, Brantley's car was parked in the driveway.

Great.

I sat inside my truck for a minute before taking a deep breath, getting out, and grabbing my tools from the back.

My heart thumped a little too hard as I approached the front door. It swung open before I could even knock, and Ellie stood in the doorway wearing nothing but a pair of Disney Princess panties.

Waell, I guess it was better than the inexplicable time Eli had answered the door wearing a superhero cape, his underwear, and red rain boots. At least this one could be explained by her getting dressed.

"Ellie!" shouted Brantley from inside. "Get back in here and finish getting dressed or we're not going anywhere!"

"It's Kawi!" she shouted, giving me a cheeky grin before running back inside.

I hesitated only for a second before I walked into the hallway and shut the front door behind me.

"I know it's Kali," said Brantley. "I can see her car outside. Will you now please finish getting dressed?"

I took a few tentative steps towards the front room door, my stomach turning as I did. Looking in, I saw that he had his back to me and was currently wrestling with Eli about which hole you are went into which hole your head went into. Apparently, Eli kept putting his head through the armhole, meaning both straps of his tank top were on one shoulder and only one arm was through.

"Daddy, where are my shorts?" asked Ellie. "Dey were here a mimmit ago."

Brantley sighed, finally getting Eli's head and arms through the right holes of his superhero shirt. He turned to look at Ellie. "I'm going to say they are wherever you thre them five minutes ago when you were having a tantrum." He raised eyebrows at her.

Ellie put her hands on her hips. "I did not had a tantwum," she said. "I was just shawing my annoyance."

"Whatever you say," said Brantley. "I'm calling it a tantrum. I don't care what you want to call it. Just go and find your clothes."

Eli slowly raised his hand pointing his middle finger up at the ceiling. Brantley tilted his head back to look up at what he was pointing at. I, too, followed the line of sight, and had to stifle a giggle when I saw what Eli had spotted.

Ellie's shorts were hanging from the light fixture.

Brantley buried his head in his hands.

I guess it been that kind of morning for him.

With a sigh, he stood and pulled the shorts from the light fixture. He tossed them Ellie's way, with a stern look for her to get dressed.

Then, finally, he turned to me, meeting my eyes. It took all for two seconds for a red-hot blush to work its way through my cheeks. Hell, if he was thinking what I was thinking in this moment—which was how it felt to be against the wall with him fucking me—then I didn't know how he wasn't blushing himself.

He glanced over his shoulder to make sure Ellie was getting dressed before walking towards me. A slow, easy smile stretched across his handsome face. "Morning," he said, his voice low.

I cleared my throat and scratched the back of my neck awkwardly. "Morning," I replied. "Is all the flatpack furniture still in the garage?"

He nodded. "Sorry. I didn't realize that what you are doing today or I would have taken upstairs for you."

I shrugged one shoulder. "It's okay," I said. "I was hoping to build their closets today."

Brantley nodded. "Let me help you carry them

upstairs before I take the kids out."

"No, no. It's okay. I can do it."

He quirked an eyebrow, smirking. "No, I'm helping you."

I opened my mouth to argue further, but the way he was looking at me told me that it would be futile. So, instead of arguing, I decided to give in and let him help me. He was going to do anyway.

He poked his head into the front room to see if the kids were okay. They'd both made their way onto the sofa and, they were, for now, sitting and watching TV nicely. He motioned with his hand to me to follow him.

I put down my toolbox at the bottom of the stairs and following him towards the door in the kitchen that led to the garage.

The boxes were where we'd left them when the delivery came and I rifled through them and the delivery note to find the box that Ellie's closet was in.

"Here, it's this one," said Brantley. He tapped the box at the very back.

I sighed. Of course, it would be the one at the back where we'd have to move about six boxes to be able to get to it. "All right." I stared at it. "It looks really heavy."

He smirked. "That's exactly why I'm here to help you.

"Are you saying I'm weak?" I raised an eyebrow teasingly.

The smirk transformed into a grin. "No. If you were weak, then my shoulders wouldn't look like they'd been in a fight with a tiger."

Once again, my cheeks flushed bright red. "Yes,

well," I paused. I didn't know what to say to that.

Amusement danced in his eyes. He grabbed a box, his biceps flexing as he moved it. "Aside from not raising my children to be assholes, I think my life's mission is to make you blush every time I see you."

"I take issue with that mission." I pushed a box across the floor.

"Why? What's wrong with it?"

"I don't like it."

"You want my kids to grow up to be assholes?"

I frowned at him. "That's not the one I was talking about, and you know it."

"I know." He grabbed a box that held Eli's dresser and stacked it against the other wall. "But, you're also really adorable when you frown, so I might make you do that, too."

"I'm not adorable. Puppies are adorable. Kittens, rabbits, hell, even baby goats are adorable." I sniffed and rested my hands on top of the closet box. "I. Am. Not. Adorable."

"Beauty is in the eye of the beholder. Personally, I don't care much for rabbits."

"Neither do I, but that doesn't mean they're ugly."

He held his hands up. "I think you're adorable. Especially right now, when you're trying to glare at me with your nose all wrinkled up."

I clapped my hand over my nose. "Can we not talk about this? I have work to do."

"We can not talk about this right now. Grab your end of the box and lift it up on three. One, two, three."

We both picked it up.

Shit, it was heavy.

"Thank you," I said as we carried it through the kitchen to the hallway.

"I said right now," Brantley continued, taking the first stair and glancing over his shoulder.

I was really taking the brunt of the weight of this box, and my arms were shaking. "What is right now supposed to mean?"

"It means we still have to have a conversation."

"A conversation? About what?"

"Well, for a start, about the fact your thong is in my washing machine."

I almost dropped the box.

He stopped. "Are you all right?"

"Why the hell is my thong in your washing machine?"

Moving again, he said, "Because you forgot to put it back on last night before you left, and I thought you'd appreciate me cleaning it for you."

I exhaled slowly. "And here I was, thinking we could avoid mentioning anything about last night."

"Why would we do that? Seeing you blush every ten seconds is much more fun."

"You have a warped idea of fun."

"Coming from the woman who uses a paintbrush as a microphone."

We reached the top of the stairs and I let go of the box. "Look," I said, putting my hands on my hips. "First of all, I did that one time. One. Time. Second, I have a large hoard of very adoring fans in your backyard who were incredibly honored to have witnessed such a fabulous display of entertainment from me."

His lips twitched. "You had one fan in the doorway who enjoyed watching your shake your ass for two minutes straight."

I blinked at him. "I might be late to the party, but we've definitely shattered any illusion of professionalism here, haven't we?"

Brantley shoved the box into Ellie's room and, then, very slowly, turned to me with one eyebrow raised. "Yes. I figured that out last night. Right about the time I was eight inches deep inside you."

I coughed on thin air. My cheeks burned again, and his lips formed a smirk.

"What's that? Three times today? I'm on fire. Like your cheeks."

"Oh my god!" I took the last two steps and smacked my hand against his chest. "You infuriating man."

He grinned, leaning against the doorframe as I passed him. "If I kissed you right now, would you slap me again? It was kind of hot."

"Now, I know you're messing with me." I pointed my finger at him. "Stop it. You have children to take out and I have a huge-ass, flatpack closet to build. There's no time for your bullshit."

He laughed as I passed him, once again, but this time, I left the room. I couldn't build it without my tools which were downstairs. I ran down, poked my head in the living room to see the miracle of the twins still sitting nicely together, and grabbed my toolbox.

Brantley was still leaning against the doorframe when I got back upstairs. His arms were folded across his chest, and his gaze followed me as I eked past him into the room.

"Are you just going to stand there and stare at me?" I set the toolbox down next to the giant box.

"Do you mind if I do?"

"Yes. If you're not going to go out, help me open this box."

"Are you this bossy to all your clients?"

"No. You should know by now you get special privileges." I pulled a pocketknife from my toolbox and sliced open the tape holding one side of the box together. "And not all of them are enjoyable for you."

"I don't know…" he trailed off. "It is quite enjoyable when you tell me what to do."

"It's a shame you don't ever do it."

He grinned. "I was only going to the store. Not some wondrous day out where they get to run around like hellions. At a push, I was going to take them to the beach tonight."

"All I hear from this is your opinion that they need to go somewhere to run around like hellions." I paused, and a shout came from downstairs.

"Daddy! Daaaadddyyyy!" Ellie's shriek got louder, and stomps on the stairs echoed. "Ewi hit me!"

Without blinking, he replied, "What did you do to him?"

"Nuffink!"

"What did you do to him?"

She mumbled something under her breath, dipping her head.

"Eleanor."

"Pushed him off the sofa."

I coughed to hide my laugh.

"Then the lesson here is, don't push your brother and he won't hit you, isn't it?" Brantley sighed. "We've covered this a hundred times."

"But it hurted me." She sniffed, giving him puppy dog eyes.

"Okay? So, let's go downstairs. I'll push you off the sofa and you can see if it hurts, too."

Her eyes widened, from puppy dog to deer in headlights. "No. I'm okay. I go say sowwy now."

Brantley nodded, watching her go.

"I can't decide if that parenting technique is brilliant or…well, brilliant," I admitted.

"Thank you." His lips twitched. "It's simple. If she didn't push him, he wouldn't hit her. After the paint fiasco, you'd think she'd know that. The stuff she does always gets a reaction."

"What about Eli? Will you tell him not to hit her?"

"No. If she pushed him, she deserved it. Eventually, she'll get the message."

"So, basically, what you're saying is that you're raising both the kid who throws the first punch and the one who always punches back?"

He paused. "That's the most accurate description of my children I've ever heard."

I laughed, opening the box fully and picking up the instructions.

At least this wasn't Ikea furniture.

I liked my patience, and I wanted to keep it today.

"That's a lot of pieces," he muttered, looking at the box.

"About normal." I paused, then looked from the box to him. "You sounded…weary. Like this is terrifying."

"I don't build flat-pack furniture," he admitted,

dropping his arms and stuffing his hands in his pockets. "I can't build it, actually."

I looked at him for a moment. "Not even, like, a table? Or a bookshelf?"

Grimacing, he shook his head. "My father always used to do it. For whatever reason, I just can't do it."

I blinked. Several times. "You can't build flat-pack furniture?"

"Nope. It doesn't matter where it's from. Whether it's a local store or Ikea…"

"First, nobody can build Ikea furniture. Well, I can, but I don't like to." I put down the instructions. "But, this? Easy. I might need some help to hold some pieces together, but honestly, it's like stacking Lego."

"More like stepping on Lego," he muttered.

"I can't believe you can't build flat-pack furniture."

"Here we go. I never should have told you that."

"I'm going to bring it up every single time you mention me blushing. I promise you that." I laughed, sweeping the instructions to the side and pulling out the first bit of solid wood. "Every. Single. Time."

He pushed off the door, smirking. "Rookie error, Kali."

"What is?"

"What you should have said is you'll bring it up every time I make you blush. Now, I'll keep making you blush, and just not mention it."

My lips parted. "No, wait. That's not fair!"

He went to step out of the door, then stopped. "You promised. You can't take it back. Oh, and by the way? I dreamed of you naked in my bed last night."

I gasped, moving forward to be on my hands and

knees as if I were going to chase him.

"What a coincidence." He smirked. "You were just like that."

I dropped back onto my knees immediately. "You rotten bastard!" I snapped through the burning of my cheeks.

He winked, and, on that note, left, shouting for the kids to find their shoes.

I stared after him for the longest moment.

That sounded like a war declaration to me.

My lips curved.

If you can't beat them…

Torture them.

23

Look, I didn't mean to go home and get changed.

Well, not entirely. It hadn't been my initial idea, but when I'd built the main structure of the closet and only had to add in the rail and the shelves, and Brantley still wasn't back, I made a flash choice around lunchtime.

In my defense, he'd started it. He was the one who'd declared war upon me and my blushing.

Yeah. He'd started it, and I was ready to finish it.

I adjusted my bra and glanced at my legs. This skirt was basically indecent—like hotpants but without the stretch of denim covering your vagina. I hoped like hell I wouldn't have to bend over around the kids.

Jesus, that would scar the poor things for life.

I slotted the rail into Ellie's closet and took a step back. The doors were open, but the pink and white closet was every little girl's dream. Complete with custom handles in the shape of a tiara. She was going to freak the hell out when she got back and saw this.

I closed the doors and gave it a push across the floor so it was against the wall. I blew out a heavy sigh, then turned my attention to the mess of packaging. My Spotify playlist ticked over to the next song, and I hummed along as the familiar tune of Ed Sheeran's *Galway Girl* filled the room.

It made the clean-up a little better. I just wasn't going to hold an impromptu concert this time…just in case.

The last thing I needed was for Brantley to come in and see me using a screwdriver as a microphone this time.

With all the trash sorted and in the opposite corner, I headed downstairs to the garage and found the box that had Ellie's drawers. I would build her furniture first, and get her room ready except for the bed before turning my attention to Eli's.

The box was lighter than the closet, and I was able to move it myself. I heaved it upstairs into her room and set it down. I glanced around for my pocketknife to slice it open, humming along to another Ed Sheeran song I didn't know the title of. I found it in the trash in the corner of the room, grabbed it, and kneeled down to open the box.

"Jesus!"

My hand slipped in shock and I sliced my finger open.

"Shit!" I immediately dropped the knife and brought my finger to my mouth. "Ouch!" I mumbled against my finger.

"Oh, shit." Brantley crossed the room in two quick strides. "I was about to tell you to warn a guy you're wearing next to nothing, but never mind. Let me look."

I shook my head and pulled my finger out of my mouth. "It's fine. It's not deep. It'll stop bleeding in a minute."

It really, really fucking hurt, though.

"Let me see." He grabbed my wrist and looked. "That's not going to stop by itself."

"How do you know?" I brought it back to my

mouth.

He met my eyes and said dryly, "I have a four-year-old son. I've seen more cuts and scrapes than you can imagine. Come downstairs and I'll get the First Aid kit."

"It's fine," I mumbled against my skin. "Really, it's my own fault."

"I won't argue with that." He stood. "Come on."

I sighed and followed him. Maybe he was right—my finger was showing no signs of slowing down its bleeding.

Just great.

"Oh no," Eli breathed, sitting at the kitchen table with apple slices. "Do you had a booboo?"

I grimaced in pain and nodded. "Yep. Opening a box."

"Opening a box?" Ellie asked, her voice getting higher at the end. "How do you cut yourself opening a box?"

"When your daddy starts shouting in the doorway and scares me," I answered honestly.

"Oh, Daddy!" Ellie stared at him. "Look what you did to Kawi."

Brantley froze, plastic tub in hand. "I didn't do anything. If I knew she had a knife in her hand, I wouldn't have said anything."

"Lies," I muttered under my breath.

He met my eyes. "Your own fault and you know it."

"You started it."

"Who started what?" the twins asked in unison.

"Never mind. Eat your fruit," Brantley said waving me over to the side. "Rinse your finger off and dry it carefully."

I did as he said as he basically emptied the contents of a hospital storage room onto the countertop. I was seriously impressed by the amount of Band-Aid's, bandages, and various other first-aid type bits he had in there.

"Were you a doctor in a past life?" I asked holding the dark red towel around my finger.

"No," he replied. "I'm a parent in the current one. You'd be surprised how often I restock this thing."

I glanced at Eli who currently had a scrape on his elbow. "Maybe two weeks ago I would have been. Now? Not so much."

He laughed, taking the towel. "You're learning fast. Rest your arm on the counter and I'll bandage your finger up."

"I don't think I'm learning anything," I said slowly, putting my forearm on the towel. "Everything just makes a bit more sense now."

"Whatever you say." He got to work on wrapping my finger.

"What are you doo-win?" Ellie asked. "Upstairs."

I turned my head to the side and offered her a smile. "I'm building your furniture, actually. I did your closet already. I was about to start your dresser when I cut myself."

"Oh no! Is my dwesser okay?"

Brantley snorted.

"Perfectly fine. Unlike my finger."

"You're the one with butterfingers," Brantley said, wrapping a bandage around my finger.

"You scared me," I shot back. "I didn't do it on

purpose."

"Can you still build my dwesser?" Ellie asked around a mouthful of strawberries.

It was nice to know where her priorities were.

I was fine, not that she cared.

"Yes, I can still build your dresser," I replied as Brantley taped my finger. "Amazing. You can do that, but not build a bookshelf."

He sighed, dropping his head back. "I could build it if I had to. But, I don't have to. You do."

"I think you're lying." I admired his handiwork on my finger before crossing my arms and ultimately wincing as I put pressure on my cut.

"Daddy can't build wego," Eli said. "He twied to build a castle for Ewwie but couldn't."

"Okay, first," Brantley waggled his finger at Eli, "There were bricks missing."

"I stole dem." Ellie grinned.

Brantley flicked his gaze to her. "Exactly. And second, I can build Lego, I just choose not to."

"Because you can't?" I offered.

"Don't you have something to do?"

"Mandatory break," I replied.

"On what grounds?"

"My finger really, really hurts."

He stared at my hand, then shook his head. "I don't know how to argue with that, so I'm not going to. I'm going to say okay and leave it at that."

Smart choice. And he said I was the one who was learning fast…

"Can I help you build my dwesser?" Ellie asked, picking up an apple juice box and sipping on it so hard her cheeks hollowed out. Trails of red juice dribbled down her chin from the strawberries.

Brantley hit a button on the dishwasher and closed it. "What happened last time someone tried to help?"

"But, there's no paint dis time," she replied.

Ha. Point: Ellie.

"Kali already sliced her finger off. I can only see this ending badly."

"I didn't slice my finger off. It's just a scratch."

"A scratch that won't stop bleeding."

"Oh my god, you're so pedantic. Whatever."

He burst out laughing. "You're feisty today. Is it that time of the month?"

"You know damn well it isn't." I put my hands on my hips. "I'm not taking this. I'm going to work."

More laughter followed me as I made my exit, and I realized that was exactly what he was trying to get me to do.

I paused at the bottom of the stairs. "Well played!"

Again, laughter.

"Ellie! Let's go!" I called, waving my hand toward her.

"Yes!" She threw her tiny fist into the air and jumped off her chair, scrambling after me as I headed upstairs.

Ellie tipped a tiny bag of the screws into her hand. Holding it out, she picked one screw off her palm and handed me it.

"Thank you," I said.

Apparently, four-year-olds liked screws if it meant they could help. Organizing all of them had kept her amused for the entirety of this build—she'd taken them all out, sorted them into piles, and then put them back in bags.

"Kawi," she said, watching me as I screwed together a drawer.

"Yes?"

"Do you wike my daddy?"

I paused mid-screw. That was a loaded question. "What do you mean?"

She shifted, then tucked some of her hair behind her ear. "Are you fwiends?"

"Sure. We're definitely friends."

"Are you fwiends who kiss?"

I blinked at her. This was not a conversation I'd ever pictured myself having. "Why do you ask?"

"'Cause he waughs wots now, and I know he doesn't have any fwends."

I tightened the screw, then set down both the completed drawer and my screwdriver.

This was one observant child.

And I had no idea how to have this conversation with her.

"Have you asked Daddy this?"

She shook her head. "I don't wanna make him sad."

"Why are you asking me?" I said it gently, because I genuinely wanted to know.

"Daddy was sad. Den we moved here." She dropped her eyes and played with the screws in her hand. "Den you came. And now Daddy is happy. And,

and, sometimes, when I'm sad, Daddy kisses me and den I'm happy again. So, I fort maybe you kissed Daddy and made him happy again."

Wow.

Kid logic.

Pretty accurate, actually.

Shit.

I took a deep breath and slowly let it go again. How was I supposed to answer that? How was I supposed to answer it in a way that she wouldn't take it and come up with some wild scenario?

Because, yes, I had kissed Daddy—and a whole lot more—and he'd already told me that I made him feel happy. But explaining that to Ellie when she obviously had some kind of hope for something would not be easy.

Maybe it shouldn't even be explained at all.

"I like your dad very much," I said slowly and carefully. "But that doesn't mean I'm the reason he's so happy. Maybe he really likes it here in your lovely new house."

She shook her head, her curls bouncing. "No. He waughs a wot wiff you."

"Maybe he thinks I'm funny. Like you think that dog on that TV show that's really clumsy is funny."

She looked up, a hint of a grin on her face. "Marshall is funny when he cwashes into the elevader."

"Right? See, maybe that's how Daddy thinks I'm funny."

The smile slowly dropped from her face, and she nodded. "Okay."

I moved the drawer to the side and grabbed two

pieces to start the next one. She was already handing me a screw. I took it and paused. There was something else bothering her.

"Ellie?" I said softly. "Is there something else?"

She looked up and met my eyes. "All the udder kids at Summer's house have a mommy."

Oh, boy.

"Yes, they do," I said carefully.

"But, my mommy is an angel." She frowned. "Do you fink I can have anudder?"

Oh.

Boy.

I started screwing. "Well, maybe. That's sometimes how it works. Did you know that my mommy is an angel, too?"

"No. When did she gwow wins?"

"I was five," I said, taking the next screw. "I was very sad, but when I grew up a little bit, my daddy met someone else, and now she's my step-mommy."

"Does she do fins like bwaid your hair and paint your nails and help you pick pwetty dwesses?"

"She used to. I'm an adult now, but she did, yeah."

"Do I had to wait until I'm big for a new mommy?"

"That's up to Daddy, I guess. He has to find someone who makes him happy and who loves you and your brother."

"Like you mate him happy?"

"Kind of like that." I stopped. "Maybe you should finish this conversation with Daddy. He will probably have more answers than me, okay?"

She frowned again, but she nodded in agreement

anyway. Thank god—that was rapidly approaching a line of questioning I had no answers for.

If I didn't stop, I knew she'd connect things. And the very last thing I wanted to do was to break her heart.

Because I wasn't even sure if I'd accepted how I felt about Brantley yet.

***

"Man, that escalated quickly," Jayda said when I was done explaining everything that had happened. She tore off a piece of naan bread and tilted her head to the side. "Did she ask Brantley anything?"

I shrugged, dipping my own bit of naan into the sauce on my plate. "I don't know. She hung around until we'd finished building, then disappeared. I put up a couple of shelves and left quickly."

"Wasn't it awkward?"

"I don't think he heard, honestly. When I was done, he was on a work call, so I just motioned that I had to leave and came here." I nibbled on the bread, then put it down and reached for my wine. "It's all…Shit, I don't know, Jay."

"It's all fucked up," she finished for me.

"Basically." I sighed and leaned back on the sofa.

She cradled her wine glass against her, nestling herself into the corner. "Are you only feeling like this because you see him literally every day, though? Like, when you're done next week, how often are you going to see him?"

That was a good point.

"And is he even someone you'd consider dating if

you hadn't met him like this? No. Because of the kid thing. And the only reason you're in this situation is because you know and like his kids."

"You're the one who told me to screw him, remember?"

"Yes," she said slowly. "But I didn't know you had feelings for him."

"Neither did I until he fucked me seven ways to Sunday."

She snorted. "Funny how that happens." She rested her glass on her thigh. "I mean, think about this, Kali. If you acted seriously on the way you're feeling right now, literally everything in your life will change. You wouldn't be stepping in to babysit because he's desperate. The kids would become your responsibility. Are you ready for that?"

"You assume I'm going to tell him that I have feelings for him."

"Well, that's the first thing you need to decide."

"I love it when you state the obvious," I said dryly. "I don't even know how I feel. Are you right? Maybe. Maybe it's just because I see him every single day right now. I don't know." I leaned my head against the sofa. "I need to figure it out."

Jayda nodded, almost grimacing as she did. "And you need to do it quick. Is it just attraction, or are you falling for him?"

"Thanks, Dr. Phil."

"You're welcome." She grinned. "One thing you could do is go on a date and see how you feel about it then."

I winced. "I haven't checked the app for days."

She raised her eyebrows.

"I haven't had a chance!"

"Because you've been getting drilled against a wall?"

I sighed. "Shut up."

24

I swept the pencil across the wall, using my phone as a reference for what the Superman logo looked like. I'd spent the last hour drilling and putting up shelves in Eli's room. The floor was coated in dust from the drilling, but I couldn't be bothered to clean it up just yet.

I used my spirit level to make sure the lines were straight for the outside of the logo. The gold writing on the pencil read 'Don't be a twat,' and kept catching my attention as it glinted in the light.

Nobody really needed twenty pencils that read 'Don't be a twat,' but I had them, thanks to my mom.

It was a good motto to live by, to be honest.

The silence of the house was welcome as I sketched onto the wall. The logo was simple, but the straight lines were killers. Still, I got it done after about half an hour of drawing, and moved to paint.

I didn't get to do this often, and it was nice. Nice to break away from the noise and occasional tediousness of my job.

I loved what I did, but there was only so many times you could do something before you got tired of it. I felt that way about painting in general, so doing the Superman logo was fun.

I'd just finished the red when the front door opened and then shut again. The twins were at daycare, and since I'd skipped out last night to go to

Jayda's, this would be the first time we were alone since…well, yeah.

I kinda hoped he wouldn't come up and talk to me, but I knew him better than that.

No sooner had I thought that than I heard him on the stairs.

I bent down and dipped my brush into the yellow paint.

"Hey," he said from the hallway. "You're not holding a knife today, are you?"

"Ha. You're funny," I replied, getting excess paint off the brush. "Just a paintbrush today."

"Am I interrupting a private concert?"

"I'm never going to live any of this down, am I?"

Brantley finally stepped into the room with a wolfish grin on his face. "No," he said. "Not even close."

I sighed and started painting again. "So unfair."

"How is your finger today?"

"Painful, but it stopped bleeding. Just a normal Band-Aid today." I wiggled my fingers in his direction.

He nodded slowly. "Good."

I got more paint on my brush and carried on. Neither of us said anything for a moment, and the silence was both comfortable and awkward. How that was possible I didn't know, but I did know that I didn't mind being around him in silence.

"Do you want to get lunch today?"

I froze. "Just lunch, or…like a date, lunch?"

He quirked an eyebrow. "Does it matter? Lunch is lunch."

"In a restaurant?"

"The Coastal? Sure."

"We'd be more likely to keep our clothes on." Welp. I didn't mean to say that out loud.

Brantley considered this. "I can order in."

I waved my hand at him. "Stop that. I'm working, and I'm determined to get finished on time so they can have their rooms in a few days."

He glanced around. "Are you really almost done?"

I nodded. "I just have to build the rest of the furniture, mostly. Oh, and put up the curtain poles."

"Wow." He cast his gaze over the room. "That'll be weird when you're done. I'm used to having you here."

I smiled. "You'll like it even more when I'm not."

He didn't respond, just inclined his head slightly in my direction. "So, lunch? Here or out?"

I twisted my mouth to the side. "Whenever. I planned to stop in an hour."

"Do you have time limit for lunch?"

"Not really. I'll just stay a bit later."

He bobbed his head. "Let's go out. I'll call the Coastal and see if Marcie can save us a table."

"Sounds good." I smiled, and he returned it right before he turned and left.

My brush hovered over the wall.

Was it a date?

Damn it.

The roar of the restaurant was loud. Apparently, there was some competition down on Rock Bay beach and the Coastal had picked up all the people who'd turned out for it. Every table was full, and I was definitely glad that Brantley had called ahead. We'd been able to walk right in and go to our table, passing the people in the front foyer who were waiting for one themselves.

Marcie eyed with me raised eyebrows, a look that told me she wanted to know everything as soon as she possibly could. She put our coffees down and, with one last glance, excused herself to another table.

Brantley's lips twisted in amusement. "She's not very subtle, is she?"

I grimaced. "About as subtle as a nuclear bomb."

He laughed quietly, opening the sugar packets she'd brought and pouring a couple into his coffee. "How much do you want to bet she's going to call your mom and tell her we're both here together?"

"Fifty says she's already on the phone." I snorted. "Whatever. People are already talking. It doesn't matter."

"It really bothers you, doesn't it? The gossiping."

"It doesn't bother you?" I questioned, then shrugged. "I wouldn't say it bothers me. I'm used to it. I do wish people could keep their nose out of my business, though."

"I guess I'm still at the stage where I'm charmed by this small town and all its little idiocies."

"Little idiocies." I laughed, finally pulling my mug toward me. "That's one way to describe it."

"Well, they are. They're kind of charming, in a really weird way. The gossip is…unusual, to me. I'm not used to everyone knowing everything."

"Yeah, well, you started that with us when you

told everyone I'd stayed late or whatever it was you said."

He frowned for a moment. I watched as realization dawned, and he laughed hard. "Oh, god. I never told you."

"Never told me what?" I narrowed my eyes.

Brantley scratched the back of his neck. "I never said that. It was a joke. I was fucking with you."

I leaned over the table and smacked his arm. "Oh my god. All that stress, and for what? You ass!"

"I'm sorry." He didn't look sorry at all. "I forgot I never said."

"Yeah, sure. Whatever."

This time, his laughter was silent. "Well, there you go. Now, you know." He sipped his coffee, eyes shining with mirth. "I did actually want to talk to you about something."

"I should have known there was a catch with this lunch thing," I said. "Does that mean it's not a date?"

"It's a half-date," he replied.

"I think I can deal with that. What did you want to talk about?"

He paused.

And I knew. I knew exactly what he was about to say.

"You heard my conversation with Ellie, didn't you?" I beat him to it.

He nodded. "I was coming up to check she wasn't being a pain in your ass. I don't think I heard it all, but I heard enough."

I swallowed. God—what if he thought I'd overstepped my bounds? Had I overstepped? Should I have just not had that conversation with her at all?

"I'm sorry," I started. "If I shouldn't have talked about it with her, but I didn't know what to say."

His brows twitched into a frown. "What? No—it's not that all. I wanted to, first, thank you for how you handled it. I could tell she came at you from left field with her questions."

I blew out a long breath and slumped back a little in my seat. "Honestly, yeah. And I knew what she was fishing for, but…" I trailed off, looking away.

"But that's not what you want," he finished for me.

Not coldly, not sadly, not anything. Just a statement.

One that was true.

Or one that was.

Was…

Maybe.

I picked at my napkin. "I don't know how to respond to that," I admitted quietly. "I don't know, Brant. That would have been true even a week ago, but I don't know how I feel right now."

He raised his eyebrows, surprise glinting in his turquoise gaze. "That wasn't what I was expecting you to say."

"Well, I…" I sighed. What the hell could I say? How could I explain feelings I didn't understand? "I don't know what to say to you."

He rested his forearms on the table and leaned forward. "You don't have to say anything to me. You don't owe me any kind of explanation, no matter how much I want one for that vague-ass answer."

I half-smiled. "There are a lot of things in my head right now. I'm basically arguing with myself a whole lot."

"Careful. I don't want you to think too hard and hurt yourself."

I stared at him flatly.

He grinned at me. A real boyish grin that sent butterflies through my stomach. "I still just want to say thank you for the way you handled her. She notices a lot, and…it's not always a good thing. For the record, you already know that what she said is true."

A lump formed in my throat. "I know."

He took a deep breath. "And I like you, Kali. I like you a lot."

My heart skipped.

"I know it's hard and it's complicated, but I wanted to make that clear to you." He paused, then scratched at his jaw. "The last thing I expected when I moved here was to find someone like you."

His words curled and curved through my body, grabbing hold of me.

The last thing I expected when I knocked on your door was to find someone like you.

That was what I wanted to say. But, the words wouldn't come.

I was saved from an immediate reply by the arrival of our food. After a quick check on whether we had everything, we were left to ourselves and I finally grew a pair and asked the question about something I hadn't realized was even bothering me until now.

"Can I ask you something?" I met his eyes.

"Anything."

I licked my lips. "Am I…" Deep breath. "Am I the first? Since she died?"

He stared at me for a moment, then nodded his

head. Just once. "I'm a father before anything else. I wasn't looking to meet anyone when I met you."

I swallowed. "I get that. I was just wondering."

He smiled wryly. "Well, I'm so glad we got to have a nice, light conversation over lunch."

I stared at him for a moment, my lips twitching, then started to laugh. "You're the one who wanted this chat."

"True. It escalated, though."

"Is that a bad thing?"

He picked up his fork and let his lips curl into a small smile. "I hope not."

Ellie stared at me. "Are you done yet?"

I glanced up into the doorway. "Nope. Not quite."

She sighed and leaned against the frame. "Oh, gosh. It's taking so wong."

I fought back laughter. "I'm sorry. Maybe three more days. Four at most. Is that okay for you?"

"Can't you do it kicker?"

"'Fraid not. I wish I could." She had no idea.

"Dat's okay." She put her hands in the pockets of her skirt. "Daddy's working and Ewi is asweep on the sofa. I bored."

I tilted my head to the side. "Okay. Did you want to help me?"

"What are you doing?"

"I'm building your toybox. See the pink lid?"

She narrowed her eyes. "Can I do some

scwewing?" Hope flashed across her face.

"Sure. Come sit." I waved her over. "Here's a screwdriver for you."

"Oh. It's pink," she breathed.

"They're all pink." I grinned and moved the toolbox between us. "See?"

"Wow." Wonder crossed her little face. "Dat's 'mazin'."

I grinned.

"How do you know which one you need?"

"Which screwdriver?" I clarified.

She nodded, clutching hold of the handle so tight her knuckles went white.

"The screws are different. Look." I picked up one of the crosshead screws and showed it to her. "If you look the head of your screwdriver, it matches the shape. See?"

She made a great show of looking at both the screw and the screwdriver.

"If you put it in, it should fit." I pinched the sharp end of the screw and held it out to her. "Try it."

She did just that, poking it. Except I'd given her one that was a size too big.

"Oh, hold on. That's too big. They come in different sizes, see?" I pointed at the screwdriver. "You need a smaller one."

"Can I get it?" she asked.

"Sure. See if you can find the next size down."

"Okay." She rifled through them, checking each one until she came to a flathead screwdriver. "It's different." She held it up.

"Yep, there are two types. I don't think I have any screws that it would fit, but not all screws have the cross. Some have one line, and that's what you'd use a flathead—that's what it's called—screwdriver for. But, if you have a cross screw and don't have the right crosshead screwdriver, you can use a flat one."

"Weawy?"

"Yep. Poke the screw with a smaller, flat one."

She got one of the small ones out and did it. More delight crossed her face. "Okay. I need a cwoss one, doe, wight?"

I smiled. "Yes, you need a cross one. Did you find it yet?"

She nodded. "You sittin' on it."

I plucked the screwdriver from next to my thigh with a grin. "Here you go." I put the screw in the pre-drilled hole and twisted it a few times. "Okay, come here." I patted my thighs, and she came to sit on me. "Now, very carefully, put the screwdriver in the screw and twist it clockwise, okay?"

"Why cockwise?"

I bit back a laugh. "Clockwise is to the right. That's how you tighten screws. There's even a rhyme my daddy taught me when I was little."

"What is it?"

"Righty tighty, lefty loosey."

"Wighty tighty, wefty woosey."

It had a certain charm coming from her.

"That's it. Turn right to tighten, and left to loosen."

"Okay. Can I do it now?"

"Sure. Do it as tight as you can."

She leaned forward and, oh so carefully, inserted the head of the screwdriver into the screw. She turned the screwdriver, sticking her tongue out of the side of her mouth. I leaned around to see her face—she wore the mask of complete concentration.

Tongue out, eyes narrowed, brows drawn together.

It was the most adorable thing.

"Dere," she said, sitting back. "I did it."

"Amazing job!" I squeezed her lightly. "Can I please have the screwdriver to check how tight it is?"

She nodded and handed it over to me.

I checked. She'd barely turned it at all, but she was having fun, so it was what it was. I tightened the screw the rest of the way and grabbed the next one. At least I was almost done.

"I do again?" Ellie asked hopefully.

"Sure."

She wore the same expression as she turned it. The sticking out tongue was my favorite part of all of it.

"Ellie, you're quiet. What are you—" Brantley stopped in the doorway, phone to his ear. "Oh. You're here."

Ellie turned to look at him. "Ewi fell asweep. Kawi said I could help."

He looked at me for confirmation.

I motioned to the fact she was sitting on my lap.

His lips tugged up. "She's not bothering you, is she?"

"No, she's helping. Look. She's doing the screws." I pointed to where she was giving it a good try at tightening it. "It's almost done. She's enjoying herself."

"Okay. If you're sure?"

"She's *fine*. If she stops being good, I'll pick her

up and hand deliver her to you in your office, okay?"

He laughed, holding up a hand. "Okay, okay, fine. I just thought… Crap. Hello?" He ducked away. "Yes, I'm still here."

His voice trailed off as he went downstairs.

Ellie made a clicking noise with her tongue. "Daddy said a bad word."

Ah. Crap.

"He did. Naughty Daddy. Can I try that screw now?"

She nodded and let me tighten it. We repeated this over and over until all the screws were in place and tight. She even held the lid in place for me while I attached the hinges.

When it was all said and done, Ellie gently closed down the lid and walked around the box. Then, she stopped in front of it, and with a huge, proud grin on her face, she met my eyes.

"It's perfeck, huh?"

"It sure is," I agreed. "You did a great job helping me. Thank you."

Even if it had taken an extra half an hour.

She beamed. I'd never seen her so delighted about anything before. "Can I help you tomorrow, too?"

"You can help me do your bookshelf when you get back from Summer's. Does that sound good?"

She nodded. "I'm hungry. Do you fink Daddy cooked me food yet?"

"I don't know, but we can find out." I glanced at the time. It was almost six p.m. No wonder she was hungry.

Ellie ran downstairs and into the kitchen. I took

the time to pack up my tools before following her, but I left the box in her room.

I went down and found Eli awake, sitting on the sofa, and Ellie pouting in front of him.

Eli looked at me. "Daddy's on the phone. He keeps shouting."

I frowned and walked toward Brantley's office. He sounded super frustrated, even though he wasn't shouting, but there was something about the "damn intern" mentioned a few times.

I rejoined the twins in the living room. "Daddy's working, isn't he?"

They both nodded.

"He probably doesn't know what the time is." I paused. "Why don't we go in the kitchen and I can get you some dinner?"

More nodding. They ran into the kitchen, and when I stepped into the room, Eli was already trying to give Ellie a leg-up onto the counter.

"Oookay!" I said, waving my hands. "Let's not do that. I'll look instead of you two trying to break a bone."

"Oh," Ellie said sadly. But, they both moved, climbing up onto the table via the chairs instead.

I stared at them.

Eh. I'd won one battle. Why start another?

I left them there and opened the cupboard. I had no idea what I was looking for. Pasta? Spaghetti? What did you feed the tiny humans?

The souls of the elderly or something?

My eyes fell on two cans of tomato soup.

Ah-ha.

"How about tomato soup and grilled cheese?" I

asked.

"Yes!" they shouted, clapping.

"Okay." Good. I could do that. "Sit on the chairs, grab a juice, and let me get to work."

Miraculously, they did as they were told.

Well. I'll be damned.

25

"Again?" I questioned.

They both nodded. "Pwease?"

That simultaneous speak was starting to get a bit less weird. Maybe.

"One more time, then you have to go to bed."

They both looked at me with wide eyes and nodded again.

"Okay, fine. You twisted my arm." I'd just opened the front cover of the book to read it for a third time when Brantley's shout of "Shit! Eli? Ellie?" sounded.

"In here," they chorused.

I shuddered.

Maybe it wasn't getting less weird.

He rushed into the front room, stopping dead when he saw us. His hair was a mess, and he had the look of someone who was both frustrated and confused.

"Hi," I said brightly. "Welcome back."

He blinked at me. "I'm so confused." He scrubbed his hand through his hair. "I don't even know what time it is. There's no way I've been on the phone that long."

The twins, bless them, nodded sagely. "Hours, Daddy," Eli said dramatically.

"We omost starved!" Ellie added.

"Oh, stop it. No, you didn't. We found food just in time, didn't we?" I said to them.

"I don't know," Eli continued. "It was cwose."

"Close! Close? Oh, yes. Look at you. You're skin and bone." I gently prodded his side and he dissolved into a fit of giggles.

Brantley blinked at us. "I don't know what's happening here."

To be honest, he looked exhausted.

"Well," I said, closing the book and putting it on the coffee table. "Me and Ellie finally got done with the coffee table around six. We came down and you were on the phone, so after some attempted Cirque De Soleil moves, we rustled up the delicacy that is soup and grilled cheese, drank some milk and found some pajamas, and read about a dinosaur who poops everything out. Twice. We were about to read it a third time when you graced us with your presence."

"Wait. What is the time?"

"Seven-thirty."

"Jesus." He rubbed his hand over his face. "I'm so sorry. I didn't even realize."

"It's okay. We're all good, right?" I looked at both twins. "We had fun."

They both nodded. "Bedtime now?" Ellie asked.

"Yes. For sure. Come on. I'll take you up." Brantley blew out a long breath. "Say goodnight to Kali."

"Goodnight, Kawi!" they sang, scrambling up off the sofa. Then, they both stopped, turned, and jumped on me. I shrieked as I caught them, and they both planted a big kiss on my cheeks.

"Fank you," Eli said.

"Goodnight," Ellie echoed.

I squeezed them both with a laugh. "Night, guys."

They grinned and got back up, running off to the

stairs again. Brantley stared at me for a moment and held up a finger.

"Will you wait for me to come back before you leave?" he asked tentatively.

"Sure." I smiled.

He looked as though he wanted to say something else, but changed his mind. He followed after the twins, and I looked at their piles of dirty clothes on the floor.

Brantley looked shattered, as if he could fall asleep standing up.

I got up and grabbed them, then ran them through the back to the utility area just off the kitchen. I put them in the dirty laundry, then returned to the front room and picked up the dinosaurs who had been attending Barbie's wedding to Batman.

Then, with my hand around the tail of a T-rex, I froze.

I stared down at the toy in my hand.

Who had I become?

Not long ago, the idea of children terrified me. They were tiny, loud hellions who shouted and screamed. They were gross and dirty and messy.

Now, here I was. I'd taken over seamlessly, feeding them and getting them ready for bed, and now, I was picking up toys. Putting their dirty clothing in the laundry basket.

The scariest part?

It felt completely natural.

Sure, the twins had been scarily well-behaved, but that wasn't the point.

A part of me…A part of me felt like I belonged here.

I took a deep breath and dropped Mr. T-rex into the toybox. He roared as he collided with a dump truck, but I muffled that by slapping the lid on top of the box.

My mouth was dry. When had I changed from a kid-hater to playing…well, playing mom? When had it happened? Was there a point, or had something changed?

Was it acceptance of feelings for Brantley?

Was it his acknowledgment of feelings for me?

Or had I just fallen so irrevocably in love with two, three-feet-tall pre-schoolers? With tiny hands and sassy grins and dimpled cheeks?

I mean, I hadn't even thought twice about getting them ready for bed tonight. I'd just done it, like I knew what I was doing, when I didn't. Not at all. I didn't know where their pajamas were. I didn't know where to put that stupid pooping dinosaur book away.

I didn't know anything.

Except for the fact I was screwed. Stuck between a rock and a hard place. Between breaking hearts and healing them.

Maybe even breaking my own.

Shit.

I ran my fingers through my hair. The band from this morning's braid was around my wrist, and I pulled my hair into a rough, loose twist on top of my head.

I needed a drink. My mouth was so dry I doubted I could speak.

I walked into the kitchen and got some water from the fridge. I drank and drank, stupidly hoping it would calm the rapid beats of my heart.

Kids.

I was in love with two kids who had stolen my heart.

And their dad was doing the same thing.

And now, after this evening, my question wasn't "could I do it?"

It was, "Am I good enough for this family?"

I didn't want to ask it. I didn't want to know the answer.

"Kal—oh, there you are."

I turned at the sound of his voice.

Regret settled over his expression, and he wiped his hand over his jaw. "I'm so fucking sorry, Kali. What was meant to be a simple phone call turned into an intern fucking up three accounts, and me having to call every man and his mother to get it sorted out again."

"It's fine," I said. And I meant it. "They weren't a problem at all. They were perfect for me."

"That's not the point. I've already asked so much of you—Jesus, I didn't even know the time. I thought it'd been half an hour, not over two." He leaned against the counter and rubbed his face. He was frustrated with himself, and it was plain to see he was trying to keep it together.

Nothing I said to him right now would change that.

So, I acted instead.

I put the bottle on the table and walked to him. He still had his face buried in his hands, so I gently reached up, clasped his wrists, and pulled his hands away.

Guilty eyes found mine.

I leaned in and kissed him.

A gentle touch, meant to do nothing more than take some of the frustration away from him.

He wrapped his arms around my waist, pulling me into him, and softly kissed me back. I didn't know if I was doing the right thing, especially after our conversation earlier, but it was all I wanted to do.

I wanted him to know that I didn't care.

That I wasn't angry or annoyed. That I didn't blame him, because shit happened.

"Point taken," he muttered when I pulled back slightly. He didn't release me, though. "Were they really good?"

I nodded. "I came down and Eli was watching TV. Apart from him trying to give Ellie a leg-up into the cupboard and them watching me cook while sitting on the table…"

"All in all, it was a success."

"Nobody got hurt, so yes."

He half-smiled, and it actually reached his eyes. "You know, it's funny. For someone who admits she doesn't want kids, you're amazing with them."

I looked into his eyes. "Your kids make it easy to be."

"Clearly, you're forgetting that time when you bathed them."

"No. I just learned the lesson not to bath them."

He laughed, and I could see the tension leave his body. "Lucky you. I wish I had that option."

I grinned. "You need to have something to eat."

"Are you bossing me around now?"

Nodding, I flattened my hands against his chest. "Yes. You need to eat something."

"Can't I just have you instead?" He slid his hands

down to cup my ass.

"Food and sleep would be more sensible," I started, my breath hitching.

"I'm sensible all day. You make me want to be stupid."

"Are you trying to say that being with me is stupid?"

Brantley paused. "See, I feel like no matter what I say here will be wrong. This is a trap, isn't it?"

I raised my eyebrows. "I don't know. Do you think it's a trap?"

"*That's* definitely a trap."

I did my best not to laugh, but I'd never had a poker face, so that attempt lasted all of five seconds before it collapsed and I burst out laughing.

"I knew it," he muttered. "I'm not hungry."

"Lies. You have to be hungry."

He shook his head. Then, with strength that shouldn't have surprised me, he gripped my waist and pushed me back toward the table.

"What are you doing?"

"Ssssh," he whispered, pushing me until my butt bumped the edge. He picked me up, sitting me on the edge, and stepped between my legs. "Shut up and let me kiss you."

"I can't."

"Why not?"

"I think I just squashed a bit of grilled cheese with my hand."

He pulled back slightly. "That's a turn-on if ever I heard one."

"Squished grilled cheese," I said, picking up my hand and confirming my thoughts. "Helping libidos everywhere."

He removed the offending, half-eaten sandwich, and did a quick sweep of the table to make sure nothing else would get in the way of what was clearly about to become a make-out session.

I was okay with this. Especially when he got a cloth wet and wiped off my hand.

"There. Now, will you shut up and let me kiss you?"

"Are you going to do it anyway?"

"Yes. And I have half a mind to end with giving you an orgasm because you deserve it."

I eyed him. "We'll see."

He grinned, then swooped. Lips on mine, hot as hell, and all too addictive. His hands massaged up my legs, over my hips. He flattened one on the table and pressed the other against my back to stop me falling backward.

His tongue flicked against my lips.

I bit his lower one.

He chuckled, making me grin. His hand crept up my back, and our bodies were pressed close together when he kissed me again. His tongue battled mine, and I felt this kiss all over. My nipples hardened and my clit ached, and I knew without a doubt that I needed him inside me again tonight.

I needed more.

I needed to make sure the way I felt was right—that I hadn't been clouded by sex. Not that having more sex was the best idea to fix it, but still.

Then, I froze at a knock.

We stopped kissing, and at the same time, turned our heads so we were facing the doorway.

There, we found two pairs of eyes, fixed firmly on us.

And I had never seen such a look of disgust on tiny people in all my life.

"Ew," Eli moaned. "That's yucky."

Brantley released me and cleared his throat. "Why are you out of bed?"

"There's a spider in my woom," Ellie announced.

"And a fwy in mine," Eli said. "Can we swap the bugs?"

"No. We cannot swap the bugs."

"Can I sweep in Ewwie's woom, then?"

"Sure, but I bet Ellie wants the spider gone."

She shook her head emphatically. "No. He's called Bob."

A spider named Bob.

How original.

"Right," Brantley said slowly. "Eli, grab your stuff and get in the opposite end of her bed, okay? Feet to feet like you used to do."

He nodded, and they both ran back up the stairs like a herd of baby elephants.

Brantley took a deep breath and looked at me. "It's like they don't want me to get laid."

I laughed and jumped off the table. "So dramatic. You just went in too early. Rookie mistake. And now you have to answer all the kissing questions."

He groaned. "The good news is that I finally have my bedroom to myself."

He looked at me pointedly.

"Oh god, no. That's a bad idea and you know it!"

"Stay." He pulled me into him. "Please. Stay with me tonight."

I wavered. On one hand, it was a terrible idea. On the other hand…

"Kali, please," he said in a low, husky voice, sliding his hands down my back.

"Fine," I whispered. "But you're cooking me breakfast."

He kissed me, smiling. "Done."

Waking up to the feeling of a hard, hot body behind mine and a heavy arm over my waist was a new one. It'd been two or three years since I'd been in a relationship and spent the night with anyone.

I wasn't sure what this was with Brantley, but as I slowly opened my eyes and wriggled, I liked it.

"Stop wriggling," he murmured, slipping his arm beneath the covers and hooking it around my waist. He pulled me right back into him, tucking my butt against his groin and tangling our legs.

"I wanna see what time it is," I whispered, leaning over and blindly patting my hand around the nightstand for my phone. My fingers connected with it. I almost knocked it off, but somehow managed to save it before it fell onto the floor.

I hit the power button on the side and winced as the brightness blinded me. Quickly unlocking it and changing it, I was able to check the time.

Six-thirty.

"Aw, shit," I said.

"What?"

"I have twelve missed calls from my mom." I

dropped my head back down onto the pillow. "And a text message demanding to know why my car was still parked outside yours at eleven last night."

Brantley buried his face in the pillow and laughed.

"Don't laugh. She's insisting on breakfast. Since this sleepover was your idea, why don't you come and explain it to her?"

He propped his head up, his elbow digging into the pillow, and looked down at me. "What exactly am I supposed to say to her? "Sorry, Mrs. Hancock. I kept your daughter at my house all night so I could fuck her senseless?""

I frowned. "A little less graphic might be the way to go."

"Just be honest and tell her you spent the night. Who's she gonna tell?"

He had a point. While my mom was at the center of every gossip circle in town, she only ever received gossip about me. She never gave it out.

"Mmph," I hmped. "I need to speak to her anyway. May as well kill two birds with one stone."

He nodded. "Now, put down your phone and come back to sleep for an hour."

"Hang on." I quickly replied to Mom's text confirming I'd be home at eight for breakfast and then put my phone down.

"Thank you," he said when I settled back under the covers.

"You're grumpy in the morning."

"You woke me up. I had a plan to wake up before you and seduce you, but now I'm awake with an uncomfortable erection."

I shifted and rolled over to face him. "That's not

my fault."

"Your bare ass has been against it all night. It's one hundred percent your fault."

"You're the one who made me spend the night."

"I didn't make you do anything."

"True, but you gave me a very compelling argument."

He hooked one arm under my neck and hugged me into him. "Mhmm. It's eight inches long and likes you very much."

"I can't say the feeling isn't mutual."

He chuckled and squeezed me. "Stop it, or I might start to think you don't want to go back to sleep."

I leaned up and blinked. "Maybe I don't."

"Mm?"

"What's the point of going back to sleep for an hour?"

"You're right." He effortlessly flipped me onto my back and positioned himself between my legs. "I can make you come at least three times in that hour."

"Ambitious," I said, running my hands up and down his arms. "You think?"

"I know." He dropped down and kissed me. His cock brushed against my clit, and I wrapped my arms around his neck, giving him the chance to deepen the kiss.

He did.

Desire built as we kissed. We'd both only had a few hours sleep, so there was no reason for me to be so awake, much less this…needy.

All I knew was that I still wanted more of Brantley.

Still both naked from the night before, he made easy work of turning me on, traveling down my body in a succession of touches and kisses, from my neck to my nipples and down my stomach. He slid down the bed, taking the covers with him, and parted my legs with a gentle grip.

He glanced up at me seconds before he flicked his tongue over my clit.

My hips twitched. It was crazy, how such a gentle touch could evoke such a reaction.

I threw my arm over my eyes as he explored me with his tongue. He was a master at it—the way he took his time yet brought me close to the brink so quickly was a miracle. He dangled pleasure in front of me only to take it away again, and I both loved and hated that.

Because, when I finally came, it was the best fucking orgasm. And he knew it, because he slid back up my body with a smug smile.

I blushed as our eyes met.

"One," he murmured, holding my gaze before going back down.

I gasped when he closed his mouth around my clit and sucked, flexing his tongue against it. It was so tender, and I gripped the sheets as heat washed through me once again.

Jesus Christ—he'd been down there ten seconds and already, I was on the edge.

A second one slammed into me. He'd barely done anything, and I was biting my lip to keep from moaning too loudly. He kept his tongue there until I stilled, when he once again leaned over me, this time, with his cock already positioned at my pussy.

He slid in easily, whispering, "Two."

Note to self: he took a challenge seriously.

Long, slow thrusts into me covered both our bodies in a thin sheen of sweat.

This time was different.

Not like the first time against the wall—and not like last night, where it'd be hard and fueled by pure lust. This time was gentle, almost sweet, and although a part of me wanted it quicker and harder, I knew it wasn't right.

I knew this was.

This slow, easy sex wasn't a raw fuck. It was raw emotion, and I felt it in the way that he kissed me as he moved. In the way his fingertips moved across my skin almost reverently.

In the way my heart skipped a beat when our eyes met and I gasped.

In his eyes, I saw something.

It was a mere flash, a shadow passing over his gaze, but before I could grasp hold of it, he kissed me again. Deeper, and he fucked me a little harder, too. Not much harder, but enough that with a raise of my legs, burying himself further inside me with each thrust.

And pretty soon…

I forgot all about it.

"Shit," was all I could say as I pulled up in my driveway.

I was an hour late, and my mom's car was sitting

there. My curtain twitched in the front room, so she'd obviously brought her spare key and let herself in.

I was really hoping to have been able to get in and shower and not have this conversation while wearing Brantley's t-shirt.

Damn it.

That's what happens when I have the great idea to have sex and fall asleep right after.

Of all the times the twins could interrupt us, waking us up would have been a great one.

We won't even discuss the fact I ran out while Brantley was struggling to explain in kid-speak why I was in his bed this morning.

On one hand, I wanted to thank my mom. On the other… No. Not at all.

I got out of my truck and walked toward the front door. Hell, I was twenty-six, and I felt like I was about to get an interrogation about where I'd been all night. Like I was eighteen and past curfew or something.

I actually felt a little shame.

Dear god.

I shut the door behind me. Mom was sitting on my sofa, legs crossed, and her hands resting on her knee.

"Well, good morning," she said without turning around.

Which was when I looked in the mirror and made eye contact.

"I'm just going to—" I pointed toward the stairs. "Yeah."

"Kali! Get back here!"

I took the stairs two at a time and slammed myself into the bathroom before she could follow me.

Luckily for me, there were two towels on the rail.

I took my time showering and cleaning up. By the time I finally stepped out from under the water, I was sure I'd never been so clean in my life. I could practically hear myself squeaking with cleanliness as I made the dash into my room to get dressed.

I'd just picked up my blow dryer when she knocked at my door. "Kali. Are you dressed?"

I started the hairdryer.

It didn't deter her. Clearly, she'd had enough of my shit, and she was coming in whether I was dressed or not.

Which was why I'd had a lock on my door as a teenager. I'd never imagined needing one in my own home, though.

"Good morning," I said brightly. "Sorry, I was late. I slept in."

She took the hairdryer out of my hands, turned it off, and put it on top of my dresser. "And just why were you sleeping in, young lady? And where exactly was that?"

I wanted to tell her there were some things parents didn't need to know about their kids, but instead I mumbled something incoherent and took a step back.

She pointed to my bed in a wordless order.

I sat down. Like a disgraced toddler.

"Explain to me why your car was parked at Brantley Cooper's house at eleven p.m. last night and was apparently still there this morning. And why you came in wearing something that looked suspiciously like a men's t-shirt."

I paused. "Do you, er…Do you really want me to

go into it?"

She waved her hands and sat next to me. "Well, I guess you broke the 'no cavorting with clients' rule."

See? That was a real line, no matter how much he laughed at me.

"Couple times," I answered. "Oops?"

Mom laughed. "I knew exactly what you were doing there. So did your father."

"Oops." That time, I meant it.

"Oh, it was obvious. Every time I mentioned him you got all dreamy-eyed. Like that time you were convinced you were going to marry Justin Timberlake when I took you to see him in concert."

"That might still happen."

She rolled her eyes. "Talk to me, honey. I can see you have something on your mind."

"Can we get coffee first?"

"Sure. I'll make us some. Come down with me."

I snagged a hair tie from the pot on my dresser, along with my brush, and followed her down. I took a seat at the kitchen table and did my hair while she made coffee.

A few minutes later, she set two mugs on the table and sat down. She didn't say a word as I toyed with my braid. She simply sat, drank her coffee, and waited.

"I know we already had this chat. Kinda," I started. "But, how did you know? That you could take on someone else's child?"

She raised her eyebrows. The surprise registered on her face for a second before she realized and smoothed out her features. "I just knew. I didn't wake up one morning with an epiphany that I was Mother

Teresa or something."

"Damn. I think that would have been easier."

She nodded once. "Very much so. This question tells me that the way you feel about a certain family has changed an awful lot."

I sipped my coffee before setting it down and wrapping my hands around the mug. I wasn't cold, but goosebumps prickled over my skin. "I don't know how it happened," I admitted. I explained to her what had happened last night, and how easily I'd settled into a role that looked after them both without blinking.

"You love them. The twins." It was a statement.

I nodded, looking into my mug. "They're easy to love. Hard work, but easy to love. But, when does that stop becoming a novelty? I did it because I could. Not because I had to."

"I disagree," she said softly. "You knew Brantley was working. You knew it was obviously something important—something that couldn't be interrupted. Someone had to look after the twins, and you did it."

"But, the responsibility. When it becomes a responsibility and not just a one-time thing, then what?"

Mom studied me for a moment. "You're afraid."

"I'm not…afraid," I said uncertainly. "I'm…I don't know. This wasn't my plan. I didn't want kids. I didn't want to walk into that house and fall in love with everyone in it." I buried my face in my hands, taking a deep breath.

There.

I'd said it.

Jumped over the cliff.

Mom gave me a moment before she gently

reached over and pulled my hands from my face. She lay my hands on the table and squeezed my fingers, then said in a low, quiet voice, "You don't get to plan who you fall in love with. I'm sorry, honey, but you don't. You don't get to plan who, how, or when it happens. You just have to go with it when it does. If you got to plan it, I never would have fallen in love with your father."

"You wouldn't?" I said softly.

"Nope. I'd just got divorced. It was my fault. I was the one who couldn't have kids. My ex-husband couldn't deal with it. And let me tell you, honey, I was furious." She squeezed my hands again as if to make me understand. "I didn't want to be around kids. I especially didn't want to be a step-parent. If I couldn't have my own children, I didn't want anyone else's, either."

"I never knew you felt like that."

"I was grieving. Unlike you, a family is all I'd ever wanted. I had the choice taken away from me. Until I met your father."

"How did you go from that? To being so angry to being who you are right now?"

"I fell in love with your dad," she admitted. "It sounds fickle, but that's all it took. It wasn't like you were a secret—I knew he had you, and although I wasn't interested at first, the way I felt about him outweighed all my anger eventually. We'd dated for months before he introduced us, do you remember?"

I nodded. "I was pissed because he wouldn't tell me anything about you."

"And you made it known." Mom laughed. "Until that point, I was still in denial about having kids. I was still angry. Then, I walked into your house, and you looked up from your homework, stared at me, then to your dad, and said, "I'm busy. I've asked for weeks, so, now you have to wait for me.'""

I bit the inside of my cheek, smiling.

I was kind of an asshole teen.

"I fell in love with you there and then." She laughed again. "And, Kali? The day I fell in love with you was the day I accepted I couldn't have children. There was no need to, because there was a child out there who already needed me, and that child was you."

The smile dropped from my face.

"And, if I'd had my own children, I never would have gotten the greatest daughter ever: you."

A lump formed in my throat. "Weren't you scared? About how your life would change?"

"I thought you weren't afraid." Her lips twitched.

"Hypothetically," I said.

"Hypothetically, I was terrified. Not only was I entering into a relationship, I was entering into a relationship with a man who had a teenage girl. Jeez." She winked. "I was afraid you wouldn't accept me. That…I don't know. I wouldn't be able to be the kind of person you needed in your life. I didn't know anything about you except what your dad had told me. It took a long time before I understood what you needed me to be to you."

I pulled my hands from hers and took a deep breath. "What if…What if I'm not good enough for them, Mom? What if I fuck up because I'm not the person they need me to be?"

"Good enough? What is good enough? How do you measure how worthy you are to someone else?"

She raised an eyebrow. "Do you know how many times your father and I felt like we failed you, yet you turned around and made it clear we hadn't? That's part of being a parent. There will always be times you feel like you're not good enough, but as long as you give it your everything, then you can't ever be any better than that."

"It's just so…different. They're tiny. They need so much more than I did when we met."

"It sounds to me like you're talking through your excuses."

I took a deep breath and let it out on a shudder. "Maybe I am. Maybe I need to talk myself into it. I don't know. I just…you're right. I'm terrified, Mom. Of so many things."

She stared at me, her eyes piercing into me, seeing right through me. "You're terrified of never measuring up to their mom in his eyes, aren't you?"

Ding ding ding, we have a winner.

I nodded. "He loved her, you know? Really loved her. How do you cope with that? Knowing that they lost someone they loved enough to have a child with?"

She folded her hands on top of each other and looked me dead in the eye. "I cope knowing that even after that, even though he sees her every single time he looks at you, he trusted me enough to open his heart to me. Your dad still loves your mom, Kali. Understand that. He'll ever stop loving her, and that's okay with me. It's a different kind of love." She paused. "And the part you're forgetting is that both of you are still young enough that you have your lives ahead of you. Just because he loved her a certain way, doesn't mean he can't love you just as much in a different one. Remember, he's the one who was hurt."

"What do I do?"

"You need to think about what you really want. He's the one putting three hearts on the line, and he's trusting you not to break them."

"No pressure, then."

"Listen to your heart, Kali. I promise it won't steer you wrong."

26

Two days later, Dad had installed the kids' beds, and their rooms were done.

I didn't know how I felt about it.

On one hand, it was amazing to see the rooms completed. All that needed to be done was bedding, curtains, and unpacking. As far as my work was concerned, though, I was done.

On the other and, there was nothing left for me to do but stare at the completed rooms with my heart in my throat.

Would I ever see these bedrooms again?

I had a choice to make, and one I knew I had to make soon. My mom had been right. This wasn't a normal relationship—there were two, little hearts on the line here as well, and as long as I kept myself in a state of indecision, I was being selfish.

Did I take the risk, or did I take the easy option and walk away?

If I took the risk, everything would change. And, in the weirdest kind of way, I was ready for it. The thought of not being around the twins and laughing at them…Well, that sucked.

The thought of not being around Brantley?

I didn't want to think about that.

I leaned against the windowsill in Ellie's room. I'd just made the choice, hadn't I? Walking away wasn't the easy option at all. If I did, I'd leave a piece of my heart here.

I'd leave a piece in the paint on the walls and the nails in the floor. In the drawers in the dresser and the shelves that held their piggy banks.

I stared around the room. A box sat at the end of her bed, and a frilly, tulle skirt poked out of the top. While Brantley had gotten most of downstairs unpacked—finally—the kids' bedrooms had, understandably, been left behind.

Pink hangers hung from the rail Dad had built into the bed. It was the entire width of the bed, and slowly, I crawled under the mid-sleeper bed and dragged the box with me.

One by one, I pulled out each costume and hung it up. Cinderella. Belle. Tinkerbell. Moana. Every costume you could imagine a four-year-old having, she had it.

I paused, fingering the satin-tulle skirt of Rapunzel's costume. Dad had listened to me—he'd put hooks on the bed under Eli's.

For his superhero costumes.

I lined Ellie's dress up shoes on the shelf beneath the rack and used a small tub to put tiaras and gloves in. Leaving the box in the middle of the room, I darted into Eli's. There were boxes in the corner of his, and damn it.

Excited, I rifled through each one until I found his special brand of dress-up.

Capes.

So. Many. Capes.

A gleeful smile spread over my face as I pulled a Batman one out. Two capes hung from each hook, and I grabbed a small tub to put his masks in. There were a couple hats that sat carefully in there, too.

I slid out from under the bed, pressing my hands against my stomach.

My heart skipped.

Seeing his capes hanging up. Knowing Ellie's dresses were in the other room. Shoes and masks and gloves and tiaras.

Imagining the smiles on their faces when they saw it.

I bit my lip.

Hard.

Something—something inside me flared to life, and these incomplete rooms weren't enough. These rooms needed curtains and bedding and rugs.

Brantley was at work.

The twins were at daycare.

I should have been at home.

Instead…

Instead, I tore open boxes. I rifled through the closet in the hall. I laid rugs and hung curtains. I plugged in lamps and fitted lampshades. I bended the legs of action figures until they were sitting, and I taped a poster of princesses to a wall.

I fitted sheets. I shook out pillowcases. I turned bedding inside out before giving the quilts a damn good shake. I buttoned the sheets and laid out soft toys. Wriggled rugs and set them in the perfect place.

Lined books on shelves.

Stacked DVDs next to TVs.

Sliced the tape on empty boxes and flattened them.

Removed them from the spots they'd occupied for too long.

More importantly, I injected a little piece of my

love for each of those kids into their rooms.

I hugged empty boxes to my chest and, standing in the hallway, I looked into both rooms.

Perfection.

Nothing more, nothing less.

Just perfection.

I stacked the last of the cardboard next to the trash can in the front yard and headed back inside. The clock said they were arriving anytime now, so I shut the door and took up my perch on the fifth step.

They wouldn't see me when they came in, but I'd be able to execute the final stage of my master plan.

Well, the next-to-final.

The final was the admission to Brantley that I was in love with his children. In love with him. In love with the*m all.

And I was.

Never mind Keeping Up With The Kardashians.

I was in love with the chaos of the Coopers.

Hammered.

Nailed.

Screwed.

Drilled.

I'd done all those things since I'd walked through that front door, but none compared to the things this family had done to me since that day.

Brantley had all but fucked me into loving him, and his kids had done the same thing so effortlessly, albeit it in so many different ways.

A car rumbled into the driveway.

I covered my smile with my hand as the sounds of Brantley getting the kids out the car creeped through the door.

I'd parked my truck a block away a couple hours ago, and instead of wearing what I normally did, a blue, floral dress hugged my body until it flared at my hips, and it did that right now. Spread over the stair I sat on as my heart beat ten million miles an hour.

I wanted to see their faces as I saw their bedrooms.

I wanted to see Brantley's face as he saw their rooms.

The door opened, and I tucked into myself.

"I hungry," Ellie said.

"Cake?" Eli asked hopefully.

"Sure." The door shut, but it didn't measure up to the tone of Brantley's voice. He was downcast, almost sad…

I stood up, biting my lip. "Hi," I said.

The twins grinned.

Brantley stilled.

"I have a surprise for you," I said softly. "You wanna see?"

They nodded their heads.

"Okay, come upstairs and cover your eyes."

On cue, they both followed me up and covered their eyes with their hands when they got to the top.

"You ready?" I asked.

They nodded.

"One…" I pushed open Ellie's door. "Two…" Did the same to Eli's. "Three! Open your eyes!"

They both threw their hands off their eyes with a

flourish. Given that they were staring into each other's rooms, they didn't move a muscle until I nudged them in the right direction.

Then, Eli gasped, and Ellie screamed.

Brantley shot up the stairs like a bullet. "What is…" His feet touched down just inches behind me, and he stopped. I moved back against the wall. The kids were already in their rooms. They waited for nothing as they tore through toyboxes and scrambled under their beds.

A deep breath filled my lungs, and I wrapped my arms around my waist.

"What did you…" he breathed, looking first in Eli's room, then into Ellie's. "Kali. What did you do?"

"Made their beds, hung their curtains…" I trailed off when Eli emerged from under his bed wearing a yellow mask and a lime-green cape. "Hung up their costumes."

Right on cue, Ellie appeared, dressed as Cinderella.

Eli pointed at her. "You damsel in distwess! I wescue you!"

She frowned, looking him up and down. "No. I wescue you!"

He paused. "Okay," he said, scampering into his room and climbing up onto his new bed. "Help! Help!"

Brantley rubbed his hand across his forehead. "I don't know what to say to you."

"Let me make you a coffee is a good start," I admitted. "I've been here all day."

He eyed me for a moment, lips twitching, before he moved to go down the stairs. We both hovered for a second to check on the twins, but seeing them reenacting some great rescue from the mighty top of Bed Mountain obviously reassured us both, because seconds later my feet touched the floor and we were in the kitchen together.

Awkwardness tinged the air.

I leaned against the table and took a deep breath. I was exhausted. Nobody had bothered to tell me how exhausting it was to hang curtains and make beds.

No—nobody had told me how exhausting the little things were.

"Did anyone ever tell you," I started, "That finding tape in your house is impossible?"

Spoon full of sugar in hand, Brantley paused. "Everyone who ever needed tape in my house."

"Okay, so, for future reference, it's on a red dispenser on your desk."

"For now. Ellie likes to hang her drawings on her walls."

"Ellie can learn to put it back where it belongs when she's done with it."

Again, he paused. Only for a second, but long enough to be poignant. "I feel like there's a part of this conversation I'm not privy to."

There was.

"There is," I said.

"Mostly the part about why you're here."

"Well, that's a funny story."

"Isn't it always with you?"

"As a rule," I agreed. "So, me and Dad got done with the beds pretty quick, and I hung around to make sure everything was done. And I just…couldn't leave."

"Sounds more voodoo than funny story to me."

"Shut up and let me talk."

"Yes, ma'am." He turned and gave me a coffee with a grin, then rested back against the counter with his arms folded across his chest. "Please continue."

I took a deep drink of coffee, set the mug down, and did just that. Well… "Now, you interrupted me. Where did I stop talking?"

"You just couldn't leave," he reminded me.

"Oh! Right. Thanks." This wasn't going how I'd planned it.

Story of my fucking life.

"So, yeah. I couldn't leave. Then, I found Ellie's costume box, and one thing led to another."

"One thing led to you completing their bedrooms almost to entirety," he pointed out.

"Right. Another." I shrugged and used my coffee mug as a shield to hide my smile. "Semantics and all that."

Brantley eyed me for a moment. "Why?" The question was short. Sharp. To the point. But, not cruel. Still kind—but so curious. "Why did you stay?"

"I told you. I couldn't leave."

"That's not an answer."

"It is if I wanted it to be."

"Kali—"

"I couldn't leave because I didn't want to," I blurted out. I put the coffee mug on the table next to me and steeled myself. "I couldn't leave if I didn't get to say goodbye," I added softly.

He took a deep breath. "Right. So, goodbye?"

I shook my head, dipping my gaze away briefly before swinging it back up to meet his. "No," I said quietly. "That's not what I meant. I—I thought about what you said. The other day, in the Coastal. And what I didn't say and what I should have said—"

He closed the distance between us. His hands cupped my face, and he kissed me right as I hesitated. "I didn't tell you enough," he said as I curled my fingers in his shirt. "I didn't tell you that I don't just like you. I didn't tell you that I'm falling in love with you, and I should have. I didn't tell you—"

This time, the cut-off kiss was mine.

I shut him up.

"I didn't tell you that I'm falling in love with you," I echoed. "That I love your kids. That your family turned me from someone who never wanted them to someone who can't imagine her life without them."

He took a deep breath.

Pulled back.

Looked me in the eyes.

"I don't know what I'm doing," I whispered. "I will never be good at what you do as a parent. I don't know if it will ever be natural or right. But, I want to try. I want to try to be enough for them. For you."

He touched his forehead to mine, smiling as he did it. "Baby, you already are. More than you know."

I let my eyes flutter shut until he pulled back. "Is it okay? That I won't be perfect?"

He stared at me for a moment, then used the fingertips that brushed my cheeks to sweep my hair behind my ears. "A few days ago, you looked after them when I didn't even know what time it is. I don't exactly have the market on perfect cornered."

Well…there was that.

"And it doesn't matter," he continued quietly.

"You'll fuck up. I fuck up all the time. It's part of this rollercoaster."

"But, what if—"

He pressed his finger against my lips and shook his head. "Don't ask it, Kali. Don't you dare compare yourself."

Tears stung the back of my eyes. "How can I not?"

"Listen to me." His voice was so soft and soothing, and his eyes were so bright and open and raw in their emotion. "You're different people. Katie will always be their mother, but that doesn't mean you can't be who you want to be to them. A part of me will always love her, but that doesn't mean that the rest of me—all of me—can't love you. Because, it can. And, I don't want you to compare yourself. You—God, Kali. You breathe so much life into me," he whispered, leaning his face down to mine. "Don't. I want to see you singing into a paintbrush and chasing me around a table until I die laughing."

I nodded, squeezing back the emotion. "Can I be scared of this?"

"Please do. I'm fucking terrified."

For some reason, it made me laugh. Knowing he felt the same as me…I don't know. It flipped a switch, and instead of crying, I burst out laughing, wrapping my arms around his waist.

His slid around me. His body shook with silent laughter, and in that moment, with my soul laid bare, wrapped around him, I knew.

I knew that we'd be okay.

Because, it was just like my mom had said.

I never wanted kids. Not until I met the two who

needed me to want them.

And, I'd never wanted to want anyone as much as I did those crazy kids.

"Voom, voom!" Eli shouted, running through the room in a flash of color with his fist raised in the air.

"Ewi!" Ellie clobbered after him, her play shoes smacking against the kitchen as she readjusted the tiara on her head. "How cand I save you if you keep wunning away fromd me?"

I glanced up and met Brantley's eyes.

They sparkled.

My heart skipped.

"Eli," I called. "Stay still and let your sister rescue you!"

"Voom voom!" came from under the table.

"Pick your battles," Brantley mouthed, releasing me so Eli could pop up between us. His masked face jerked between us before he grinned and took off, heading for the stairs.

"Okay," I replied. "You fight this one, then."

"That's not what I meant." His lips twitched.

"Ewiiiiiiiiiii!" Ellie cried.

I cradled my coffee with a smirk.

Brantley sighed, strolling out of the kitchen. "Eli!"

Epilogue

One year later

I stared at the party spread in front of me, then down at my stomach.

I looked fat.

Not even pregnant-fat, just fat. The horrible, awkward moment where people would stare at you in the store as they figured it out.

Too pregnant to hide it, too small to confirm it, my mom kept saying.

Although, if she touched my bump one more time, I was going to karate chop her head off her fucking shoulders.

Hands slid over my waist and across the pudge. "Look at that," Brantley murmured, drawing my body against his. "You finally passed the fat stage."

I looked down again. I even tilted my head to the sides. "Does this mean your mom will stop questioning her existence if she can see the bump?"

"Yes. She'll probably touch you a few times."

"Nope." I shoved his hands off me and pointed my finger at him. "I am not an interactive exhibition at a museum! I'm going to change!"

"Kali!" he laughed, following me up the stairs. "I'm fucking with you!"

"Nope! Between my mom and yours—nope!" I threw my hands in the air. "I am not doing this." I tore my shirt off over my head and threw it on the bed. "It's bad enough I can barely work because of safety regulations on a whole bunch of shit," I continued. "Now, I can't even host a birthday party without my fat being fondled? Nope. No way. I spent three hours in that kitchen today. Three. Hours! You know the last time I spent three hours in the kitchen?"

"You were trying to hide the fact you were binge-eating yogurt and cookies. Together."

"You don't get to judge me." I jabbed my finger through the air. "I was hungry!"

He raised his eyebrows and smiled.

"I did not spend three hours in that fucking kitchen to have people poke my fat."

"That fat is our daughter."

"Still fat!" I poked my bare bump to prove my point, and got kicked harder than I ever had for my troubles. "Hey!" I said to my stomach. "What was that?"

"Did she kick you?"

"Kick me. Try to break out. Same difference."

He came over and rested his hand on my stomach. "Do it again," he said softly. "Poke her. Gently."

I prodded the front of my stomach, and she kicked. Right where his fingertips were.

A smile spread across his face. "She's telling you to get off her. Just poke her every time a mom touches you."

I was torn between grinning that he'd felt her and glaring at his suggestion. I decided to pull my t-shirt over my head instead.

I'd bought it especially for this mutual meeting of our parents.

Brantley walked around me and read the shirt.

"Hands off the bump," he read.

"I wanted one that said, "Touch me and I'll cut you like a fish," but they didn't have that on Zulily."

He rubbed his hand over his face. "Just as well. Is everything ready? They should be back any minute."

"Everything except my patience."

"You're testy today. Did Eli eat all the yoghurt again?"

I stared at him.

"Yet still so very, very beautiful," he tried.

I still stared at him.

He laughed, drawing me close. "Come on, fatty. I know for a fact there are cookies in the kitchen. I hid them high up where the kids couldn't get them."

"And I just fell in love with you all over again."

He kissed me, fighting a smile.

Downstairs, the door slammed open. "Mommmmmmmmmy!" Eli shouted.

I sighed. "There go my cookies."

Brantley cupped my face. "Quick, distract them in the backyard, and I'll get them for you."

"I just swooned," I said, kissing the corner of his mouth and heading for the stairs.

"Mommy! Where are you?" Ellie shrieked.

"Coming!" I shouted. "Let the fat lady walk!"

Brantley's laughter chased me down the stairs.

Ellie frowned as I came into view. "You look fat today."

"That's not nice!" Eli shoved her. "Mommy looks pretty."

"We're not fighting." I waved my hands and crouched down to them in the hall. "Where are Nanny and Granddad?"

"In the car," Ellie said. "You really do look fat today. Can I touch it?"

"You," I said, "are allowed."

I stood so she could. She even got the hint of a kick for her troubles.

Her eyes widened. "What was that?"

"Your sister has your attitude," I replied.

"That was weird." Ellie backed off. "Daddy! Mommy's stomach hit me!" She ran upstairs.

Eli touched my stomach, too, a look of mild curiosity on his face. That quickly changed to sadness. "Why won't she kick me?"

"She likes you." I grinned, resting my hand over his. "And you know the best part of having two sisters?"

"There will be nothing good about having two sisters," he said somberly.

"No, there will be." I gently took his hand from mine and bent down. "You're guaranteed to be my favorite boy. Them? Who knows."

He grinned, his bright eyes sparkling. "That sounds fun."

I returned that smile of his and kissed his nose. "Happy birthday, buddy."

He hugged my neck. "Thanks, Mommy. Can I go eat some of that food?"

"Don't touch the cake," I warned him.

One thing they hadn't grown out of was their love for superheroes and princesses, and I'd managed to incorporate that into one cake.

All right.

I'd paid someone to, but it was basically the same thing.

Wasn't it?

"Go down," Brantley said from the staircase. "And get a drink, then."

I laughed as Ellie scooted past me to the fridge.

He looked at me. "One day," he said. "One day, we will be child free."

"Eighteen years and five months," I responded.

"Shit," he muttered. "Shoulda thought of that."

"Before or after you threw me over the sofa?" I wrapped my arms around his waist and looked up at him.

He settled his arms around my shoulders and pursed his lips. "I wasn't thinking straight when I threw you over it, so…"

I buried my face in his chest and laughed. "Can I have my cookies now?"

He kissed the top of my head, laughing, too. "Sure thing, baby."

He released me, still laughing.

A lot of things had changed since I'd met the Coopers.

The ring on my finger? That had changed. So had the fact my uterus was incubating a tiny human being. So had my name—I wasn't Kawi anymore, I was Mommy.

The one thing that hadn't?

Brantley still laughed.

Every day.

Sometimes with me. Sometimes at me. But, always because of me.

If I'd have known how everything would change when I walked through the door, I probably never would have. My family quadrupled overnight.

Christmas got bigger and more expensive, and responsibility rained on me.

I'd come into this house to fix bedrooms.

What I'd done was fix a family.

And, I'd never been so damn happy.

Well…Maybe when I got my cookies.

The End

Enjoy MISS FIX-IT? Try Being Brooke or Mixed Up! Details at www.emmahart.org.

Make sure to sign up for Emma's newsletter to get early cover reveals and exclusive excerpts! http://bit.ly/EmmaAlerts

COMING SOON:

Miss Mechanic, a sexy, standalone romcom, now available for pre-order everywhere. Coming December 12th!

Two mechanics.

One rivalry.

He'll prove her place isn't under the hood--it's over it.

About the Author

Emma Hart is the New York Times and USA Today bestselling author of over twenty novels and has been translated into several different languages. She first put fingers to keys at the age of eighteen after her husband told her she read too much and should write her own.

Four years later, she's still figuring out what he meant when he said she 'read too much.'

She prides herself on writing smart smut that's filled with dry wit, snappy, sarcastic comebacks, but lots of heart... And sex. Sometimes, she kills people. (Disclaimer: In books. But if you bug her, she'll use your name for the victims.)

You can find her online at:
www.emmahart.org
www.facebook.com/emmahartbooks
www.instagram.com/EmmaHartAuthor
www.pinterest.com/authoremmhart

Alternatively, you can join her reader group at http://bit.ly/EmmaHartsHartbreakers.

You can also get all things Emma to your email inbox by signing up for Emma Alerts*. http://bit.ly/EmmaAlerts

*Emails sent for sales, new releases, pre-order availability, and cover reveals. Each cover reveal contains an exclusive excerpt.

Books by Emma Hart

The Vegas Nights series:
Sin
Lust

Stripped series:
Stripped Bare
Stripped Down

The Burke Brothers:
Dirty Secret
Dirty Past
Dirty Lies
Dirty Tricks
Dirty Little Rendezvous

The Holly Woods Files:
Twisted Bond
Tangled Bond
Tethered Bond
Tied Bond
Twirled Bond
Burning Bond
Twined Bond

By His Game series:
Blindsided
Sidelined

Intercepted

Call series:
Late Call
Final Call
His Call

Wild series:
Wild Attraction
Wild Temptation
Wild Addiction
Wild: The Complete Series

The Game series:
The Love Game
Playing for Keeps
The Right Moves
Worth the Risk

Memories series:
Never Forget
Always Remember

Standalones:
Blind Date
Being Brooke
Catching Carly
Casanova
Mixed Up
Miss Fix-It
Miss Mechanic (coming December 12)
The Upside to Being Single (coming January 30,' 2018)

Made in the USA
Lexington, KY
18 March 2019